MW00881226

FORGOTTEN MONSTER
By J. Emery

Edited by V. Duncan
Cover designed by Natasha Snow

First Edition August, 2019

Print ISBN: 9781081582302

FORGOTTEN
MONSTER

J. EMERY

TABLE OF CONTENTS

Content Warnings

- Depictions of fantasy typical violence including injury, blood, threats of harm, and death (minor characters, not graphic)
- Mentions of suicidal ideation, depression, anxiety, and PTSD
- Mentions of fatal illness
- Depictions of sex and sexual situations

PRONUNCIATION GUIDE

Taisce: TASH-kah

Ciaran: KEER-an

Saracque: sah-RAHK

Éthys: AY-tis

CHAPTER ONE
IN WHICH THERE IS MUCH FIGHTING

"You have the wrong man," Sef said, tugging back against the guards who held both his arms. With straw clinging to his long, honey-colored hair and caught in his month's growth of beard he looked more unkempt than usual, but a crooked smile accompanied the plea. It might still have been charming if they had bothered to look at him.

Instead of answering, the guards picked him up and bore him from the dank cell and into the equally dank passageway with his toes dangling above the floor. His shackles clacked like chattering teeth.

"I tell you, it wasn't me. There's been some mistake."

"We'll let the gallows decide that," said the guard at his left.

"That makes no sense at all. A noose kills everything."

"That's the idea," said the guard on his right as they rounded the corner.

Ahead rose a flight of squat stone steps that

bowed down at the center from centuries of reluctant heels. A short trip up and then: the hangman.

Sef wouldn't have minded if the journey was a bit longer. A dozen extra miles or even a few days' hard ride perhaps. Not that he feared death. He didn't. He feared the part that came before the dying. And luckily he had foregone the grayish gruel his jailers had offered as a final meal because suddenly there was every chance that Sef was going to be sick. If he made it to the gallows, an empty stomach would be the least of his worries.

The guards carried him up the stairs as if he weighed no more than an empty sack. His toes scuffed each step as he rose higher and higher.

"I feel unwell."

The guards set him atop the final step and steered him towards the iron gate without a word. Through the artfully curling metal rails the courtyard was visible, all pale flagstones and towering walls bordering it, teeming with onlookers already. Many of them gathered under the trees to hide from the early morning sun while they talked. The rougher lot stood in the full sun growing damp with sweat. There were women in their bonnets and men checking watches, if they had them, or the sun, if they did not. Waiting for the snap of his neck.

Well, they wouldn't see it. Of that he would make certain.

Sef swallowed around the sudden lump in his throat. His plan had been to disappear from his cell in the dead of night, like a proper phantom, another ghost story for mothers to scare their children with at bedtime. *Say your prayers or Sef will steal your breath.* But the joke had gotten well out of hand. The cell walls had been etched with sigils to ward against magic. He'd been to so many villages and edge towns, so many cells, but none had caused him as much difficulty as this one. Who did such a thing? Using magic to catch magic. *Really.* You couldn't trust anyone to be honest anymore, even the law.

Somewhere Iolan was laughing at him, wherever the souls of cunning women retired to after their deaths. He could almost hear the deeply musical sound of it. Perhaps someday he would be able to laugh too. Today was not that day.

The gate creaked as it swung out, lending an extra air of gravitas to the moment. Then he was out and into the open air.

It had been days since he'd felt unobstructed sun on his face, felt the wind in his hair. He wished he could enjoy it, but every step beneath the cloudless blue sky brought him closer to the wooden platform of the gallows. Though he couldn't see it through the crowd, he knew it was there, with a noose made just for him.

He could only drag his feet so much before the guards yanked him forward again, rougher each time, until he finally tripped and hit the ground face first. He landed hard, knocking the wind from his lungs and setting stars dancing in his eyes. By the time his vision had cleared they'd pulled him up again and had continued his death march.

The people crowed with excitement at his arrival. It made him feel sick. Always did now.

Another step. One foot in front of the other. Someone in the crowd threw a rotten cabbage. It missed by half a dozen feet, exploding against the cobbles like a vile smelling bubble. As if his roiling stomach wasn't bad enough. Sef breathed through his mouth as they passed, but the stink clung to him. It had barely dissipated when they reached the gallows. Just looking at it he could feel the tightening of rope around his neck. The memory was one of his less pleasant ones, though he had worse. Much worse.

There were only six short steps up to the platform. He let himself fall over the first, barely catching himself with his shackled hands before he could break his nose against one of the steps. That was as much freedom as he was allowed. The hangman escorted him from there as the guards fell back to stand at attention beside the gallows. It was difficult to tell if they were keeping watch over him or his morbid spectators. Not that any of them seemed likely to intervene on his behalf. The executioner wore the same humorless expression of executioners the world over. Sef winked at him anyway and tried to smile, but his lips froze midway. They settled into a wince instead. He'd been hoping for a miracle to save him somehow. Luckily he knew how to fabricate his own.

Once he was shuffled into place beside the noose they began the proclamation of his crimes so the crowd knew how best to hate him. Sef barely listened. He was well aware of all the things he'd done. He had no need of a reminder.

"You have been convicted of thievery, forgery, impersonating an official of the kingdom, and the use of restricted magic craft. For this you have been sentenced to hang from the neck until dead," read a sour faced official with skin the color of old parchment. Not once did he glance towards Sef.

Sef nodded along. They hadn't gotten everything, but they'd gotten enough. He might have swung for far less. Especially the magic. It wasn't *strictly* illegal in this country anymore, but no one seemed to care about that. They still carried on as though it was.

A riot of shouting began in the midst of the gathered spectators. At first it was hard to tell it from the usual noise of the execution-hungry rabble. Then it formed itself into identifiable words, most of them "Stop!" The shouts rang against the walls of the courtyard.

The hangman ignored the noise, but the crowd was already turning, seeking out its source, Sef along with them. A stone wall of a man pushed against the crowd, heading towards the source of the shouting with a blue cloaked figure dragging behind him. And such impressive shouting it was. Not just loud—loud enough to interrupt the execution for a few moments—but it rang with the kind of bred-in authority one only found in the aristocracy. The voice itself was pompous enough to grab and hold anyone's attention, but then Sef picked the man out of the crowd and could look nowhere else. Even at the distance Sef saw him. Knew him. Recognized him. Sleek bronzed hair pulled back into a tail and a mouth that favored frowning. If Sef drew close enough he knew the man's eyes would be the color of liquid gold. Then the hood was slipped over Sef's head, cutting off everything but the rough lattice of burlap that stank of old sweat and fear.

"Say your prayers, boy," said the hangman, chuckling under his breath. It was the first thing he'd said. He threw the loop of the noose over Sef's head and tugged it tight. The rope bit into Sef's throat when he swallowed and again when the hangman tested it to be sure it would hold.

"I don't pray," Sef said.

~~*

Taisce certainly thought that the town of Ciaran made an impression. Unfortunately it wasn't a good one.

And that was before a thief bumped him and stole his purse with such startling ease that Taisce only stared as the thief disappeared into the crowd of early morning marketgoers. It wasn't until his companion Finn ran past shouting "Stop, thief!" that Taisce took up the chase himself. The first few steps over the hardpacked street reminded him of why he had stopped running in the first place. Pain shot up his leg from shin to thigh. His kneecap felt like it might pop free. If that purse hadn't contained all of his traveling money, Taisce might have given up the chase before he'd taken a dozen steps. Or left the matter to Finn. The big man was certainly much better suited to physicality in the heat. Unfortunately he was also quite slow. Even running at an uneven stagger, Taisce was able to overtake him with ease.

The thief slithered in and out of the shifting masses, leading Taisce and Finn on a chase through the center of the sun-bleached town. It hardly even seemed as though they were trying to lose their pursuers, only lead them about by the nose. Irritation lent speed to Taisce's feet and he almost closed the gap between them as the thief turned onto another street. This one opened onto a large courtyard paved in mica-flecked stone and populated by what seemed to be half of the citizens of Ciaran all at once.

Taisce stumbled to a stop before he collided headlong into a slow moving line of shopkeepers and servants come straight from the day's washing. Some of the women hadn't even bothered to take down their bundled up skirts. Spindly and unexpectedly pale ankles stuck out above their dusty shoes. All around the courtyard stood people of all ages in ragged groups, even children. Most of them seemed to be idly chatting and their voices mixed together in the courtyard, the sound bouncing off the stone walls of the bordering buildings. One of those buildings, a short, squat, and rather dingy looking pile of brick, held an equally dingy looking clock above its doors. The sound of its movement was lost among the crowd but, as Taisce watched, the minute hand slid another mark closer to the hour. An excited murmur moved through the crowd in response.

"What is it?" Taisce asked one of the nearest loiterers. "Is there something happening today?"

His question earned a curious look from a few of the washerwomen. One of the shopkeepers, a man with slicked down hair and a voluminous mustache, pursed his lips in what might have been disdain. "Hanging's today," said someone else. "It's posted all around. Haven't you seen?"

He hadn't. Though that certainly explained all the official papers he'd seen tacked up to the boards he'd run past in his chase. Taisce nodded and turned away. He had no stomach for that sort of thing though it was possible he might have felt differently if it was his own thief climbing the steps to the gallows instead of some unknown criminal.

He searched the crowd, looking for the familiar shape of the thief and their cloak, a cloak that was much too warm for the early summer heat. They should have been easy to pick out. They should have been quite a lot of things. Slower would have been nice. And less given to nabbing purses in crowds. Taisce would have approved of that too. Finn had finally caught up and stood beside him, looking through the crowd. Not that he could see much more that Taisce could. For all his added bulk Finn was still a good two inches shorter than Taisce and the people of Ciaran were very good at standing tightly packed together. Taisce was about to give up the search and try pushing through the crowd instead when he spotted a bit of movement off to one side of the courtyard. "There!" he shouted.

Finn was off in pursuit before he'd finished pointing. Taisce cut around the other side of the courtyard, hoping that he might box the thief in that way.

"I need that purse, you little vagrant," he muttered under his breath as he made his way through the crowd. It was easier said than done. His legs ached and he'd already been elbowed and kicked by half a dozen people. One of them almost slapped him in the face as he passed, arms flapping in some kind of argument. "Of all the days. I hate this city." He stumbled and fell against someone. He put up a hand to catch himself.

It was met with a shrill cry that he might have taken for terror if not for the angry red color of the woman's face. "'Scuse you!"

"My apologies," Taisce said, already sliding past.

A hand in his collar pulled him up short.

"Hey, you. You call that an apology?" Taisce turned to see who was addressing him and looked up. And up still more. The man was easily the size of the stuffed bear in Father's hunting lodge and just as broad. Just as hairy as well. The man's bushy sideburns nearly covered his ears and his beard could have served as a waistcoat. Taisce tried to pull away, but the man still had a hold of his collar. The fabric was practically tearing already.

"Generally, yes." He reached up to pull the man's hand free of his collar.

Instead he was pulled in another direction to the

sound of rending fabric. His collar.

"My lord!"

Taisce turned to glare at Finn's return, prepared to berate him for the ruined collar. It wouldn't have been so dire if Finn wasn't a horrid seamstress. It would go unfixed until he'd returned home now. "Finn! What *do* you think you're doing?" he cried as soon as he saw the familiar, broad face.

Finn's tight-lipped grin cut across his face in a slash. "My lord. Look who I've found, my lord."

Taisce glanced at what he'd been presented with. A young woman. The face was completely unfamiliar, smooth with youth, and dominated by large eyes of such a pale blue they were almost white. But the hair. The red hair was unmistakable as was the blue cloak. He'd last seen it disappearing into the crowd with his purse.

"You!" Taisce stabbed one finger at the thief, eyes searching their person for the stolen purse. It wasn't clutched in a hand or slung over a belt in easy reach. "Where is it? Where is it?" He tugged at the folds of the thief's clothes in search of hidden pockets.

"Hey! We ain't done yet," bellowed the bear man.

Taisce had completely forgotten him already.

"Take care of that matter, would you, Finn?" he said before continuing his search, patting down the would be thief with increasing roughness. "Where is my purse?" he asked in a lower voice. "You couldn't have had time to hide it. I've chased you over half of Ciaran. Where is it? Where could it be?"

The minister had finally finished the reading of

the proclamation. Atop the gallows, they slipped the rough sack over the condemned man's head. Taisce turned away again. There were enough curious eyes already. He didn't need to add his.

The crowd surged forward, throwing Taisce hard against the thief. He flinched back.

The thief smirked and drew a small bundle from a pocket. The fuse burst into flame. A cloud of bluish smoke enveloped them and Taisce felt rather than saw the thief, and his purse, slip through his fingers yet again. He swore as he blundered towards the unpolluted air outside the effect of the smoke bomb and collided with a woman whose skirts were tucked up in front. He coughed, eyes stinging, and her colorfully patterned skirts swam in front of him.

"Have you seen a thief—a girl—a... have you seen someone with red hair come by this way?" he asked, palming tears from his eyes.

The woman stared at him. Slowly she shook her head, pressing her three children behind the protection of her skirts.

Taisce offered a polite smile as he turned away.

Every glint of sunlight felt like a dagger to his eyes. He'd lost the thief again and now he could barely see. If he'd had the luxury, he would have regretted coming to this place already.

A fresh cry went up from the crowd and Taisce whirled, half expecting the bearded man to be after him again. Belatedly he realized that the cry hadn't come from a single mouth. It had come from many of them. The noise grew as heads all around the courtyard swung towards the gallows like compass needles finding north.

At the center of the yard, the noose swung empty. The executioner had dropped to hands and knees beside the trap door and helmeted guards circled the platform, weapons at the ready.

"What is it? What has happened?" Taisce asked. They'd only finished the proclamation a few moments before. He couldn't possibly have missed the whole thing in such a short time.

A man beside him spoke up. "He's vanished."

Taisce turned back to face the gallows. "Vanished? Was it magic? How did he manage it?"

The man shrugged, tucking a hand into the pocket of his waistcoat and worrying the chain of his watch with one thumb. "Don't know. I saw nothing, sir." He withdrew with an uneasy glance at Taisce as if he expected him to give chase for being left unsatisfied.

Taisce frowned. It was none of his concern, really. Just one more reason to leave Ciaran as soon as possible if they weren't even able to contain their own criminals.

"My lord!" Finn burst through the crowd. "I lost the thief, my lord." His square-jawed face was streaked with dust and sweat. He'd earned a split lip from his fight with that great bear of a man and, when Finn tugged at his ear, Taisce noticed his scraped and bloody knuckles. At least the fight hadn't been one sided. Good.

"No matter." Taisce ground one fist into his right thigh, at the ache starting there after pounding around town. "With luck we'll find that thief along the way. Now come. We still need to search this terrible town after we arrange lodging."

Taisce led the way back towards the main thoroughfare without checking to be sure Finn followed. He knew he would. And Finn overtook Taisce before long, moving with an ease that Taisce had trouble matching now that the chase was done. It was enough to let Finn part the crowd for him a while, to let himself slow to an easier pace. There were so many people about that he felt almost claustrophobic. Watched. He glanced around, trying for casualness, but there were no obvious culprits. No one made themselves known, betraying their position with a self conscious move. Just in case, Taisce quickened his step, even thought it sent fire up through his leg.

Around them, the crowd was split between fearful chatter at the disappearance of the condemned man and a return to their daily routine. Housewives herded children back to their homes and shopkeepers bowed greetings to passing customers as they reopened their stores for the day's business. Taisce smiled at the simpering apologies given to grannies and spinster aunts. It was like music to his ears. It had been so long since they had been to town. Any town. Even the stunted commerce of this backwoods city was something to relish. His time in the wilderness with nothing but the rocks and trees for polite conversation had left him rather disenchanted with nature. He missed people and their quaint chatter. Their petty complaints. It had been months since he'd last observed Father's holdings. It was something of a chore, but he regretted its loss now.

Regrettable or not, he couldn't deny his current task. No matter his opinion on it. He only hoped he could complete it and return home before Mother's health failed completely.

"We've arrived, my lord," Finn said with a half realized bow. If he'd bent all the way down he would likely have bashed his head into something. It had happened more than once. What Finn lacked in manners he made up for in enthusiasm.

Taisce looked at the building he'd indicated.

It was unimpressive by his usual standards — would never even have been up for consideration by his usual standards — but it wasn't a cave or a bed of moss stretched out beneath a tree so it already seemed an improvement over their most recent sleeping arrangements.

The place called itself *The Wounded Lamb* — hardly a favorable endorsement with its wooden sign depicting a blood-streaked lamb awaiting the final mercy of death. Taisce considered the rest of the building. The rough white exterior was clean and the smell coming from inside was only mildly offensive.

He pushed open the door.

The interior of *The Lamb* seemed unnaturally dark after the glaring sun on the street and it smelled of spices, spilt ale, and years of body odor. Luckily the fresher scent of cinnamon was enough to partially blot out the more unpleasant ones.

"Are you sure this is the place?" Taisce asked, attempting to speak and breathe through his mouth at the same time.

"We're the only decent inn to be had in this city," said a burly man that Taisce hadn't even noticed. He hovered in the shadows behind the counter, scrubbing away at the scarred wood. His skin was so sun-darkened that he seemed to be made of the shadows in which he stood.

Taisce stepped closer. The floorboards creaked wearily beneath his boot heels. It was a sentiment he could sympathize with. "A room for myself and my man."

"Just the one?" The innkeeper looked between them and then gave Finn a more thorough inspection from head to toe. "You sure he'll fit?"

"Yes, very clever," Taisce said tightly. "But I'm quite sure he'll manage."

"Half a croy a night then. Up front." The innkeeper put out one square palm to accept it.

Taisce froze.

He turned to Finn. "Pay the man."

Finn's eyes grew as wide as full moons. He shook his head and, looking ashamed, patted his pockets. "You have not paid me since our departure, my lord," he whispered.

"Right," said the innkeeper. "Out with you."

"You don't understand," Taisce began, standing his ground beneath the innkeeper's impressive glare.

"No money, no room."

"I can assure you, you will receive our payment with interest. I am a highborn son. My word is my bond."

"Don't care. Out."

"But—"

"Leave on your feet or get tossed out on your asses." The innkeeper gave a sharp whistle and a man parted the curtain at the back of the room. He gave the impression of a large tree stump come to life. His smile, when it appeared, was missing several teeth.

"If you would only listen, I'm sure we could sort this out peacefully," Taisce insisted.

~~*

Later, sitting in the dust outside *The Wounded Lamb*, Taisce sighed. "I was very much looking forward to that bed." He dabbed a knuckle against the blood on his lips, scowled, and—after a moment's hesitation—wiped his finger on the leg of Finn's pants. One more smudge there wouldn't hurt anything and he'd lost his handkerchief. "What shall we do now?"

He hadn't expected much of an answer from Finn and so wasn't surprised when he only shrugged and went back to tightening the buckles on his pack. At least they hadn't lost their supplies in the scuffle. Of course, without funds they were unlikely to make it much farther. They were weeks from home. Too far to turn back in search of help. "Do we have an agent in this city?"

Taisce looked up at the cloudless sky, searching his mind for the names and locations of Father's associates. They were few and far between at this distance, but there was still a chance.

"Clotsfield," Finn offered unexpectedly. "There's Brannigan and Felix both."

Taisce hummed, working out the distance in his head. "That's... at least two days' ride and back north a bit. No one closer?"

"The local Saints would have us. They take all comers," Finn said hopefully.

A charity shelter.

Taisce shook his head before he'd finished. "I can't be seen frequenting a Saints' refuge. My reputation would never recover." He caught Finn's veiled look at the state of his clothes. His shirt was torn and his trousers were smudged with what he sincerely hoped was mud. He couldn't be entirely certain after this morning. He glared back. "This is road dirt, nothing more. Come along. We still have work to do in this horrid town," he said, regaining his feet. He put a hand to the wall of *The Lamb* to steady himself. "Have you my coat?" It would cover his torn collar at least. He'd meant to put it on earlier in a show of propriety, but the morning heat had made him hesitate. If only he could have continued to go without it.

Beside him, Finn gave another tug on his worn leather satchel before he stood. Taisce's coat emerged from the pack wrinkled but in otherwise good repair. With it removed, the satchel sagged pitifully. Nearly empty.

When they had set out, it was full almost to bursting. Taisce's sister Adeline had secreted candies and a handsome sheaf of writing papers among their supplies. As if they would need such things where they were going. Still, she had insisted on letters to keep her apprised of his progress and an additional promise of mementos upon his return.

Some might have made a grand show of sending him off. Father had simply taken him aside and pressed a dagger into Taisce's hands. It was a familiar blade, sheath studded with cabochons of cat's eye, serviceable but not often used. He'd seen it before, arranged with others upon his study wall. Then he had clasped Taisce's other hand, turning it to look at the signet ring there. "And keep that hidden from all but our people. No one is to know," he had said in a whisper so fierce it was a hiss. "Just find him."

Mother had sent Taisce off with the faintest warmth of a kiss upon his cheek.

Taisce pressed a hand to his cheek now. The ghost of her kiss still lingered, bringing more comfort than his father's dagger ever had.

"We must go," Taisce said, nudging Finn when he seemed inclined to start poking about in his satchel again.

They had many more miles to travel before they rested, but their journey would be a fruitful one if he had to overturn every rock in his searches. The kingdom could only hold so many hiding places.

CHAPTER TWO
IN WHICH THE TWAIN SHALL MEET

"Surely you can do better than that," Sef wheedled, leaning against the counter separating him from the pair before him.

The lady smiled back, resettling her ample bosom over her crossed arms and shaking her head. Sirena was always a series of whispers, the rustle of skirts and the swish of shining satin. Today she was dressed all in burgundy with an abundance of ribbons and ruffles along the bodice. Sef wondered what occasion had compelled her into what was surely one of her better dresses. Even her black hair was in careful curls that the summer heat had yet to wilt. She tipped a kind look at him before stepping back, deferring to Ando without a word. Ando would be nowhere near so easy to sway. Everything about him was severe, from the top of his clean shaven head to the tips of his shoes. They gleamed with fresh polish. If a thing could be done, Ando could do it with more skill and probably without removing his coat. The list of those who had seen him in shirtsleeves was short and did not include Sef. He was also entirely immune to Sef's charms. Damn him.

"I'll give you one night. No more. You bring trouble wherever you go and I want none of it this time either," Ando said. He pressed a finger into the wood of the counter to further his point. Then he raised a suspicious, if belated, eyebrow. "You were due to be hanged today, weren't you?"

"I got lucky is all," Sef said, smile weakening. "And thank you so much for your concern. I'm touched. But I couldn't have timed it better if I had planned it. There was some kind of scuffle in the square and I slipped the noose while the guards were distracted." He rubbed at the back of his neck. There hadn't been time for delicacy and now it itched with rope burn. His gaze swung around the room and, even though it was too hot for the damn thing, he tugged the stolen blanket he'd swaddled himself in closer about his face. *The Lady's Stallion* was known to attract a less savory sort, the most lucrative business in a town so corrupt and the reason Sef was so familiar with it, but that made discretion even more necessary. If there was no honor among thieves then they wouldn't balk at returning him to the gallows in exchange for a bit of reward money either. Sef leaned closer. "Have you heard, is there talk of a reward yet?" he asked in a whisper.

"Fifty croy says the Guard," Sirena volunteered.

Sef slumped. "Is that all? Even with a guilty conscience I couldn't be bothered to turn myself in for that little." It was a comfort as much as it was a blow to his pride. He was worth far more but better *they* didn't know that. The wrong sorts might decide to take an interest in him. But only fifty croy...

He leaned back against the counter on his elbows, eyeing the trio sitting at a table in the far corner of the inn's main room. They hadn't looked in his direction yet, but that didn't mean they weren't watching him. The haggard old man in the chair beside the window had been snoring for the last half hour while Sef spoke to Sirena and Ando. Seemed an unlikely rat there. The rest of the room was empty this early in the day, most of the occupants probably sleeping off last night's hangovers. Sef thumped an open palm on the counter. "Well, I'll see myself to my room then and thank you for your troubles." Ando's hospitality was best snatched up before he could change his mind. Fickle man.

Sef turned to head up the stairs.

Ando cleared his throat. "You get below stairs until you're a paying customer. The cellar should be quite comfortable this time of year." His mustache twitched in amusement at the look Sef shot him.

"All this time I thought us friends," Sef mourned, but he corrected the direction of his departure. It wasn't the first time he had slept on an earthen floor and it was still better than a broken neck.

The cellar was just as luxurious as he expected. Low ceilinged and dark was perhaps the most polite way he could describe it, but the dirt floor and stone walls did offer a pleasant coolness in contrast to the gathering summer heat in the streets. He'd nearly sweated himself into a puddle on the trip through the back alleys on his way here and he had already smelled horrid enough before that. A month in jail would do that to a person.

Luck had saved him from a broken neck earlier, but he had no plans of tempting her by making himself an easy target for further misfortune, especially not now when he was within reach of the man with the gold eyes. Sef was sure he'd seen him before. Not just his eyes but the face that went with them. The face that appeared so often in his dreams contorted with fury, eyes flashing bright with delicious malice. If he was a poetic sort Sef could have gone on for hours about how it felt to have those eyes upon him, how he shuddered in something akin to pleasure as the blade pierced his chest and his blood ran out. Over and over. Dream after dream.

He'd spent decades in love with that dream, so much so that Sef had started to wonder if it was only a fantasy concocted to keep himself sane. His mind had played enough tricks on him in the past. Why not this one too? But now he'd finally seen his dream attacker—and lost him again in the crowd in the courtyard.

Sef swore, kicking at a lumpy sack of potatoes.

He had seen the man, had been close enough to choke the life out of him, before he vanished again. It was the worst kind of game. Sef wanted to be out searching, not trapped in a cellar attacking vegetables. But he couldn't. His golden-eyed prize had shown himself when Sef was at such a disadvantage. If he traipsed about the town square asking questions mere hours after a thwarted appointment with a hangman he might as well march himself straight back into a cell. Someone would recognize him. And then clang would go the cell door. Or creak the noose. He couldn't do that again.

He brushed a hand over his cheek. The sweaty heat made his beard itch and lent him an aged look he would never earn any other way. Without it maybe...

It would be a start at least.

Sef bounded up the stairs two at a time in search of Sirena. He found her in the kitchen, humming to herself in a low, melodious voice. If Ando kept the guests in order, Sirena saw to everything else about the inn from the linens to the books and all of it with a song and a smile. Before he could surprise her with a hug, she turned and tapped a finger to her lips. "Hush. There's people with business up front."

Sef shriveled, shrinking back into the farthest corner of the room at her words. He pointed a finger at himself. She nodded. Then she shoved him towards the nearest closet, blocking him in with an assortment of brooms and mops before slamming the door in his face.

The closet was stifling. Whether it was the heat of the day or hiding from the Guard he couldn't quite say, but in moments he was drenched in sweat again.

Outside the door, he could hear Sirena clanging pots as she resumed her work with enthusiasm.

Heavy footsteps entered the kitchen. The clanging stopped. Sef held his breath.

"We're looking for an escaped prisoner, ma'am. About yea tall," said the muffled voice of one of the city Guard. "Pale haired. Bearded. He was still in prison linens when he escaped. Tattoo on the back of his hand."

Without thinking, Sef covered his right hand with his left, as if the mark there would give away his hiding spot somehow.

"A prisoner?" Sirena asked in mock surprise. "What's he done, sir? Nothing too terrible I hope." Sef could almost picture her, wide eyed with concern. He had seen her play this part for people in the past and, if Sef hadn't known the truth of the matter, he would have believed every word she said.

"He's done enough to earn himself a stretched neck. Best stay clear if you do see him."

"I've seen no one like that," Sirena said without hesitation. For that Sef would be eternally grateful. He knew few enough people who would cover for him without expecting payment for their silence. He pressed his hands together and tried to listen with his heart pounding hard in his ears. He couldn't go back to a cell. Not now. Couldn't.

On the other side of the door, the Guard's voice grew louder and Sef's heart stuttered. He closed his eyes, lips moving in silent prayer. Couldn't. Couldn't.

"Do take a biscuit before you go," Sirena called to the Guard, luring him back to the other side of the kitchen with the promise of baked goods. Eventually it grew quiet again.

"It's clear," Sirena said from outside the door, making him jump.

He waited another moment to be sure, eyes still closed, senses searching for anything that might give away her lie. There was nothing.

Sef burst from the closet, knocking brooms and mops out ahead of him. A bucket tipped and rolled over the clay tile floor with an uneven clunk. "You've saved me." He smiled.

"Give your gratitude to Ando as well." She returned his smile, but the glance she cast towards the door was as nervous as Sef's had been. It would be just as bad for them if Sef was found there. Worse even. They didn't have his abilities. The thought stung.

"One night and I'll never darken your door again," he said with all the sincerity he could muster. Then he stooped to put the brooms and buckets back where they belonged. He'd collected a dusting of red clay on his shoulders from being crammed in with them. He brushed it away.

As he did, his eyes snagged on his hand. He hadn't paid attention to his hands in so long. They'd become spindly fingered. Dirt beneath his nails. He grimaced and the tattoo on the back of his right hand seemed to glare back, still as fresh and sharp as the day they'd done it. The loops and vine-like tendrils of the script that ran between the tendons, outlining the center disk. It was meant to be beautiful. Meaningful. He tugged his cuff over it. The movement nearly tore the ragged cuff clean off.

His appearance hadn't mattered when he was in a filthy cell, but in Sirena's warmly lit kitchen he could see just how dingy he looked. When he turned, his distorted reflection frowned at him from the shiny back of a hanging pot. His rough, uneven beard. His sun-bleached hair standing out at his temples like a bush aflame. It all had to go. They were looking for a filthy prisoner dressed in rags. He needed to be something else and quickly. "Might you have a razor?"

Sirena chuckled. "I'll shave you. I suspect you're liable to slip and slit your own throat if you try it yourself." She nodded at his shaking hands. "When was the last time you ate?"

"A very long time," Sef said, finally regaining his smile. "And nothing so nice as a plate of your butter biscuits."

"You always know just what to say. Maybe I should have married you instead of Ando."

"I heard that," Ando said. A second later, he appeared in the doorway, boots thudding on the tile. He folded his arms and leaned against the jamb. "Trust you heard the town Guard's visit?"

Sef nodded. "I am in your debt." He paused. The next words were tougher to digest than he had expected. "I'll not trouble you again after this."

Ando pursed his lips before he nodded back. "It's best that you don't."

Sef turned away in search of biscuits and said no more.

~~*

Barely an hour later, he was a much changed man.

Sirena had hustled Sef off to the upstairs bath and forced him into a waiting tub without a peek or a blush. He almost felt slighted by her lack of interest. When he'd finished she set to work on grooming his hair and beard. It had taken all his concentration to sit still while she wielded the straight razor and scissors. Even in her capable and trusted hands, the nearness of the cutting edge unnerved him. One never knew when it might slip.

He kept himself occupied with studying the cracks in the walls and trying to find some sort of pattern there. One wall seemed to hold a Tree of Life in its faded, gray plaster while the other was speckled with so many cracks and chips that he found it impossible to make any sense of it at all. However he did spot the name Peter scratched beneath the window. He doubted Sirena would be pleased that someone had carved her wall like a lover's tree trunk.

He shifted on the stool and Sirena smacked his shoulder. "Stay still. We're nearly finished."

Sef blew out a long breath, shivering as metal grazed the back of his neck.

Out the window, the city looked parched in the midday sun, everything bleached pale from its rays. No color stood up against the sun for long. They were almost at the edge of civilization. A few days farther south and it would all dwindle back to sand and dust, but here the town still bustled with sluggish energy. Shutters were thrown back to accept the warm breeze and the clattering noises of life echoed up between the squat buildings and down the narrow alleys.

The city of Ciaran sat low to the ground, most buildings reaching their greatest height at only three stories. It made the sky seem that much farther away, arching high overhead, streaked with thin, parched clouds. If he didn't know any better he would have thought it was a peaceful place. Ciaran had gotten clever about hiding its more questionable tendencies. It kept those tucked away like pilfered jewels.

Not that he could see much of anything from the window of the bath. His view mostly consisted of rooftops and stucco walls bordered by the distant ridge of the horizon, when he would have preferred to be inspecting streets full of faces. He only needed that one.

"You'll do," pronounced Sirena, setting aside the razor and clapping her hands together to clean them of stray hairs. She swept at the nape of his neck with a cloth. He pushed it away.

"Do I look like a dead man?" Sef asked. He rose from his stool and leaned towards his reflection in the basin. His hair was short again, barely curling against his neck and his jaw was perfectly smooth. Sirena was certainly much better with a razor than he was.

"Why don't you use the mirror?"

Sef shrugged, but she was already holding the hand mirror out to him. He barely glanced at his reflection, instead running a hand through his hair until he'd worked it free of her attempts at flattening it into submission.

"You'll ruin it!" She attacked him with her comb, smoothing down his unruly hair a second time.

He allowed it, biting his lip the whole time. He would fix it again when she'd left. It wouldn't stay flat for long no matter what she did, but he'd rather not go about looking like a banker even for a few minutes. Especially not in this town. Someone might try to rob him.

"I found you proper clothes. They're not finery, but they'll do better for you than prison rags. Make yourself decent." It was the first she'd said of his ongoing nakedness. He'd started to wonder if she'd completely forgotten about it.

"I am ever in your debt," Sef said, dropping a quick bow as she closed the door behind her.

He gathered his worn clothes and held them up to the light streaming in the window. They'd become so threadbare that he could see through the fabric as if it were lace. Maybe Sirena could use them for cleaning rags. They certainly weren't good for anything else.

What she'd laid out for him was as simple as she'd described, but the clothes fit and that was all that concerned him. He'd thinned after his recent travels and even more recent stint as a prisoner of the town of Ciaran. The trousers sagged at the waist, slipping down his narrow hips. Only the shirt he'd tucked into the waist kept them from slipping even lower. It was lucky that Sirena had thoughtfully provided him with suspenders—obviously borrowed from Ando's wardrobe but still serviceable despite their size difference. There was no waistcoat or overcoat, but that suited him fine. It was too damned hot to wear so many layers. He would sweat clean through his new shirt and look just as shabby as he had before. It wouldn't do at all. He'd rather go about half naked than that.

Sef finished his toilet slowly, splashing water in his face just for the feel of it, and ruffling his freshly shorn hair. It felt cool on the back of his neck. Exposed. He shuddered, imagining the rush of an axe blade at the chopping block. That was one pleasure he was content never to have. He much preferred the way Ciaran did things in that regard. He splashed another cupped handful of water in his face, dampening his hair until it was plastered against his forehead. Sirena would scold him again, but it would dry quickly enough in the summer heat. Until then it would be a welcome comfort. He felt overheated all of a sudden.

There was a comforting silence from the rest of the inn when he left the bath, but he crept along like a thief. Some habits were hard to break. To move about freely was an unexpected privilege after days in shackles and he still expected to hear their tinkling music with every shuffle of his foot.

Sirena and Ando had returned to the front of the inn, speaking in low voices, and Sef backed out of the room before they could spot him. Instead he kept on down the stairs to the cellar. A wave of cool air kissed his skin as he ducked through the low door. It was the best room after all. Private certainly. By the dim light spilling down the stairs he inspected his lodgings. The walls were of smooth stone and the floor was solidly packed. In the corner sat a shelf of the dwindling autumn stores with other odds and ends. Old, chipped crockery. Baskets of candle ends and burlap sacks that he didn't care to poke through. Nothing of real interest. Nothing of use. Pity.

He pulled a crate free and upended it for a stool in the center of the room. He wanted to enjoy his cleanliness for as long as he could. Sef settled atop the box and hugged his legs to his chest. Closed his eyes. Another chill ran over him, snaking around his shoulders and up to his neck like a clammy hand. This was the part he always hated.

Shadows sat thickly behind his eyelids, inky dark and cold. With an effort he brought forth the half remembered look of the man he'd seen earlier, paired it with the gold eyes from his dreams. In his mind they glowed bright as liquid fire. It was difficult to concentrate on opening his senses with fear clawing at his stomach. Maybe he'd lost it. Used it all up. Maybe last time had been the last of his already limited power. He shoved the thoughts away and tried to cling instead to his target, to those eyes.

He barely felt it as his consciousness popped free and sailed like an arrow. A moment later he was there. His target drifted before him like mist, but his eyes were bright as the sun.

It was the first proper look that Sef had gotten of him, unconstrained by the waiting hangman, and he saw now that what he'd taken for a full grown man was almost closer to a boy. His face still bore a youthful innocence even though his mouth and his manners were those of a much older sort. His hair was unexpectedly long, pulled into a tail at his nape, tightly wrapped and tied with a ribbon. The color of his hair was hard to place watching from this shadowy distance, not pale, not dark. Beside Sef's target walked a man twice his size. A bodyguard no doubt or something similar. He looked moneyed enough for that. Sef barely spared the bodyguard a glance. He had little interest in servants as long as they stayed out of the way. No. The man—the boy—he was the one Sef studied, eyes closed, feeling the space around him. It hummed with his energy and the energy of the people who had passed before him. As they walked, the boy flicked his long hair over his shoulder with an irritated shake of his head and Sef's attention followed it. What would it feel like to run all that hair between his fingers?

"He was lying. I'm sure of it."

Sef smiled at the voice. It felt warm despite the agitated tone. He reached for it, trying to pull closer. They wouldn't feel him even if he attempted to touch them. Without flesh he was barely the wind.

"We must go back," the boy went on, stopping midstride as if he meant to do just that.

"But my lord—"

"Not another word." A pause. *"Where else can we go? That wretch stole my purse."*

A sigh passed through Sef's mind like a summer breeze and the voice wavered. *"We'll have to camp outside the city again tonight in that case. I trust you haven't forgotten how to fish."* More quietly he added, *"How I long for a bed."*

"My lord, you look unwell. You should rest."

"I'm fine. Leave me be."

Another weary sigh followed. The squeeze of fingers massaging an aching head. The crunch of pebbles beneath boot heels. Golden eyes swept the area, barely registering the battered door of the business they had just exited. But Sef noted it. The brass sign was just as scuffed as the door and the finish had been worn down by years of the harsh swing between the blazing summer sun and the frigid winter wind. *Jeremen Hallow, Esq.* it said in raised letters caked with grime.

Sef knew the place. The man was a local lawyer, not well respected but known to many for more unsavory reasons. Sef himself had sold the man half a dozen forgeries before he'd been caught in that ill timed scuffle that had sent him to the gallows. Though, he mused, if not for the days gobbled up by the jail cell he may well have been miles from Ciaran when his young lord arrived. It made the time no more enjoyable, sitting in filth and fear for his neck, but he began to consider it as dues paid towards a future benefit. He hoped. It had been so long since he'd had anything that he could call promising. He was hesitant to mark this as such either, but the thought already glowed in him like a coal.

Sef turned his attention back to the watery image of the pretty lord and his dog. What were they doing roaming the streets? Neither of them *seemed* the type to while away their time in gambling or forgeries. Sef knew the look and they didn't have it.

"There must be something. Something else that we have missed... Every indication pointed in this direction. He must have passed through this city. Lord Dunn said..."

The voices grew fainter and the young lord's final words wavered and disappeared.

Sef let them go. He'd already gotten what he needed and the effort to concentrate was becoming increasingly difficult. The small noises from above stairs, of creaking floorboards and friendly conversation, and the muted sounds that seeped in from the street, pulled his attention back. Some could hold such a trance for hours, if not days. He was not one of them and never had been. He let it run off him like water, but the last echo of the lord's voice rang in his head. Sef liked it. He'd waited so long to hear that voice and it was everything he might have wished for—had he dared to do so. Higher than his with the fresh pucker of privilege and something else. Hope, perhaps. It was a feeling Sef recalled like a distant friend. As he sat, legs tucked in tight, already starting to sweat despite the chill in the air, he wondered if it might be a friend he would be getting more familiar with. He prayed it was so.

Of course, before hope came preparation.

Sef hastened through the back alleys, hiding from the sun as much as the Guards that might lurk on the main thoroughfares. He'd spent enough time in Ciaran to know that they were just as likely to run him through as they were to drag him struggling back to the gallows. An unresisting corpse was so much easier to drag.

Just past noon was the worst time of all to be out. The sun had already done much of its work to warm the city to baking temperatures and the people wandering the streets were few. Those that braved the heat moved in slow waves at they fought against the bright sun. While he watched, a young woman swayed into the man strolling beside her. It was no ploy on her part. Her lashes fluttered and her cheeks had gone ruby red. The couple hurried into the shade of a nearby building to recover. Before he turned away, Sef saw the man fanning the girl's flushed face with an unexpected tenderness. He held her gently, as though she were precious, pressed a hand to her cheek. Sef couldn't hear the words said, but the attitude was all endearments and concern. The girl roused herself quickly and pulled away. Whatever his feelings, it seemed she didn't share them.

Sef frowned, good mood quashed.

He hurried through the sunny cross street, scooping up the hat the man had lost in the rush to find shade. It was a tidy little thing with a band of deep red satin, dark as dried blood. Sef popped it atop his head and gave it a stylish tilt. He was sure it suited him just as well as it had the man. Probably better. Red had always been a favorite color of his and one really should have a hat this far south, where everything was made of glaring sun in the summer. Then he put extra speed in his step. The trip from *The Stallion* had been short, but he'd wasted enough time already.

Sef located the door of the less than honorable Mr. Hallow without trouble. He didn't bother to knock. There was nothing of interest for him there and Hallow couldn't be trusted to offer assistance even if Sef was only worth fifty croy. The young lord had moved on, but he couldn't have gotten far in an unfamiliar city with the heat slowing him even further. After a moment's hesitation, Sef turned left and headed on. He'd learned a healthy respect for instinct over the years. It generally led him to what he desired.

He'd barely gone two streets more when he saw them. On the left, a hulking man with a head of hair so closely cropped that he was nearly bald, and on the right the man Sef wanted. He could tell even from behind with that fine and shining hair. In the light, the bronze color flickered with hints of sun-bleached gold and copper. Sef imagined running it through his fingers again, letting it slip between them like molten metal. Would it be soft as silk or coarse as boar bristle? Perhaps it would sear his fingers like the metal it resembled. He hoped there was time to satisfy his curiosity.

Sef brushed a trickle of sweat from his forehead, replacing the hat before cutting to the side of the walk closer to the shops and the slip of shade they cast. The men ahead of him made no such efforts. They walked down the middle of the hardpacked street as if nothing could disturb them. The man with the beautiful hair kept in the lead, the large man at his flank like an ever faithful hound.

Sef trailed them in silence. They walked with confidence, never moving aside though people would jostle them as they passed, but Sef noted the sway in the slighter man's step. It was faint. Easy to miss. But from this distance Sef picked out the way the young lord favored his right leg. His limp grew more pronounced with every step until there was a noticeable drag in his foot. He stumbled, catching himself quickly, as the duo turned off the main street.

Sef raised his eyebrows. He could guess at their destination already. They wouldn't be welcomed there.

~~*

As he had suspected, they made their way to a tavern that lay along the edge of town, bordering the canal that fed a thin stream of water to the town during the cooler months. In the full heat of summer it would be dry as picked bones, but for now it still held a bit of water in its rocky bed. It sparkled like tumbled glass.

The tavern was decidedly less attractive. The exterior was bleached the same shade of dusty pale to match the rest of Ciaran but the inside was dark and overheated and gave off that curious, overpowering reek of sour sweat and piss that seemed to crop up wherever people were packed together for long periods of time. Or maybe the smell was just from the cheap liquor they sold. Sef had never been able to stomach a glass even at his poorest and most desperate. Still, he blessed the darkness of the place. Darkness and discretion made it so much easier to hide.

The two he had followed in had no such compulsion.

Before he'd even settled against the wall where he would go unnoticed they had begun making a spectacle of themselves. Sef couldn't hear the exchange with the woman behind the bar but he didn't need to. The boy did most of the talking, gesturing tightly, and growing increasingly agitated. Whatever it was that he argued for, it seemed to be quite important. He was also completely thwarted. The barwoman shook her head and her own fist clenched and thumped against the bar. By the end of the argument—for that's what it had clearly devolved into—she looked ready to throw the pair out into the street. She would have assistance from many of the nearby tables. And if pockets were picked in the process, well, that was life.

Sef kept a wary eye out but he really had no desire to get into a fight so soon; it didn't matter how pretty the boy's hair was. The practice of magic might be technically legal again but the distrust was centuries old. This far from the civilizing influence of the capital and polite society a show of magic was more likely to earn one a jail cell than praise. And that was the best outcome. Maybe if favors had been offered he would have considered removing his remaining sense of self preservation. But only then.

The moment passed.

No one seemed particularly inclined to take the first step towards turning the argument into more than harsh words, with the air inside the bar rapidly reaching oven-like temperatures. Sef tugged the collar of his shirt open, fanning his face with one hand, and tried to unearth more patience for the task at hand. He doubted he would find much. Patience had never numbered among his few virtues.

After an exhausting amount of time, the boy ended the fruitless conversation with an exaggerated huff—*that* Sef could see quite clearly even from across the room—and swept towards the entrance. He was still wobbling a bit on that leg too, Sef noted.

Sef hung back to let them leave ahead of him. Then he slipped out too.

The return to the street felt like a blessing even with the sun bearing down on him. He could breathe again without the thick stink of rancid sweat choking it.

His relief lasted only a moment.

The young lord and his dog had turned alongside the canal, no doubt heading towards their next argument. It wouldn't take long to find one with their manner. The pride that had kept the young lord's spine straight as an arrow inside the tavern had relaxed. Now he looked exhausted. His shoulders slumped in the heavy fabric of his coat and his right leg was hesitating more severely than before. It was that drag that had him tripping over a loose stone in the road. He stumbled sideways. Straight towards the edge of the canal.

Though he shouldn't have been able to cross the distance quickly enough, Sef did it. The dog had barely turned to catch his master before Sef was beside him, stopping his fall and cradling that head of bronze hair against this chest. He brushed a thumb over an errant lock. It was as soft as he could have hoped. Sef had dreamed of this man, this face, so often that finally holding him felt like finding a missing piece of himself. Sef pulled him closer, tighter.

The dog cried out. He reached down to pry his master from Sef's hands.

"He's sick. He should be out of the sun," Sef said, turning away from the attempts to detach him. He had to fight the urge to snap at the other man and tighten his grip even more.

A second later, the lord groaned and pushed against him and, though Sef tried to hang on, he was left holding nothing but air.

CHAPTER THREE
IN WHICH EVERYONE HAS A STORY

Taisce landed on the ground hard enough to knock some of the sense back into him. His head swam with the heat, but he knew he'd fallen and then he'd been hotter still, wrapped in unfamiliar arms that clung too tightly. He squinted into the face of the man whose arms and lap he'd been occupying until a moment ago. The sun at his back cast the man's face in shadow and, though he seemed to be smiling, there was something off about it. Taisce didn't trust that face at all.

He hid behind a fresh handkerchief a moment, patting away the sweat rising at his hairline. His blood felt ready to boil and the added insulation of his coat wasn't doing anything to help with that. He wished he could throw it away.

"Are you all right?" asked the man. His voice was pleasant with the lilt of some lingering accent which Taisce couldn't quite place. Perhaps it was something he'd heard before, a long time ago. It certainly wasn't the voice of a local. They had a straightforward drawl. This man's voice curled around words like they were treasures to be guarded. It put Taisce in mind of candlelit bedrooms and hoarse whispers, the kind that made lascivious promises. And kept them.

As soon as he'd thought it, Taisce carefully set the imagining aside. It had no place in his current plans.

The man stood, throwing himself into harder shadow as he eclipsed the sun, and held out a hand. "Do you need help rising?"

Taisce eyed the open palm presented to him. It was ungloved despite the man's formal hat. The rest of his clothes were plain and unadorned. A simple shirt, slightly open at the collar. No coat. He was a collection of mismatched pieces, both proper and not. Though the most improper thing about him, Taisce decided, was the smile that hadn't yet left his face.

"Finn, help me up," Taisce said. His eyes didn't leave the stranger until he was vertical again.

The stranger accepted the slight without comment, but his smile cooled a few degrees.

Once they were on an equal footing, Taisce studied the man's face. The thin nose and finely cut cheekbones. Heavy lidded eyes the color of algae. While Taisce scrutinized him, the other man made no secret of his own appraisal, staring in a way that might have been unnerving if not for Finn at his back. "You should be more careful," he said with a nod towards the canal at their side. "You'd crack like an egg if you fell in there. I've seen it happen."

Taisce followed his gaze. The canal was narrow and, in wetter months, he was sure it would be surging with rainwater and runoff, but now it was quite dry. The trickle of water running through it would hardly quench the thirst of a potted plant, let alone an entire town. No wonder everything was made of dust. Taisce felt hollowed out himself. The sun overhead was brutal, worse than he had been expecting when they had first set out for town early this morning. It kicked off the high walls of the buildings in baking waves and the glare was like needles to his eyes. Why was this entire town built out of gleaming white stone?

Another wave of dizziness rocked him. The stranger put out a steadying hand, but Taisce sidestepped his grasp and ran into Finn instead. "Thank you for your assistance." His nod was meant to be a dismissal, but either it was missed or ignored. He strongly suspected the latter.

Their eyes met again and Taisce shivered. There was something terrifying and hungry and almost wonderful in that man's gaze. Like Taisce was a feast and he the only guest. All he needed was to be invited in.

After a moment, Taisce turned away. He had a task to complete. The sooner he did, the sooner he might return home. Back to his life. Back to the stability of a roof over his head and a meal awaiting him when he woke. The rigid structure of the day's business. Ledgers full of figures. That was what he needed. Not this man, no matter what his mouth and his eyes might promise.

"Come, Finn. We have business to attend to."

"Yes, my lord." There was a shuffle as Finn collected the pack that he'd dropped when Taisce fell. He shrugged it onto one shoulder.

"Best take care to stay out of the sun from now on... milord," the stranger said with a pointed pause. He swept a lazy bow, tipping his hat but not removing it. His eyes still held a slyness when he smiled. "I hope you find what it is that you seek."

Taisce stiffened, half turned already to depart. Was it so plain that he was seeking something? His curiosity got the better of him. "Have you come across a man by the name of Brenton? Rupert Brenton? He may have been... accompanied by a man and woman."

"When might this have been? If I'm permitted to ask, that is."

Taisce scowled at his impertinent tone and got a laughing smile in return. "He was seen heading in this direction three weeks ago."

The stranger whistled. "A long time. Very long indeed." He shrugged, looking away. "I can't say that I have heard of him, but I've been many places and met many people. After a while they run together unless I've some reason to remember them." He glanced at Taisce again, lingering on his eyes before his gaze drifted to his lips and then lower again.

Taisce felt a fresh wave of heat that had nothing to do with the sun. The man could not have made his intentions clearer had he spoken them aloud.

"Then I'll be on my way," Taisce said abruptly. "Thank you." He made a stiff bow to the man and turned on his heel. Bouncing off Finn yet again ruined his attempt at a dignified exit, but he told himself that it was better than staying and making a greater fool of himself.

Taisce's leg pulsed with pain like red fingers digging deep into the muscle whenever he put weight on it. He needed rest and the padding of a mattress beneath him, but the soft earthen floor of the nearby forest would have to suffice. It was the best accommodation he was likely to get until they'd made it to Clotsfield. If they headed that way. He'd seen no sign of the red haired thief since this morning so any hope of recovering his purse was dwindling.

His limp grew stronger, only exacerbated by the stranger's open regard. Taisce glanced back once, hoping that he was mistaken about being watched. But no, as he'd suspected, the man's unreadable eyes were still on him. Taisce straightened his coat and held his spine as straight as he was able even though it pulled at the muscles in his hip and down his thigh. He wouldn't be cowed by the man no matter how he looked. Or how he looked *at* him.

Beside him Finn grumbled. "Strange man." He had tossed more than a few looks of his own over his shoulder.

"Very."

They walked on in silence, cutting into a shadier street as soon as they were able and resting beneath the covered arch of a closed business. Taisce squinted through the boarded up window, but it was hard to tell what the place's function had been. Perhaps a tailor. He thought he spotted the ghost of a straw stuffed mannequin near the back wall.

"We'll have to try again tomorrow. For now, we'd best make our way back to the horses," Taisce said eventually. Hunger and nausea clawed at his stomach, and he still felt lightheaded. The day had been a disaster. His purse stolen. Swooning into the arms of a man whose name he didn't even know. The only thing worse would have been passing out full stop in the street and having to be carried away.

"What about food, my lord?" Finn asked hesitantly. He swiped the sweat from his brow with the back of his hand before catching Taisce's look. The next time he tugged out his handkerchief to mop at his forehead. It was a wasted effort. Sweat already streaked his shirt and plastered it to his broad back. Taisce plucked at his torn shirt collar. He was just as sticky with sweat. The layered fabric of his coat and waistcoat felt as tight as an over-cinched corset around his ribcage, constricting his lungs.

"We can find something in the forest surely. Berries or the like. Fish," he suggested. He fanned himself harder. If he were one of those dandies back home he could have had a fan on a beaded cord around his wrist. He envied them now. His hand alone hardly stirred the air.

"As you say, my lord." Finn sounded less than eager at the prospect. "Are you certain you can make it that far on foot?"

Taisce shot him a razor edged look. "I've told you already. I'm perfectly fine."

"But your leg—"

"Is none of your concern," Taisce said. "Let's go."

~~*

Sef hunkered in the alley nearby and smiled to himself. Milord wouldn't make it far in his current condition but he had spirit, misguided though it was. Sef admired that.

After they'd languished in the shade a while, the pair shuffled off again. It was clear from their attitudes that they hadn't found whatever answer they'd been seeking. No wonder. And coming to a border town like this without water or provision, it was asking for trouble. That was none of Sef's concern. He had no interest in teaching them the ways of the world. All he wanted was the answer to the question that had been his only companion for so many years. What was so special about this boy? Surely it wasn't just the beauty of his hair or his frowning lips. There were plenty of men with eyes like flashing gold coins. There had to be something else. Something deeper. If Sef had had any doubts they vanished the moment he had laid hands on him. There was something different in him. Something he couldn't name. Sef would find it even if he had to crack the boy open to do so.

He shadowed them through the streets at a safe distance. Sef had expected them to take lodging somewhere within Ciaran. It was clear they were exhausted. Instead they collected their horses from a stable on the edge of town and ambled off across the plains. The lord nearly fell from the saddle when he mounted but he regained his balance, sitting tall as they shrank into the distance. There was only one shelter in the area, a forest a few miles distant made up mostly of papery birches and tumbled rock.

Sef dug into his secondhand pockets and swore. He didn't even have a scrap of paper. But no matter.

He curled his hand into a loose fist and blew into it. A few whispered words and a press of power later a little beacon hovered in his palm. It shone with a thin blue light, a tiny flicker like a sputtering candle flame. Feeble. But it would suffice. He tossed it into the air where it tumbled about like a dust mote until he gave it another push to send it on its way. It would follow the departing pair as long as Sef needed, his guide in the event that they moved on. It was invisible to any without magic—the majority in this area—so he had little worry that it would be spotted and it was unlikely that anyone had felt it either. Such a small spell didn't make many waves. After this morning it was wise to be cautious. He preferred his neck just the way it was.

After the flame fluttered out of view, Sef turned back to the city. He'd never cared much for the place, but he might have to upgrade his opinion of it. It had brought him an unexpected treasure.

Sef perched on the curved wall that stretched around the city like a protective arm. It was little more than a blocky fence but it seemed to make the townspeople feel more secure all the same. Nothing of Ciaran extended outside the wall's embrace. Even the cobbled walk tapered off after a dozen steps, fading into the ground, rounded stones buried beneath the scrubby grass of the plain.

No. Sef didn't like the place at all. He longed for the jade green of tall, reed-like grass. The thorny vines and delicately colored roses of the gardens. He longed most of all for a tree with twisted branches and twisted roots, a tree big enough to swallow him body and soul.

He closed his eyes. He could almost smell the dew. But there wasn't anything for him now in the place he'd once called home. There wasn't anything there at all. His home had faded into so much less than legend. All of its grandeur stripped away. It was barely a bedtime story now and so was he.

He had no place in this world. No amount of screaming would cure him of his sickness. Waiting would not bring his peaceful end. He had tried and failed and tried again so many times that it hurt even to think of it. His past was an exposed wound, unhealed by time.

Let this be your downfall, she had said. And so it had been. Sef had fallen in all the ways it was possible to fall. He had hurt in all the ways he was able. Still there was no end to it. He had given up hope that there would ever be an end for him.

But now, this boy. He had poured hope back into his heart and Sef realized now how much he did not want it. To hope was even more painful than to wish for nothing at all. Even now he ached to follow the boy, to throw himself at his feet, and to crush him in his hands until Sef understood the meaning behind her words and the dreams that drove him mad with vague promises of release.

Iolan.

He should have known better than to love her. His family had warned him, his brothers counseled him. They had told him to stay away from her. But Iolan was clever and beautiful and she wanted him and that had been enough for Sef. They'd met at court, him the useless third son and she the comely stranger. Like something out of a children's tale. Even her hair as black as ebony, always in ringlets that caressed her cheeks, was like a story. Her beauty hid a wit as sharp as daggers. So very smart that she put him to shame.

Sef should have stayed away from her.

He stretched the stiffness from his muscles. He'd been a fool. He was *still* a fool. It couldn't be anything but foolish to set his hopes on a ridiculous young man with hair and eyes that glowed like precious metal.

Too bad he hadn't gotten the boy's name. There was so much Sef could do with a name. A few syllables could give the world if one knew how to ask properly. People were so careless with their names these days. They tossed them around like they were rubbish instead of hoarding them like the treasure they were. Once upon a time he had hoarded his own. Once he'd been a story so oft told that he'd heard his own name whispered around more than one campfire, told to warn off unwary travelers.

The soul stealer. The monster. That's what they used to call him.

It wasn't true. He had no use for others' souls when he could barely abide his own. He'd liked the stories though. They made him feel a little less alone. His stories lived on with him as long as they were told. His terrible twin.

But they spoke of him less and less now. One day even the stories would die and leave him.

Sef swiped the sweat from his brow and dropped from his perch on the wall.

This side of town was abandoned for the moment, but that wouldn't last. The hunters would return from the plains before the sun had set, the Guard would take up their posts as lookout, and the unscrupulous would stir from their hiding spots when night finally fell. Best he wasn't around when they did. He'd had enough trouble from Ciaran. Tomorrow he would leave it and, gods willing, never return.

~~*

Taisce groaned. No matter how he arranged himself or how he stretched, the ache in his leg remained. He'd been too hard on it today. Running was something best left to those who wouldn't have to regret it for days after. In the middle of the clearing, Finn crouched over the makings of a fire. It should have been started already but he'd been gone longer than expected, searching for anything edible to bring back to camp. In the end, he returned empty handed and Taisce added hunting to the list of things Finn was ill suited to.

The bright orange of sunset had already dribbled away, leaving the sky a wash of deepening purple. It was the most color he'd seen in days. Everything had turned to yellow and brown and white since they'd left the low lands. Taisce had never thought he would miss the marshes and the scattered villages of farmers, their sprawling fields of pale green crops waving as he passed.

A wave of homesickness hollowed his stomach. He missed Blume's network of streets with their dark cobbles and the narrow houses that huddled together like children sharing secrets. The air heavy with soot from a thousand chimneys. It was dirty and dark compared to Ciaran but it was home.

When he was young, he'd spent most of his time alone, wandering the streets of nearby Blume or the forest that bordered the family estate, learning every dip and curve of the earth, every secret hiding place. He'd enjoyed it. Finding something to call his own.

Then a broken leg and a string of feverish, bedridden months had put an end to his ability to freely wander, and responsibility had stolen the time when he might have tried anyway. At first he'd chafed at the tacked on studies, the hours spent at a desk, but in time he found new places to explore. There was an order and a fresh set of obstacles to overcome. He took to it easily once he saw it that way. Instead of reading shadowy crevices or the bark of trees, he read books. He learned how to move goods like they were chess pieces. He sorted business transactions, the tax on textiles, and the cost to rebuild their damaged chapel, numbers marching down ledger columns like ants returning to their hill. These were tasks that should have fallen to Rupert as the eldest but he was too busy to be taught. His mind and his nights were occupied with studies of a different nature. Magic had barely been legalized a year before Rupert latched onto it.

It was absolutely unheard of for a nobleman's son to take up the hobby. There were research societies of course, closed drawing rooms and private libraries for its followers, all of it very proper sounding on the surface. Magic might be technically legal once more but that couldn't change centuries of poor reputation. It was still a practice that drew the attention of only the most perverse scholars and the most unscrupulous of practitioners. Decent people knew to stay away. Magic was a poison. If it wasn't, it never would have been outlawed in the first place.

Taisce had warned Father that it would come to no good—Rupert was too easily led—but he hadn't listened. As expected. Father was willfully oblivious to Rupert's failings, to his weak character, and to the growing shadows in his eyes.

"He'll learn in time," Father had said. "A young man needs a taste of freedom before he can understand his responsibilities. And when he's ready you will be there to help him into his proper place."

The conversation had concluded with a slap on the back that jostled the wire-rimmed glasses on Taisce's nose. Father didn't even acknowledge Taisce's reluctant agreement before he'd thundered from the room.

But that hadn't been the end of it at all.

Rupert came home later and later, carrying strange books and bringing even stranger people. There were men in battered top hats and ladies wearing loops of clicking beads and charms around their necks. Their clothes were dark and loose as if made to cover more than just their person. They would sit up until all hours, lounging about the sitting room and talking in lowered voices whenever Taisce came near, following him with dark eyes as if they knew his thoughts. Other times they retired as one behind the locked door of Rupert's apartments. Taisce learned to mistrust them all quickly. They had no business in his house. They had no business dragging his brother into whatever strange games they were playing at.

One night he woke to find one of the men, a dashing sort with a well groomed mustache, and a lady he'd never set eyes upon perched at the foot of his bed. Drunk and confused probably. The dagger Taisce had begun keeping beneath his pillow was enough to keep the woman at bay. She scrambled backwards and nearly fell to the floor, curled hair flying around her, but the man looked at the blade in Taisce's hand and smiled. "I won't hurt you, lad." As he spoke, his eyes flickered with unnatural blue light despite the darkness of the room. He had paused on the edge of the bed, one leg bent to support him, the other foot still flat on the floor. He made no move to retreat. If anything, he leaned closer.

"Get out." Taisce pressed the tip of the dagger to the man's throat. Any harder and it would draw blood. Taisce had sharpened the blade himself just to be sure.

The dapper man's smile only grew at the obvious threat but he finally withdrew. "As you wish. Dreadfully sorry to have disturbed you." He waved a hand and the woman came to his side. They left arm in arm. Silent as ghosts. Just before the door closed behind them, the man turned back and bowed low, eyes on Taisce the entire time. Taisce's heart had pounded in his chest. He knew what lay in the depths of those eyes. But he would never stoop to sharing lovers with his brother, not even if the man had presented himself properly.

From then on, Taisce made sure to lock his door at night.

He saw the dapper man many more times and always the man would pause and tip his scuffed hat with its emerald green band. But he never said another word to him. Never approached him again.

And then one day, Taisce woke to find the house in a panic.

Rupert had disappeared in the night. He'd taken a few things, trinkets mostly, the leather bound journal he kept with him at all times, and a hefty sum of money which he referred to as his "inheritance" in the letter he left behind in explanation. There was no possibility of the letter being a forgery. It was definitely Rupert's extravagantly looping hand that slanted across the page. He never had learned to write in a straight line.

"How could this happen?" Father tore the letter in half and tossed the crumpled pieces at the servants that stood beside the door of the drawing room. In the corner of the room, mother had wilted a little further into the cushions of the chaise she sat on. She pulled her blanket around her as if its warmth could keep out the unwelcome news in the same way it chased off the chill. His sister Adeline had been the last to show. She had the misfortune of poking her head through the partially opened door just as their father launched into the rest of his tirade.

"Incompetents! Was no one watching him?" he yelled, looking everywhere at once until none of them were sure to whom he spoke. A vase filled with the last of the season's tulips was his next unfortunate target. He swept it to the floor with a crash, trampling the delicate bouquet beneath his boots and tracking the water over the polished wood floor. Mother flinched as if he'd trampled her along with her favorite flowers.

"What happened?" Adeline asked, sneaking up beside Taisce. Her large, wide-set eyes gave her a perpetually surprised look that was only accentuated by the current situation. Her auburn hair was already escaping its hasty braiding. She must have done it herself when she heard the noise.

Taisce guided her back into the hall and closed the door before he answered. "Rupert has run off."

He should have been surprised but he couldn't even pretend it. It had been years since he'd thought well of his older brother, but whatever his feelings, Taisce couldn't be happy about Rupert's disappearance. Until Father decided otherwise, Rupert was meant to be the head of the house, the heir, and he'd run into the night like a fugitive. It was shameful. At least if he'd done it for love—in the heat of some misguided romantic fantasy—then Taisce could have seen some sense in it. But Rupert was no romantic. He had made no secret of the fact that he was disinclined to marry.

"It makes no sense."

Adeline snorted. "He's probably run off with that man." She paused, brow furrowed in thought. "Norland. The dashing one with the wicked smile." She tossed off a smile of her own. It was far too knowing for a girl of sixteen.

Taisce hissed at her in horror. "Impossible."

"Don't pretend you haven't noticed him. Are you jealous?" Adeline raised an eyebrow.

"Hold your tongue. That man is not to be trusted. Tell me you haven't gotten too close to him." He was tempted to take her by the shoulders and shake her until sense returned to them all.

Adeline shook her head.

"Good. He's as corrupt as the rest of them. That's what magic does. That's why it's dangerous. Look what it's done to Rupert."

At that Adeline sobered. She shrank back into the girl he'd once had tea parties and traded ghost stories with. The wicked sparkle in her eye dimmed and she looked down. "Won't he come back? He has to come back, doesn't he?"

Taisce looked into her eyes and had no answer to give.

~~*

"My lord."

Taisce woke with a start. The sky was still the bruised purple of predawn. Too early to move on. Finn nudged him again with a gentle hand. Before Taisce could say a word, he noticed the finger pressed to Finn's lips.

"What is it?" Taisce mouthed. He wondered if Finn could even see him in the dark.

His answer was more obscure gesturing. When Taisce shook his head Finn finally spoke, albeit in a whisper. "Heard something." He pointed into the trees where there was another crackle of movement in the brush.

Taisce scrambled to his feet, though his leg seized up at the sudden movement. He almost tipped onto his face. Finn was already up, waiting on him, but he moved off towards the far end of the clearing immediately when Taisce waved him off. For such a large man he moved soundlessly. Like a specter. Taisce was not quite so successful but he managed to cut into the trees with only a little unnecessary noise.

The noise had come from somewhere further into the woods where the trees made a thick curtain. Careful of his footing, Taisce picked his way through the underbrush, trying to find a safe path among the rocks and roots in the darkness. He was no outdoorsman and it was hard to know if he was even headed in the right direction.

He spotted Finn ahead in the trees, hiding his mass behind a trunk too thin to truly conceal him, and closer: the source of the sound they'd heard. The doe was enormous and an unusual silvery white, larger and finer than any Taisce had ever seen with his own eyes. It would have been a prize worthy of celebration. The doe paused in its rambling and looked towards him. She stood tall, head raised at a proud angle. Beautiful. Black eyes stared into his before the doe bounded away into the trees.

Finn stepped from behind his tree, smiling and shrugging at his mistake as he turned back towards their camp. Taisce turned to do the same just as a shadow dashed through the nearby trees. He didn't see the blow coming. He saw only an explosion of stars as he toppled sideways.

CHAPTER FOUR
IN WHICH TAISCE SHOULD HAVE COME BETTER ARMED

Sef woke to a horrible pain in his head though he'd done nothing this time to deserve it. It pressed against the backs of his eyelids until he was sure his eyes bulged from their sockets. He dug the flat of his palm into his aching eyes but it did nothing to relieve the pressure. It didn't seem fair. He'd been an upstanding citizen since his escape from the gallows and this was how his head repaid him.

In the night, he'd rolled free of the burlap sacks he'd laid out as a makeshift bed. It was lucky then that he'd had the foresight to remove his new clothes. Brushing the dirt from his body was easier than cleaning a white shirt. Sirena would have his head if he dared ask her to wash it for him after only one day.

As if his thoughts had drawn her out, the door to the cellar swung in and Sirena appeared in the doorway carrying a sack in one hand, a wooden tray in the other. The tray was immediately more interesting, especially once he spied the biscuits piled on it.

"I see your time in the local jail has done nothing for your modesty," Sirena chuckled. She turned away from him but her gaze snuck back as Sef slipped into his trousers.

"You caught me unawares. I wasn't expecting visitors so soon," he said, wobbling on his feet and nearly falling into the dirt. Now that he was upright the horrible throbbing rhythm of pain had grown more insistent. It was quickly becoming an entire symphony. He felt along the back of his head but there was no sign of nocturnal injuries there. His hand came away clean. No sign of blood. He found only a smattering of cellar dirt.

"You're looking pale this morning." Sirena set the tray atop the crate he'd put in the center of the floor and left the sack beside it. "I've brought you some supplies for your journey."

"You're too good to me."

He started on his first biscuit while he shrugged on his shirt in the hopes that a bit of food would ease the shaking in his hands. It didn't. His whole body felt as though it was vibrating, eager to be moving.

"We'll miss having you here."

Sef shot her a surprised look. Then he laughed. "No, you won't. Ando will be glad to be rid of me."

Sirena answered him with a musical laugh of her own. It was the most beautiful thing about her. Her laugh was as gentle as the tinkling of bells. Sef closed his eyes. He'd often thought he could have fallen in love with her on the basis of her laugh alone. So few laughed with her abandon. He would be sad to do without it.

"Perhaps I'll come back someday," Sef said. "Since you won't tell me the recipe for your biscuits."

She shook her head with mock sternness. "It's a family secret. You know that. I'm sworn to protect it with my life. Besides, you have no oven of your own. Perhaps if you did..."

Sef looked down at his hands. He'd finished his biscuit and crushed the second to crumbs in his fist. He let the crumbs fall to the floor and brushed his hand off on his leg. "I had best be going." His gaze again fell on the sack she'd brought for him. "And what's in there?"

"Provisions. Food, mostly. I thought it might keep you from a cell for a few weeks at least if you're careful."

Sef saw what she meant when he pulled open the flap on the rough sack. Inside was a parcel of fruit, a small loaf of bread still warm from the oven, and beneath that a smaller leather purse. He could tell by the weight of it that it was filled with coins. "This is too much."

"Hush. Ando doesn't know it's there." She pressed her lips together and for a moment she looked like the woman she would become in twenty years. Old, wise, and achingly kind. Sef looked away.

He closed his hand around the purse, squeezing until it hurt. From anyone else he would have taken it without comment. He wished he could turn it down, hand the purse back to her and be on his way, so she might think better of him once he'd gone, but he'd learned to accept kindness wherever it was offered. It was always a rare occurrence. So he bowed his head and dropped the purse back into the sack, its weight dragging it back beneath his other provisions. He saw now that she'd tied each bundle with colorful ribbon. It was a very Sirena touch. "Thank you."

He paused before wrapping Sirena in a weak hug. With any luck he would not see her again. It made him quicker to turn away. Lingering had never done him any good. Then he slipped out the door. The sky had barely been touched by light and was still dark as a fresh bruise.

So early in the morning Ciaran had a deceptively placid look, like still water hiding a deadly beast. The back alley dealers were sleeping off last night's activity, the white cobbles were free from the clatter of hooves and boot heels, and the air hung with the light scent of fresh baked bread and morning sweets. In the morning, Ciaran was almost beautiful.

Sef looked up at the narrow windows of the squat, two story buildings. They had a certain charm unlike anything he'd seen further south. This was one of the last generally respectable towns for quite a while. The battered robin's-egg blue paneling of *The Stallion*'s door stood out against the rest of the stark white buildings. He gave it a nod before he turned left towards the shortest path out of town. He kept on nodding to every building as he passed, and even that infernal canal, saying his farewells. This could well be his last chance to make peace with the place.

It had nearly gotten him hanged, but if it had led him to his fondest wish he would bear it no ill will.

He glanced down into the canal. It was full of long shadows this time instead of water. He grumbled and pressed his thumbs to his eyes. The pressure in them had lessened but the pain still lingered, spreading through his head and seeping down his spine. A voice whispered in his ears, a far off echo.

"Oh bugger."

He knew that voice, maybe not as well as he hoped to, but he knew it, and he knew then what the pain in his head might mean. He ran.

His sack of provisions banged against his side, probably turning to mush already, but he paid it no mind. He'd been foolish to waste so much time dawdling this morning.

Behind him a Guard called out but Sef ignored his cries. "It's always the Guards at the worst time." When the Guard yelled again, Sef swatted him like the insect he was. It took more concentration to knock the man backwards than it normally would have and it made Sef's head ache worse but he couldn't have anyone following him through town and calling more attention. The Guard bounced over the cobbles like a skipping stone on a pond. It might have been amusing on any other day.

Sef kept running. By the time he sighted the city wall he was in such a frenzy that he nearly forgot to steal a horse.

~~*

Taisce hit the ground hard, whole constellations of stars bursting before his eyes. The surprise stunned him as much as the blow had.

"Get the big one." The voice belonged to a woman but it was impossible to see which of his attackers had spoken when Taisce's head was in the dirt.

He tried to rise. Before he'd gotten more than a few inches between him and the ground he was pressed back down by the weight of a foot on his spine.

"Hold it there, my rich darling," said the same voice that had spoken a moment ago.

From deeper in the trees there was a cry and a crash loud enough to be a falling tree. That would be Finn then. Taisce scowled. Father had sent him as protector and assistant but so far the man was proving to be positively useless.

Taisce tried again to lift his head, spitting grit out of his mouth. "Who are you? What is it that you want?"

A chorus of laughter rose up around them. The sound was higher than he would have expected from the band of brigands. All women. The knowledge did him little good. With their numbers it didn't matter who or what they were. He was sorely outmatched. Taisce turned his head to the side, resigned to leaving his cheek pressed against the forest floor. His new vantage point only offered a view of booted feet and the forest of legs surrounding him. As he watched, two sets of legs broke off from the group and headed back the way he had come.

Camp.

"More thieves," Taisce spit. The word was quickly becoming one of his least favorite. "I should have known."

"If you were smart you would have stayed away. You stink of money," said the woman, obviously the leader. She was the only one who had said a word yet. Her voice was low and pleasantly accented, her diction almost too precise for a low life. He'd expected them to speak as they did in novels, in broken phrases and sneers. Yet another assumption proven incorrect.

"We have no more money. You're wasting your time here," Taisce said, displeased at his sad state as much as at having to admit it. And to a thief of all people. He didn't know how much worse his situation could become but at least there was no one else to witness it.

Another round of laughter went up among the assembled thieves. The leader ground her heel into the small of Taisce's back until he winced. "See, that's where you're wrong. *You* may not have money as you say. But there must be others who would pay handsomely to keep you in one piece."

"Got it!" called another voice. There was a rustle of fabric and papers as they dumped the contents of his pack into the dirt. His books, his folded shirts, everything fluttered out in an untidy pile. A thief crouched beside it still holding his emptied pack in one hand. He would have recognized that mass of impossibly red hair anywhere—the thief from the market.

"You!" He struggled to rise up on his elbows.

The leader stomped down, slamming him back into the dirt. "You'll stay still if you know what's good for you. I would much rather collect on you while you're breathing but I'll make an exception if you give us too much trouble." She slid her foot up to rest between his shoulder blades. The toe of her boot pressed against the base of his skull.

He bit his lip to keep his retorts inside. Until he was sure of their intentions he would pretend to be docile. This was no time to be hasty.

Rough hands pawed through his papers and the book from Adeline. They'd even riffled through his clothing before they were through. Finally the red haired thief whooped and held something aloft. "We've got a winner."

Taisce didn't need to see it to know what it was. He could picture it clearly. The thick gold band of his signet ring. The face carved with a wreath of reedy leaves and a hippocampus with its tiny equine head tossing and a curved tail in miniature. He had only the one ring and he'd hidden it in a small pouch in the bottom of his pack.

"Give it here," the leader ordered. As she inspected the ring, she hummed quietly to herself. "I'm not familiar with this house. Where are you from, my boy? It can't be around here."

"What does it matter? You'll get nothing from my

family. I've run away," he added, thinking quickly. "They've disowned me."

The leader tutted. "You're a poor liar." She gouged the squared heel of her boot into his back again.

"I'm not lying! Why would I be here, in this miserable place, if I had anywhere *better* to go?" It wasn't difficult to infuse his tone with the proper level of scorn. It was no less than what he truly felt.

"Boy's got a point," said another of the thieves.

There was a long silence while they considered his words and every second that ticked by made him itch to take action. They hadn't bothered to take his knife from him. He could surprise the leader and perhaps buy himself enough time to escape. But where was Finn? Had they left him where he fell or dragged him off somewhere? Taisce had heard nothing from him since they had been attacked. There was no way that Taisce could carry him if Finn was injured and he wouldn't even consider the possibility that they'd done worse to him. If he couldn't locate Finn quickly, Taisce would have to escape alone. Perhaps he could come back for him later. His mind sped through the options, putting pieces in order, plotting his course through the woods. Ciaran was certainly out. He would have to head farther north. But the horses... He didn't want to abandon them either.

"Hey!" Another of the thieves jabbed him in the side with the staff she carried. "She asked you a question."

"What?"

"I guess nobility doesn't mean what it used to," the leader chuckled, "but this one may still prove useful." She leaned down to be sure she had his full attention. It was a struggle to breathe beneath the added weight of her boot bearing down on him. "Name your house."

Taisce hesitated. He could lie, it would be easy enough, but his proper name was there in his papers if they troubled themselves to look. He glared at the ground beneath him. "Brenton."

She repeated it thoughtfully. With each repetition her foot tapped against his skull. He could almost feel the moment the pieces clicked together for her. "Well, well, well. The wayward son has graced us with his presence this day! How very fortunate. I've heard about you, first son. You're younger than I pictured. Prettier. I was expecting something a little less haughty."

A murmur went up around them.

"Show us a trick!" cried one of the assembled women. She was quickly joined by her fellows.

Taisce stilled. They knew of Rupert. They knew of his travels and his obscene interests, perhaps even more than that, but he'd trapped himself with his lie. Asking more risked giving away his true identity. But he had to. He had to.

"What do you know of me?" He stumbled over the question. Never before had he wished to be Rupert and he didn't like pretending to be him now.

"We know you're a fool!" called out one of the thieves that circled him but the leader shushed her.

"Though she's not far afield. Only a fool would go chasing after bedtime stories."

"I don't know what you're talking about," Taisce barked. "I don't chase stories."

The leader laughed, a hearty chortle that had her leaning even harder on him. Much more and he might smother. "Our young prince is a schoolboy after all. He believes in demons and their treasure. Does he also believe the sprites leave coins beneath the pillows of obedient children?" She spurred him with her heel, all humor dried up. "Or perhaps he's not who he says. Where are your traveling companions, lordling? You travel with only one man, by the looks of him a servant. Where are your fine companions?"

"Gone."

"'Gone' he says. I don't believe that, do you, girls? Who would give up such fine bait? I think we've caught ourselves a liar instead of a lordling. Mayhap you stole the ring from the real one."

There were noises of agreement from the others and she seemed to be enjoying playing for her crowd. Taisce tensed, waiting until her weight shifted. He rolled then, grabbing the leader by the foot she'd held him down with and wrenching her legs out from beneath her. His dagger was in hand before she hit the ground. He pressed it to her throat.

Now that Taisce was in a position to notice, he could see how much older she was than the others in the clearing. Most of the other women looked to be about his age or younger but her skin was leathery from exposure and a life of labor, pale eyes outlined with black kohl, silver streaked, brown hair pulled back into a thick braid. Once upon a time maybe she'd been beautiful but the marble hardness in her eyes made it difficult to tell. All he saw now was stone.

"This blade is perfectly sharp. If you try anything I could send you on to the next life with no trouble," Taisce said, focusing on the silver edge of his dagger.

She smiled up at Taisce and the assurance in it made him feel like his blade was pointed back at him. "You could try it, my boy. But you won't."

"How do you know?" He glanced up at the red haired thief still holding his pack. "I'll thank you to put my things back in order." Then he wrenched his ring from the leader's fingers and pocketed it.

"If you were going to, you would have already," she said. Her smile cooled until it matched the icy light in her eyes. "You seem like a practical lad. I can see the books about you. So tell me... how likely is it you'll reach safety before one of us catches you?"

She gave him a moment to consider it but he didn't need it. Taisce had seen eyes like hers before but never on a human. Father had taken them to a circus once when they were children. Rupert found it thrilling. He'd shouted along with the rest of the crowd, cheering at the antics of the painted clowns and the acrobats. Taisce didn't. It was all theatrics. He knew that clearly even at such a young age. There was no danger. Each thrill was manufactured. But when the lion tamer appeared, Taisce was terrified.

The tamer was merely another actor, repeating a meaningless script. But the lion... Taisce looked into its eyes, he saw its sharp teeth, and he understood. The lion tamer had no control. He had not tamed the beast. He never would. One day the beast would tear him apart.

Those were the same eyes looking at him now.

"It's too bad you're of no use to us after all *and* a liar to boot, but you've been more entertaining than I expected, lad, so I'll do you this favor. I'll give you a sporting chance," said the leader. "Run."

He did.

Taisce kept his dagger in hand, using it to slice aside the thinner brush as he passed. Finn wasn't where he'd expected to find him, where he had last seen him in the clearing with the white doe. At the time, Taisce had thought it was a happy omen. Now he was not so sure. Behind him the thieves made a racket in the trees. They urged him on with cries and the stomping of feet. "Hide yourself well, little prince," bellowed the leader. "We want this hunt to last."

The glee in her voice was chilling.

He ran, playing his role as fox well despite the ache in his leg. Once he'd run faster than the wind. He remembered it like a dream. Now his gait was clumsier but it was enough for him to keep moving over rocks and under tree branches, putting distance between him and his pursuers. He looked up into the thin arms of the trees. There would be no asylum there. Even if the birches would hold his weight he would be spotted straight away.

His gaze swept the forest. The terrain was unhelpfully sparse. No caves, no fallen trees offering temporary shelter. His horse would have made escape easier but there hadn't been time to circle all the way back to camp and collect it. Someone had undoubtedly been posted there to stop him. All he needed was a place to hide, something to cover his trail until they moved on.

He headed towards the stream he and Finn had passed the day before. The trees were thinner there, more scrub and rocks than lush greenery. He stumbled in the brush, tumbling end over end into a narrow ravine clogged with leaves and water smoothed rocks to break his fall. He lay stunned, looking up through the lacy canopy of leaves and branches. The sky was a pale, humorless blue. No clouds. No birds. He had missed the rising of the sun.

The silence made it easy to pick out the growing sounds of pursuit.

Taisce scrambled back to his feet. *Keep going. Move faster*, he thought, willing his body to make it so.

He kept to the side of the ravine, hoping the overhanging bank would shield him from their search. Rocks slid beneath his feet and his progress dwindled to a crawl as he tried to keep his balance on the uneven ground.

A shower of gravel rained down on him when they reached the bank above. "Yoohoo!" called one of the thieves. She tossed down a large rock. It could easily have cracked his head if Taisce hadn't avoided it.

Behind him, another thief slid down the bank. Her descent was much more graceful than his had been. She slid on her heels, bringing pebbles and loose dirt with her like a wave. In her wake came another, the woman with the staff. She held it aloft, pointing at him with the carved head as if marking him. Taisce turned away and kept going. His grip tightened on his dagger. He might be forced to use it soon.

A shrill whistle sounded as an avalanche of rocks began ahead of him. He scrambled up the opposite bank to avoid it. Wisely it seemed. More of the thieves had dropped into the ravine in an effort to flank him. That made five of them at least. He couldn't remember how many there had been in the clearing. Everything had happened so quickly. Had there been six? Seven? More? He didn't know.

As if in answer, something flew past his shoulder and lodged in a tree ahead of him. He barely glanced at it. Another knife flashed past, catching his opposite sleeve. He dodged left to avoid another attack if it came and headed deeper into the trees.

They were herding him like an animal to slaughter. The cackling laughter behind him was proof enough of their intent. He was running as fast as he could but his limp was only intensifying as his leg cramped. They could have caught him already if they'd wished it. He growled. If they meant to kill him there was no need to taunt him this way. Glancing behind, he found his hunters had disappeared again, drawing back into the trees like specters. He entertained no delusion that they might retreat and leave him be. They would show themselves again. He needed to hide before they did.

He climbed up the next hill, leaves clinging to his damp clothing and boots, and almost rolled down the other side. Pride was the only thing keeping him upright but despite it he would be crawling on hands and knees if he didn't rest soon. He lunged at the first cover he found. A tangle of vines and dried grasses with a fallen tree making a partial roof over it. It wasn't much but he'd found nothing better. He crawled beneath it. The vines tugged at his clothes and caught in his unbound hair.

No sooner had he hidden than the sound of running steps met his ears. Taisce curled his body in tight, dagger at the ready. They shuffled through the leaves, beating at the saplings and bushes with sticks and stomping their feet as if he were a rabbit that could be made to bolt. The group moved closer. Taisce closed his eyes. When they passed by, he held his breath, ears straining for the sound of attack. But they passed and the forest fell silent again. He waited.

An ill-timed snicker gave them away.

Taisce scrambled for freedom, catching himself on the whip-like branches of the small plants ringing his hiding spot, just as a hand reached through the vines. The first grab missed him, instead snagging his torn collar. He wasn't so lucky the second time. Five fingers buried themselves in his hair, blunt nails scraping his scalp like talons. They tore him free, bringing vines and leaves with him. The woman with the staff blocked each of his wild swings. The carved head of her staff came down across his knuckles and his knife dropped into the dirt. Taisce cradled his throbbing hand to his chest. He could barely even feel his fingers.

Another stinging rap from the staff sent Taisce to his knees. With the fist in his hair and one on his uninjured arm for leverage, the second thief held him there. They whistled for the others.

The leader only took a moment to appear. As she cut through the trees, she flashed him a pleased smile. "You were an adequate fox. We could use entertainment like you more often."

"Let's keep him," said one of the thieves at his back but the leader shook her head.

"Someone may come looking for him even if he is a fake. Best that we're elsewhere when they do."

"You really mean to kill me?" The words slipped from his mouth before he could stop them. Saying them made it feel real in a way that it hadn't before. Fear squeezed his lungs.

His question seemed to amuse her. "Did you expect us to invite you to table for tea? I would much prefer the money to accompany your safe return, but I don't believe in unnecessary risks. You could be who you say you are or you could have stolen that ring and that name. I can't chance it but if it's any consolation to you, my fraudulent lordling, I am a little sorry it comes to this."

"It isn't."

84

"I suspected as much." She gave him another smile, bigger than the last, and shrugged. The knife she pulled from her belt was longer than seemed practically necessary, Taisce noticed, and had a strange curve to the blade. He disliked it immediately, liked it even less as she approached him with it. He leaned backwards, into the hands that held him, as far as he was able, in an effort to put more distance between him and that knife.

Taisce fought for words. He wouldn't plead for his life so they could laugh at him. He wouldn't. He bit his lip, eyes on the knife.

Something moved in the trees and the thieves froze. The leader looked past him and the smile fell from her face, replaced by something else entirely.

"What have we here?" asked the newcomer. He led his horse into the circle of thieves as if it were the most natural thing. Taisce could barely see his face, shadowed by that same silly hat, but he recognized the voice immediately. The man dropped to the ground, guiding his horse the last few steps of the way. He barely glanced at the weapons pointed in his direction before his gaze settled on Taisce. "You again." He tipped his hat.

Taisce struggled against the hands holding him down, embarrassment at being caught this way staining his cheeks a burning red. He dropped his eyes. There was no reason to expect he would help.

"It seems I've interrupted something." The man chuckled. Taisce didn't have to look up to know the comment was addressed at him. Taisce could feel the heat of his eyes.

~~*

Sef patted a hand along his stolen horse's neck as his gaze skimmed over the collected thieves before him. They stared back with open distrust, gaze shifting away as he met it but never leaving entirely.

They held the boy in the middle of their loosely formed circle. His long hair flew about his shoulders and dirt smudged his cheeks, his forehead. He was panting with exertion, shirt stretched tight over sweat slick skin, and pulse throbbing in his exposed neck. A cornered animal. Sef licked his lips. The boy was truly beautiful. For an instant, Sef was glad of the time it had taken to reach them but another moment and he might have been too late. At that thought, he turned on Selma, their wretched leader, and saw her jump. He remembered her well, though she'd been years younger when last they'd met. And if he remembered rightly he'd given her the scar that peeked from beneath her collar. From the look in her eyes, he was correct. He'd expected never to see her again after that, had hoped it really. Too many questions. Too many loose ends. Yet here she was, in his way once more. Her mouth drifted open and a single word fell out. "Young."

Sef showed his teeth in a smile. "What was that, my dear? I couldn't quite hear you."

He held her pale eyes with his. A shock of anger ran through him, lifting every hair on his body, and he knew by the way she blanched and took an almost imperceptible step backwards that his eyes had flickered. If the others in her group had seen it they gave no sign.

"Nothing at all," said Selma. She produced a smile full of bravado for him and sheathed her knife. "We've finished here." Her eyes slipped sideways and she gave a jerk of her head at the young man on the ground. The hands holding him sprang free as if he'd suddenly grown hot as the sun and they stepped away, retreating into the protection of their group.

Sef's prize wobbled to his feet, favoring his leg, and quickly propped himself against a nearby tree to watch the proceedings with careful eyes.

Selma cast another look at him, brow furrowing. "Perhaps we'll meet again, lordling. Another day. We'll finish our game then." She gave a flippant salute before the thieves turned and disappeared into the woods.

Sef turned back to his prize. The young man drew back against the tree trunk like he meant to shrink right into it. He studied Sef as if he were a specimen, running his eyes over every inch of him. Sef let him take his measure again. He didn't mind the touch of those wary eyes. Not at all. They recognized him but only as a new oddity, not in the way that Sef had first feared. Finally the boy's attention dropped to the ground, searching. A knife lay in the dirt inches from Sef's foot, half buried beneath the leaves. It was finely crafted, with inlaid stones in yellow and red, almost as fine as one Sef used to own himself. The blade was a welcome weight in Sef's hand when he picked it out of the dirt and, for a moment, he was tempted to test its edge on himself. But it was unwise with his young lord still watching.

Sef presented the dagger with a bow. "You'll be wanting this I expect," he said. He met the boy's eyes once more. The look in them was different than it had been yesterday, filled with mistrust, but finally he reached out and snatched the knife from Sef's hand.

"Thank you," he said in a voice so faint it could have been the wind in the trees.

"Are you hurt?"

"I'm fine. Thank you."

It was an obvious lie. Sef knew the sound of pain when he heard it. He gave the boy's leg a pointed stare. Only a day ago he'd been limping about town and they both knew it. There was no sign of blood. An old injury, Sef suspected.

In answer to the unspoken challenge, the boy stiffened. "It's nothing." Then he shook his head. "They were afraid of you."

It wasn't a question. A question would have been easier to deflect. Sef's smile turned into a chuckle. "I'm just a traveler. I don't even carry weapons." He held out his arms in demonstration. There were no hidden pockets to conceal weapons. No coat to secrete them. He was even without a waistcoat, a problem he would soon fix. Sef missed the feel of a well fitted silk waistcoat. He wanted to end things well dressed. "So you see? I'm completely harmless."

"They intended to kill me," the boy insisted.

"Unlikely. There's much better money to be had in kidnapping. No one pays for a rotting corpse," Sef said. A moment too late he realized his mistake. The boy went almost as pale as Selma had been earlier. Another fright and he was liable to bolt. Not that he would get far when he was already exhausted. "Where's your large friend?"

Gold eyes widening, the boy shook his head. "I don't know."

"What's your name?"

The question earned Sef another look, haughtier this time.

"You've got one, haven't you?"

"Of course I have." Sef waited patiently for his answer to arrive. Eventually it did. "Taisce."

Sef nodded, testing the sound of it on his tongue. It fit well. He held his hat to his chest as he swept into a low bow. "You're welcome to call me Sef. Levregne."

He'd wondered if the name would spark the recognition that his face did not, but he was disappointed. Taisce looked at him the same as he had before: with something between fear and disdain. It was an interesting combination.

"And where are you from?" Sef asked, curious despite himself. He set his hip against a warped tree and folded his arms. "Surely not from around here. You're much too pale."

Taisce glanced at his muddied hands before dusting them on his equally dirty trousers. It did no good but the attempt seemed to make him feel better.

Then he set to rooting about in his pocket. When he'd found what he sought, he slipped it onto his finger with a sigh. A gold ring. Sef itched to inspect the crest on it. "I'm traveling to Clotsfield."

Sef scowled, wiping it away quickly and replacing it with a smile. "What a happy coincidence. So am I," he said. "But first, perhaps we should find your friend?"

Taisce said nothing. His expression was as blank as a slate, giving nothing away. In the silence, Sef considered how best to persuade or, if necessary, force the boy to accept his help. But in the end it wasn't necessary.

Taisce nodded and turned with an abruptness that left Sef scrambling to keep up. The boy loped unsteadily through the brush. It was a wonder he could move at all, let alone at such speed.

"Hold up," Sef called.

"What is it?"

"I have a horse," Sef said, pointing at the animal in question, "and it's clear you can barely walk. It pains me just to watch you. Get in the saddle."

Sef expected an argument and again he was surprised. "Very well," Taisce said, somehow making it sound as though he was doing Sef a favor by accepting. He trudged back, eyes avoiding Sef's as he boosted himself onto the horse's back. Without another word, he set off, again leaving Sef to catch up.

"You're welcome," Sef muttered but if he was heard there was no sign.

CHAPTER FIVE
IN WHICH SEF IS AN UNWELCOME TRAVEL COMPANION

After an initial burst of nervous speed, Taisce let the horse keep its own pace, guiding it back the way he had come before. It seemed much farther now that he wasn't fleeing like a game animal. Had he really run so far? But his leg insisted that he had and he was not one to argue with it.

He shifted in the saddle and glanced back. Sef walked with a silent grace that made him seem more phantasm than flesh and blood. His hair was cut into a neat style better suited to a dandy than the tradesman his clothes suggested he was. He didn't speak like a common man, didn't act like one. His manner was rough, true, but he was educated and he stood tall. Proudly even. And somehow Sef had managed to frighten away a group of thieves without using a single weapon.

Sef's eyes rose at his inspection and Taisce turned away. Sef might be a mystery but the smiles he shot Taisce were easy enough to decipher. It wasn't the first time a man, or a woman for that matter, had looked at Taisce that way. He was not a fool. Sef wished to bed him. The only thing that remained to be seen was whether Taisce desired the same thing.

"It's just ahead," Taisce said. He spurred the horse on, scattering his thoughts beneath its hooves. This was not the time. Finn was missing and they were still two days' ride from assistance. His only thread leading to Rupert had frayed and split. Not one person in Ciaran had had any information to offer. The closest he'd come had been the thieves' unwitting assistance. If things remained this way, Taisce would be forced to return home to Blume a failure, goal unreached. He couldn't let that happen.

They broke through the line of trees into the clearing where he'd last seen Finn and found the place empty and unremarkable. Taisce slid to the ground. He was no tracker but perhaps Finn was still nearby. He swept the perimeter of the area, looking for clues, but everything looked the same to him.

A shadow fell over his shoulder as Sef came to his side. "Your friend is not here," he said simply. Then his eyes shifted along some unseen path. He pointed. "He was taken that way but I doubt they went very far. That much dead weight would be impossible to bear long."

"Dead weight?" Taisce echoed.

"He was unconscious. They dragged him."

Taisce looked in the direction Sef pointed and frowned. In this, he was at Sef's mercy. He wasn't sure it was a position he wished to be in. "Can you find him?"

"It's possible."

Taisce turned on him. "What does that mean?" he demanded.

His answer was another of those disconcerting smiles. Sef cocked his head to the side. "It means I'll require payment. Milord." As the title rolled off his tongue, Sef tipped his hat in a salute.

His smile held no trace of irony or humor. If anything it was the rudest excuse for a smile that Taisce had ever seen. Taisce bit down on the many retorts that sprang to mind. At least this was familiar territory. The exchange of goods and services, bartering, these were things he understood. "Very well, if your requests are reasonable. But you don't see a croy until we've reached our destination."

Sef raised his eyebrows. "All the way to Clotsfield, hmm? And what's to stop you from knocking me upside the head in the night and running out on your debt?"

"I'm a man of my word."

"We'll see the truth in that," Sef said. Something clouded his previously merry expression but he nodded. "Gather your things then. Let's see if we can't locate your ineffective bodyguard."

~~*

They swept the clearing together, gathering the scattered supplies from Taisce's pack. He dropped to the ground to replace everything, organizing it with a care born of hesitation more than necessity. Perhaps he had been too hasty in accepting Sef's help. What did he know of the man aside from his flirtatious eyes? Ciaran was a dangerous place.

"Second thoughts?" Sef asked.

Taisce kept his face carefully blank. "No."

"Your leg bothering you then?" He nodded at Taisce's leg stretched awkwardly out in front of him.

The ache had set in fully while Taisce fiddled with his papers and trinkets but it was no business of anyone else's. "It's fine." He shoved the last of his things into the bag, closed the flap, and cinched it tight.

"I could soothe it for you," Sef offered as suddenly as he'd said everything else. "Temporarily at least."

"And what would *that* cost me?" Taisce fired back just as quickly. He pressed a hand to the tree he'd been sitting against, using it as a crutch to stand. He slung the bag over his shoulder. "I doubt you have any medical supplies in that sack of yours. What could you possibly do?"

Sef laughed and held out a hand. With a whispered chant, his outstretched fingers burst into transparent blue flame. He squeezed the fire into his palm, extinguishing it with a hiss. "I can do plenty."

"Magic," snorted Taisce. "I should have known."

"What's that?"

"Magic is for vagrants and liars. Our deal is off. I'll find Finn myself. Good day." Taisce turned on his heel and wobbled back towards camp and his waiting horse. He'd spoken the truth—he wanted no part in any magical trickery—but he winced all the same. If Finn was still in danger, Taisce had no idea how he would find him. Or how he would free him if it came to that.

When he reached their rough camp, he found another surprise. Finn's horse had been taken.

The thieves? Taisce shook his head. No. They would have taken Taisce's horse first. It was by far the finer and, anyway, why take one horse when they could have both? It had to have been Finn. Taisce peered into the trees hoping to make out a trail, broken branches, something, that would point him towards Finn. He wished he had paid better attention during those hunting trips of his youth. He could have used some measure of tracking skill right then.

"You're brave to turn your back so carelessly on a vagrant such as myself, milord," called Sef. He sauntered up, following his words through the forest. He glanced around the abandoned camp. "I suspected as much. You two are an awkward traveling pair, aren't you? He's gone after you already. We must have passed him in the forest."

"I retracted my request for assistance. Leave me be."

"For a noble, you're also lacking in manners. We have the same destination; we might as well travel together. There is safety in numbers, especially for you. I may even reconsider the price of my services."

"I will find my own way."

"Do you even know the *way* to Clotsfield, milord?" Sef asked. He faced Taisce's jittering horse, smoothing a hand over its neck and giving it a gentle pat. "You're a lovely beast, aren't you?"

Face burning, Taisce trudged back to his horse and pulled the reins from Sef's fingers. He *didn't* know the way. He'd plotted their course on a map weeks ago but Clotsfield was never meant to be included in their journey. If not for that damned thief...

They'd only had word of Rupert from as far south as Ciaran and Taisce had entertained the hope that his brother would still be there when he arrived. Maybe after some careful thought, Rupert would have reconsidered his sudden abdication of duty. A part of Taisce had hoped it would be that easy, that they would talk amiably for once and Rupert would turn away from magic and come home without a fight. He had imagined Rupert taking up his place in the family, the one that Taisce had been filling for years while his brother wasted his life in magic and debauchery. That was the goal that he had kept at the fore while they traveled. It had gotten him this far.

But an even deeper part of Taisce had expected it would not be so simple. That part had been resigned to never seeing his brother again and, really, wouldn't that be for the best? Taisce had been running much of their family's business all these years, ever since he was fourteen. He had negotiated trades and settled disputes. He was better suited to the task than he had any reason to expect Rupert would be. Rupert had no head for figures, no patience for diplomacy. An unhappy portion of

Taisce's heart wished to give up the search altogether. Let his brother remain lost if that was what he wished. It would be best for all concerned. But pride spurred him on. This task was more important than any other Father had ever entrusted him with. It would be his proving point. He would not fail at it.

The only path left to him was Clotsfield and the hope that Finn would think to follow him there. After that... he would think of some new way to divine Rupert's hiding place. Whatever it took, he would do it.

"I can find my own way," Taisce repeated coldly.

"Do you have any provisions at all?"

Taisce wouldn't dignify that with an answer. He struggled into the saddle. He had an excellent knowledge of edible berries and other things for which he could forage in the woods. That would serve him well enough until he made town and found father's men. Brannigan and Felix, Finn had called them. Surely they would resupply him.

~~*

Sef let Taisce ride ahead in momentary triumph. He was caught between irritation and a begrudging admiration for the boy's audacity. He was a proud one, even with his long hair tangled and his face smudged with dirt, even fresh from danger. He didn't even know how much danger surrounded him. Without someone to guard his unwary head, Taisce was sure to get himself killed and between the two of them, Sef would prefer to be the one doing the dying.

Of course for that, he suspected he would need the stubborn boy. The feeling grew within Sef the longer he spent around him. There was something about Taisce. Not his looks, though they were undeniably pleasant. Sef could have found twenty people who were better looking, without that pinched expression of disdain that Taisce seemed to wear whenever he saw him. So it certainly wasn't the boy's looks that drew Sef. It wasn't even the unusual color of his eyes. Those gold eyes had sparked his interest but they weren't what kept it.

That was more difficult to put into words. Sef could hardly approach him without feeling like he'd been set ablaze. As though a lantern glowed within Sef's chest. He'd lived so long, but he couldn't remember ever feeling this way, so alive. The thought startled a chuckle out of him. If all went right, this man, this boy, who made Sef thrum with energy would be the one to undo him. Maybe it was fitting. Iolan was not without her wicked sense of humor.

It was an interesting question. Had she planned this? It didn't seem possible. She was a first rate seer but surely seeing so far past her own death was beyond even her capabilities.

Sef had spent years studying her curse, picking it apart from every direction, trying to unravel its hidden meanings but it was for nothing. After a while he became convinced that she had meant only to tease him, to give him hope where there was none.

But perhaps this meant Iolan had more tricks than even she knew.

He set off after Taisce. With the boy out of sight, he felt ill at ease, as if someone might steal him away once more. He wouldn't allow it. Not now. If it meant following him to the ends of the world Sef would do it. He would do anything if it meant getting what he wanted.

Sef's heart was pounding with anxiety by the time he finally spotted Taisce again through the cover of trees. He must have ridden ahead at a hearty pace to have gotten so far. At least Taisce seemed to have some sense of direction. Sef had no desire to herd the boy the entire way to Clotsfield.

Taisce flung a glare over his shoulder, face dark with anger when he heard Sef coming up behind him. "Don't follow me."

"I've told you already. Clotsfield is my destination as well." It was a lie, but the boy didn't need to know that.

"Then take another path to get there."

"Are you always so unfriendly with your acquaintances? It may have escaped your attention, milord, but this is not your land and I am free to come and go as I please. Unless you plan to use that dagger of yours, I believe you're stuck with me."

The next look Taisce aimed at him was baffled as much as angry but he didn't say another word. Instead he spurred his horse down the trail a little faster.

Sef didn't mind. It left him free to follow in silence

and he had no objection to studying Taisce's silent back while they traveled. It was a sort of forgotten pleasure to mark out the lines and planes of him, to study the contour of his back and imagine how Sef would reproduce it with charcoal. And, he admitted to himself after a moment, to know that further arguments lay in their future. Traveling companions were a hazard he hadn't allowed himself in some time. Keeping secrets was easier when he had no one to share them with.

When he'd given Taisce's figure a thorough consideration, Sef turned his attention to the woods around them. He knew them well after so many years spent in the middle country. He knew the silence, the frail limbed birch trees, and the others whose names he'd never bothered to learn. They made up for their thin bodies with quantity, sometimes growing so close together that they closed up the infrequently used trail and Sef could barely maneuver his horse through at all. Their progress grew slower and slower as the greenery thickened.

The sun had shifted outside the canopy of the trees and with it so had their course. He was quite certain that Taisce was unaware of the fact that he was heading northwest now, farther into the forest, instead of the slightly southward course that he needed. At this rate, they would never reach Clotsfield in the specified two days. Sef smiled to himself.

A few birds twittered in the treetops, joining the steady hum of the earth. After a while, Sef began to nod off in the saddle. The rhythmic sway of the horse's gait. The rustle of the leaves. The wind playing through the newly shorn hair at the nape of his neck. He hardly realized it was happening before it did.

And by then it was too late.

He knew where he was immediately. This dream, this memory, was the closest thing to home that he had left. Her dark eyes shimmered with their own light, flashing pale blue despite the flickering yellow light of the lamps, and Sef spread his arms to welcome the pain that was sure to follow. It was the only time he welcomed such pain. He would never do the same while he was awake. But the pain he expected was delayed as the blade hung in the air, waiting for his acknowledgment. It was a thing of beauty, burnished gold, a red jewel set into the pommel. He'd thought once that it would be an honor to be felled by such a blade. Better to give his life to such a beautiful weapon than to some withering disease. The memory mocked him now. He'd barely thought it before the knife pierced his chest.

Sef jerked in the saddle, nearly falling from his horse. He squinted against the sudden brightness around him. "Where in Strena's name are we?"

Ahead of him on the trail, Taisce jumped at his question. "I thought the silence might go on forever." From his tone it was impossible to tell if he was glad or not. He didn't answer Sef's question either.

Sef glanced around again, trying to make sense of

their shifted surroundings. The trees had thinned again, letting heavy shafts of sun through their branches. It seemed that while he'd been lost in his memories, Taisce had turned them even farther off course. "Why are we heading north?"

"I heard voices. We nearly walked right into their camp."

There was no need for Sef to ask who 'they' were. The answer lay in the tension tugging at Taisce's shoulders and the sudden redness of his ears. The thieves then. Surprising that they would have made their camp somewhere so easily found. Usually they had more discretion than that. Then again, there were few travelers in the area this time of year, with the summer heat nearing its peak. Perhaps the thieves' camp had grown lax.

Sef rolled the tightness from his shoulders. The sun had already inched its way overhead and settled itself in the sky to their left. They'd been riding for hours while he drifted. He picked at his shirt. Sweat collected at the back of his neck and between his shoulder blades, pasting the thin material to his skin. It would have been nice to strip it away. "We should stop a while."

"I need to reach Clotsfield," Taisce said, his usual stubbornness reasserting itself.

"No matter how fast you ride, you won't reach it today. Tomorrow is unlikely as well. Where's the harm in a little lunch? I'm sure your poor horse would agree."

Taisce sputtered. "The thieves' camp."

"I see no signs of them here and as long as you keep your voice down they would never even know if we *were* close. Come along. Before you fall right out of your saddle." Sef slid to the ground.

"I think you were the one most in danger of that," Taisce muttered but he reined in his horse all the same.

Sef found he'd chosen a pleasant place for their meager picnic. The shadows of the trees painted the ground in blue and sun-baked gold and there was a cluster of crumbling rocks, the remains of an ancient wall, running along one side of the clearing. Sef pressed a hand to the stones. They were cool to the touch. Old. He could feel it in their subdued hum. This was a good place. He smiled up at Taisce, still sitting stiffly in the saddle. "Do you need help getting down?"

Taisce opened his mouth to speak then pressed his lips together. He looked away.

"Very well then." Sef settled along one end of the fallen wall and reached into his bag. The morning's activity had been none too kind to his provisions but a bruised apple was better than no apple at all. He dusted off one of the lumpy little fruits with the corner of his sleeve before setting it on his knee. Another search through his bag produced a strip of the jerky he had found in the cellar of *The Lady's Stallion*. With the apple it would make decent meal. It was better than any of the moldy bread or gruel he'd had in jail anyway.

And still, Taisce stayed in the saddle. Sef could

feel his eyes on him.

"Your pride does you no favors. Is your quarrel this time with the delay or is it the fact that you have no provisions?" Sef said, nibbling on the bruised side of his apple first. It was pleasantly sweet but a bit mealy with age. No doubt it was one leftover as unsuitable for Sirena's pie baking. He took a larger bite, juice splattering his lower lip. He licked it away as he glanced up at Taisce. "It's no secret. I've seen what was in your bag. Or rather, what wasn't."

The boy was beside himself, looking this way and that as if in search of some avenue of escape. Finally he sighed, hands fisting on the reins. For a moment, Sef thought he intended to ride on alone and he readied himself to stop the boy. He needn't have worried. Instead of making his escape, Taisce threw his good leg over the saddle and dropped to the ground with a bitten off gasp of pain. He faltered, only keeping vertical because of the horse at his side. Sef returned to his apple. He had offered to help once. He wouldn't do so again.

Apple finished, Sef leaned back against his perch and let the uneven stone dig into his back like kneading hands. While the stones worked his muscles, he gnawed on his stringy piece of jerky. It tasted of venison. Pity. He would have preferred beef or pork but they were so hard to come by in this area. Still... if he closed his eyes he could imagine it was a sumptuous feast at an enormous oak table laden with food on embossed gold chargers. An entire boar surrounded by root vegetables and ripe fruit. Tureens of steaming soup. And servants bustling about, keeping his goblet and his plate full. The noise of courtiers vying for his attention. His smile leached away as the memory faded beneath the taste of old venison jerky.

Taisce slid onto the rock wall at a safe distance, one leg stretched out in the grass.

"Hungry?" Sef asked without opening his eyes. He didn't wait for an answer before holding out the remaining scrap of jerky. He'd lost his taste for it anyway. The meat sat untouched in his hand so long that he finally cracked an eye. Taisce had grown redder than before. Embarrassment suited him. "You don't plan to faint again, do you?" Sef teased.

The jibe had the desired effect.

Taisce snatched the jerky from Sef's outstretched hand, fingers brushing over the sensitive skin of his palm. Sef stiffened. He had the strangest urge to close his hand around those fingers and pull the boy in tight. He wouldn't be unwilling. In fact, Sef was reasonably certain that he would be all too receptive. As if to prove his point, Taisce's eyes danced over Sef's hand before sliding up to his lips. The heat in them mirrored Sef's own. Then it was extinguished. Taisce turned away, facing the horses. "How much farther is it to Clotsfield?"

"That depends."

Taisce grumbled, turning back to glare at him. "On what?"

"There's a town just south of here. Senter. We'll reach it by tomorrow afternoon if we turn that way now. It adds half a day in travel but it's safer to keep out of the wilderness where we can."

"I must reach Clotsfield. No extra stops."

"It's an unwise idea to be out here at night, milord," Sef said, mockery leaking back into his voice.

"Nonsense. Finn and I camped in these woods just last night."

"And we've both seen the results of that. You nearly got yourself killed before breakfast. There are worse things than thieves hiding in the woods."

"Then perhaps we should have ridden on instead of stopping to laze about in the sun," Taisce snapped.

"You're welcome to leave whenever you wish, milord. I believe you were the one who told me not to follow you," Sef said. He had no intention of letting Taisce out of his sight but Sef couldn't resist the urge to irritate the boy. Watching him sputter in indignation was far too entertaining. He felt like a puppet master swinging the young noble about like a marionette on a string.

Taisce stood, moving with more ease than he had earlier. Apparently a bit of rest had eased the ache in his leg. Sef let him get as far as his horse before he called out. "Wait."

Taisce sighed. "What is it?" he asked without turning around.

"Perhaps your large friend will seek refuge in Senter. Have you considered that?"

"He'll go to Clotsfield."

"Are you sure?"

"Yes."

"Then I'd best come with you. You would never make it through a night without me."

"I'm not incompetent!" Taisce rounded on Sef when he came up beside him.

"No. Of course not." Sef gave him a pleasant nod. "Shall we go then?"

~~*

Taisce rifled through his pack for the third time though it was becoming increasingly difficult to see in the dying light of sunset. His matches were gone. He looked at the stacked bundle of unlit branches and kindling that should have been their fire. Then he looked at Sef. The useless man lounged on the ground beneath a tree and his hat sat in the grass beside him, an apple perched atop it. Taisce eyed the little fruit. His mouth had been watering ever since the apple had made its appearance.

His stomach had become a deep pit, made even deeper by the oppressive heat of the afternoon. He was hungry. He couldn't remember ever feeling so hungry. He'd found no berries in the tangled mess of trees they'd passed that day, nothing to harvest to make himself a meal. The scrap of jerky Sef had given him earlier had hardly been enough to stave off the pangs of hunger that stabbed at his stomach but Taisce still regretted leaping upon it like a dog after a treat. He closed his eyes. He'd resolved never to stoop to such a thing again but pride did nothing to fill his stomach and when they'd stopped for the night, Sef hadn't even tried to tempt him with whatever food he kept hidden in his sack. Taisce had seen him sorting through wrapped parcels earlier and told himself he did not want to know what was inside of them. But as the afternoon wore on towards evening he was having a harder and harder time reminding himself of that. He was so very hungry.

Sef looked up and caught him staring. He arched one eyebrow. "Is there something amiss with the fire, milord?"

It was perfectly obvious what was 'amiss' with the fire, Taisce thought, but he held his temper in check with an effort. "I can't find my matches."

"I see," Sef said and went back to sitting in silence.

"Might I use yours? Or a flint perhaps if you have one?" Taisce prompted, jaw tightening around the words.

"You could do that," Sef said, "if I had any. Alas I do not."

Taisce threw down his pack, care forgotten for the moment, and shot to his feet. "Are you intentionally being unhelpful? You've been sitting there without a care this whole time. How am I to start a fire with no flint? Why don't you assist me?"

"Because you didn't ask me to." A smile broke across Sef's face, only serving to make Taisce angrier, but before he could say a word, Sef interrupted him with a raised hand. "Is that all it would take to make you happy?"

"What?" Taisce barked.

"A fire. Do you want one?"

Taisce gaped at him. He looked down at the stacked firewood and then back at Sef. "Of course not. It's just that I enjoy arranging sticks into pretty patterns," he snapped. "What kind of question is that?"

Sef leaned forward, setting his elbows against his bent knees. He tipped his head. "Do you want a fire?" he repeated. "A simple yes or no will suffice."

Taisce glared but he might as well have been looking at a wall for all the good it did. Sef's expression didn't change. Taisce bit his lip. He felt as if he were walking into a cleverly disguised trap. "Yes."

"Very well then." The fire leapt into life, reflected in the dim blue glow of Sef's eyes.

Taisce jumped back at the sudden flare of heat in the ring of stones at his side. The fire had nearly singed his outstretched fingers. Then he turned on Sef again, his hands curled into shaking fists. A hiss escaped through his teeth but it dwindled and died at Sef's sudden nearness. He'd closed the distance between them so quickly that Taisce could almost have believed in that moment that he was a ghost. Logic seemed frequently to abandon any area in which he set foot. "What? What is it?" Taisce asked.

"You're a strange one," Sef said, and his lips parted in another of his enigmatic smiles.

"Strange?" Taisce looked around for who or what Sef could be addressing. There was nothing behind him but the vast wilderness they had traversed earlier that day. When he turned back Sef's smile had faltered. It hung crookedly at one corner and finally fell away. The expression left behind was decidedly less pleasant. It reminded Taisce uncomfortably of his mother's pale face. The look she had when her pain flared up and no amount of blankets could warm her. It had no place on a young man's face at all. "What's this foolishness?"

Then even that look was gone, replaced by the careful mask of amusement Sef had worn all day. He took Taisce's hands in his, uncurling both fists with ease, and set something in them. Taisce looked down. He recognized the ribbon wrapped bundle as one from Sef's pack.

"What's this?" Taisce hesitated to pluck free the colorful ribbon.

"It's a gift. For the entertainment," Sef added over his shoulder as he started off into the trees.

Taisce's grip tightened on the thing in his hands. It gave slightly with the pressure of his fingers. "Where are you going?" he demanded.

Sef didn't answer.

When Sef had disappeared into the forest, Taisce finally unwrapped what he had given him. In the middle of the cloth sat a small loaf of bread coated in toasted seeds. Taisce wished he could throw it after Sef, especially considering the man's attitude. He acted as if Taisce was a toy, a pet, to be treated with indifference and scorn and, occasionally, amusement. He hated it. But that didn't mean he needed to act foolishly either.

Taisce pressed the oval loaf between his palms even as his stomach churned inside him. It took almost more restraint than he had just to keep from ripping great hunks from the bread with his teeth and swallowing them whole. Taisce turned in a circle, eyes searching the darkness beyond the fire. Wherever Sef had got to, it must have been far enough to cover the sound of his movements. With any luck he wouldn't return for some time.

Taisce dropped to a crouch, wincing as his leg twinged, and pulled his pack to him. He'd thrown it carelessly earlier but the contents seemed to be unharmed. He was glad. One finger brushed along the folder of stationery that Adeline had foisted upon him. The papers were wrinkled from their earlier mishandling but they were otherwise unharmed. He moved the packet aside, making a nest at the bottom of his bag. Into it he placed half of the loaf Sef had given him, again wrapped in the square of fabric for protection. That could very well be the only meal he had tomorrow. It would have to last. Taisce made quick work of the other half, chewing the dense bread with relish. All too soon it was gone.

By the time Sef returned, Taisce had settled atop his folded blanket beside the fire with a sheet of paper and his pot of ink. It was a miracle the glass bottle hadn't broken with all the mistreatment it had gotten. Adeline had provided the ink herself, red of course, to make his 'dry letters more romantic' she'd said. If he'd lost the little bottle, he didn't know where he would have found more. Taisce didn't look up at Sef's approach, giving all his attention to the effort of writing his letter by the weak fire light, but he heard the man stop at his side, could feel his eyes as if they carried the same weight as hands pressed to his flesh. His pen scratched over the paper without interruption.

"Are you feeling more reasonable now that you've eaten, milord?" Sef asked after Taisce had ignored him for the space of many minutes. He'd written nearly half a page during the silence, filling the paper with his carefully measured penmanship.

"I threw it away," Taisce lied.

"You what?" The coarse ground crunched beneath Sef's feet as he spun to look behind him. "Why would you do such a thing?"

"I am not here for your entertainment or your pity," Taisce said, eyes still firmly on his paper. He could feel his face turning as red as the ink he wrote with. Hopefully Sef would attribute it to the heat of the fire. If he noticed it at all.

Sef spread his thin blanket on the opposite side of the fire and stretched out, one booted foot crossed over the other. "Well played, milord," he said in a low voice.

Taisce ignored him. A drop of ink fell across his words, blotting out a large portion of what he'd just written. He crushed the paper and tossed it into the fire. When it caught, it blossomed into a glowing gold rose, petals unfurling and quickly turning to ash. He would have to write his letter again tomorrow. Taisce collected his supplies quickly, the ink bottle clinking against his pen as he wrestled everything back into his pack.

"They knew of him," Taisce blurted suddenly, voicing the thing that had been troubling him all day. "The thieves. They knew of Rupert, not directly, but they recognized his name. They knew about his *companions* even. How could they know of him when no one in Ciaran did?"

"Come again?" Sef said. He propped himself up on one elbow. Through the heat of the fire he seemed to shift and twist like a snake.

"Of course you wouldn't remember," Taisce said, wondering at his own petulance even as he said it. He didn't know why he should be surprised. Yesterday he had been a stranger to Sef. They were still strangers. "In Ciaran, only yesterday. Do you not recall my question even a little?"

"Perhaps if you gave me a reason to do so."

Again, Taisce bit back the many retorts on his tongue. "After we... met yesterday. I asked you if you had heard of a man named Rupert Brenton," Taisce reminded him. "You said you hadn't. Just as everyone else in Ciaran had. Yet the thieves this morning, they had heard the name. They recognized it. I traveled here after receiving information that Rupert was in the area but if he didn't go to Ciaran, then where? Where else would he have gone? What could he possibly be after in this miserable place?"

"And it's impossible that he made town and managed to lie low," Sef said. He lay back.

Taisce shook his head even though Sef wasn't

looking at him. "Why would they? They would have no idea I'm looking for them. This is the closest I've come yet to finding them." He hoped his bitterness didn't show in his voice but it was hard to be sure. He chewed his lip. "If not Ciaran, then where?"

"There are many equally unsavory cities to be found, milord, if that's what they're after. If that's all you have, you would do well to give up your search and return home before you get yourself into further trouble."

"No!"

Sef slanted a curious look at him. "Is this your lover that we're after?"

"Nothing of the kind," Taisce snapped. He regretted even bringing it up again. He hadn't thought of the questions it would elicit. The less Sef knew, the better. Taisce would not put his family's reputation in danger because of his own loneliness. He turned to face the fire until his skin grew tight from the heat but it didn't seem to penetrate any deeper than that. He still felt cold as ice. Taisce wrapped his arms around himself. "Forget what I said."

"As you wish."

~~*

The next day passed uneventfully with Taisce lost in a fitful silence. He could hardly even be cajoled into answering Sef's repeated suggestions to turn towards town and spare themselves another night in the forest. Sef found himself missing the boy's haughty repartee of the day before. When the boy didn't talk, Sef was left to his own thoughts and very few of them were pleasant.

Sef cast a longing look towards Senter as they climbed a ridge that brought it just barely into view. The soaring spire of the chapel stood up against the horizon though little else was visible around it. A bed would have been nice. Sharing a bed with Taisce would have been even better. But the boy refused to be swayed and Sef couldn't make him obliged to go to town either. Not without tipping his hand. It was much too early for that. If Taisce knew what he traveled with he certainly wouldn't be so willing. That left them with no other option than to spend the night beneath the sleepy canopy of the trees and the equally unpleasant things lurking beneath its placid surface.

Night fell with barely a warning to precede it. With the sun, their last opportunity for a restful evening disappeared as well.

Taisce seemed completely unfazed by the shift in the forest's mood while they rode. But Sef noticed. He had been this way many times over the years, but it never failed to unsettle him. The wolves would be out tonight. He could feel them prowling in the distance. It was only a matter of time before they plucked up their courage and came nearer.

The moon hung heavy in the sky, ripe as late harvest fruit. As Taisce and Sef collected firewood for the night, the trees shivered around them. Taisce was walking more easily now but it was hard to say if that was an act of spite or not. His expression was much less difficult to read.

"Are you always this disapproving?" Sef asked when he could stand it no longer.

He was answered with an icy stare and more silence.

"I'll take that as a yes, then. Perhaps your lumbering friend wasn't kidnapped at all. Perhaps he escaped," Sef muttered. "I would were I him."

Sef turned just in time to see Taisce stiffen in that now familiar way of his. His pinched, squinting expression grew even tighter with the effort it took to contain his anger. All of that was what Sef might have expected. He had already spent hours learning all the ways to set Taisce off like a flare. Less expected was the flicker of light that hid in Taisce's eyes. The force of it hit Sef like a slap in the face. A second later it was gone as if it had never been. But he hadn't imagined it. He knew he hadn't.

"You..." Sef dropped his armful of kindling, nearly tripping over his own feet as he latched onto Taisce. When Taisce tried to pull away, he held him still.

"What *has* come over you?" Taisce cried, giving another tug at his captive arms. "Let me go."

"Hold still a moment." Sef peered into Taisce's face. "Do it again," he commanded.

"Do *what* exactly? Have you lost your mind?" Taisce pried himself free, brandishing his collection of firewood as a weapon before him.

He didn't know.

Sef looked into his face. It was so open, so painfully oblivious. Taisce didn't know. And Sef couldn't tell him, not like this when he would only sneer the way he did at any mention of magic.

He turned away to collect the firewood he'd dropped. "Nothing. Nothing at all."

Sef didn't know why he was so surprised. Magic was far from uncommon and the boy's magic was incredibly weak, unpracticed, and untamed. It would be better suited to parlor tricks the way it was. But with training... What could it be then? Sef snuck another look at Taisce over his shoulder. Even now, Taisce stormed about their hastily assembled camp, throwing kindling. He was angry, yes, but there was nothing secretive about his manner. He didn't know he had a secret to keep. But Sef did. It thrilled him. And that flash of magic, the feel of it, the almost tangible quality of his latent ability, it couldn't have been a coincidence. Sef had felt its like before. He still felt the effects of that particular magic every day. There could be no mistaking it. Now, more than ever, he was sure that he had not found the boy by accident.

Taisce would give Sef his freedom. Whether he wanted to or not.

CHAPTER SIX
IN WHICH IT WOULD HAVE BEEN WISE TO LISTEN TO SEF

Sef stared into the weakening orange flames of the fire. The shadows it created leapt over the silent clearing, expanding and contracting like a living thing. It felt as if he'd trapped himself in a giant's massive lungs.

He snatched up a twig from the ground, testing it between his fingers. It was still green at the center, pliable, and he peeled the thin bark from it while he studied Taisce. The boy slept soundly with his back to Sef. How very trusting of him. Strangely so, considering that Sef had done his best to torment him for the last two days. Sef could have peeled the flesh from Taisce as easily as he did from the twig in his hand. Nothing could have stopped him if that was what he desired. The boy really had no common sense at all, but having him silent and unaware in the midst of sleep was not such a bad thing. It gave Sef a proper chance to think, to size the boy up.

He rose and moved to the other side of the fire.

Taisce's face was cast in shadow but the fire

offered almost enough light to see. In slumber, Taisce seemed even younger, face unlined and unmarred by his usual concerns. Not that he had many lines to call his own during the daylight hours. A few nestled around his eyes, the product of years of smiling or perhaps squinting. Possibly both, though Sef had yet to see a single smile from the boy. Sef guessed his age at three and twenty. Old enough to think he was worldly but not old enough to be so.

What had his life been before he set off on this fool's errand of his? Pampered certainly. The boy could barely survive in the woods, though he sat his horse well. A city dweller then. Maybe the occasional bit of hunting, but not much. He didn't have the rough features of an outdoorsman. Not part of the working nobility either. Much too haughty for any kind of menial labor. Much too soft for the toil of hard work. The contents of his pack had provided few clues either.

Sef's fingers itched to reach out. They wanted to run through the silky hair curling over Taisce's shoulder. He had unusually fine hair for a man. Another sure sign of a life of ease. Not that Sef felt inclined to complain about that. He could only imagine how it would feel to wrap that mass of hair around his fist, tugging, using it as leverage to bare Taisce's throat to his lips. Sef could play that lithe body like a harp string. Given the chance, he could tease it into making such beautiful, hungry sounds. It was an all too welcome thought.

Sef caught himself before he bridged the gap

between them. His attentions wouldn't be welcomed this way. Not so suddenly, in the dark, on the hard ground. And there was another reason for his hesitation. Sef had been without a lover for some time, a problem he longed to remedy, but looking to Taisce to ease that ache... it seemed the surest way to magnify his problems, not lessen them.

He sat back, toying with his cuffs, still watching Taisce. In the fire light, he seemed to glow. Sef allowed himself another moment of contemplation. He would've been wise to take his own advice and stay alert. There were beasts in the darkness tonight.

As if on cue, a distant howl broke the silence.

Sef tensed, waiting for the answering cries of its pack. He didn't have to wait long. The howls came from all around. The monsters had ringed them already. Sef should have been paying attention, not mooning over a sleeping boy. He'd hoped to deflect their interest in some way, to move camp if necessary, but by now the wolves had surely caught their scent on the wind. It promised to be a long night if they had. They were never kind to trespassers.

Sef resettled himself on the ground, pulling into a loose crouch. There'd been a time when he felt a kinship with the inhabitants of the forest, the wolves, the deer, even the ugly little rodents running through the moss and mud. But not tonight. Tonight he planned to kill anything that came near. With relish.

He rolled the tight muscles in his shoulders. He'd kept himself reined in for far too long. Too much time spent in cities among people who could never see him for what he was. He hoped it wasn't a decision he would come to regret tonight. It had been a silly pointless game. He was a prince of a forgotten kingdom. It made him little better than a common peasant. Even the thieves had better pedigrees these days.

There were no more howls to signal their approach but Sef could feel the wolves drawing closer, circling like a whirlpool, pulled on towards their prey at the center. He cast another glance at Taisce. The boy still slept as soundly as ever. The fire had painted him in flickering gold to match his eyes. He moaned in his sleep, the quiet low of a dreaming child, and rolled onto his back. Sef forced his eyes away. If he didn't watch himself, he would do something he would regret come morning. Assuming they made it that far.

Pacing seemed like a much smarter choice.

Their camp was barely more than a break in the trees and the ground slanted down to a nearby stream that summer had thinned to half its size. It had seemed a decent spot in case of attack. Staying the night in a proper bed with a roof over their heads would have been better.

Sef had the childish urge to kick Taisce as he circled around the clearing again. It was the boy's fault. Everything was his fault. Sef could have been sleeping the undisturbed, dreamless sleep of the exhausted. Instead he was obliged to keep sentry duty until the sun finally crested the mountains on the horizon.

And Taisce slept on.

Sef paused, standing over the boy, trying to puzzle him out. Was he really so oblivious?

The fire crackled, dimming as it ate away at a green piece of wood. Sef glared at it with a muttered "*Inse*" and the flames leapt back to vigorous life. Again shadows danced thick along the trees. Their spidery fingers lapped at Taisce's sleeping form and made his ring twinkle in the darkness. Sef crouched to give it another look.

The signet ring was plain. Old. A simple gold stamping of a sea-horse with some kind of leaves bordering it. Sef's hands hovered over the ring before he finally drew them back and rested them on his knees.

In the woods to the north of their camp, something large rustled. It was close. Very close. Where there was one there were always more. It wouldn't be long now.

Sef stood again, brushing the dirt from his pants. He neatened his shirt even though there was no one to appreciate his efforts. Then he threw another handful of dry branches on the fire while he waited, watching them sizzle and flare up like a pyre. His mouth twisted into a scowl. He hated fire really. Burning was a terrible way to go.

"Come on then," he muttered. "Let's get on with it."

They didn't need to be asked twice.

The first wolf leapt from its cover at the top of the hill. Sef had expected it.

He threw out a hand, hissing the words he'd memorized before anything else. "*Inse mo.*"

The wolf barked with pain, ablaze with bluish flame as it dropped from the air like a stunned bird. It writhed as its fur charred and the flesh beneath singed.

Sef smiled.

Then three more wolves hurtled from the darkness, coming at him from all directions.

~~*

Taisce woke slowly, stretching and wincing at the stiffness in his leg. How he longed for a bed. He would never forgive that thief for putting him through all this extra trouble. He made another lazy stretch and the leaves rustled beneath him as he rolled gingerly to his side.

The clearing was empty.

He sat up. The fire had died to ash, not even sending up a curl of smoke anymore, and overhead the sky was the brilliant blue of late morning. He had slept the whole night and half the morning without intending to. He might even have lost more time if he hadn't been woken by... What was it that had woken him? Sef was nowhere in sight.

Taisce fought free of his blanket, stumbling upright on legs that were hardly any more wakeful than he was. Sef's bundle lay on the opposite side of the cold fire, untouched. His horse was still tethered to the tree beside Taisce's. He wouldn't have gone far without his horse. Taisce's eyes swept the clearing again.

The air hung heavy with the stink of smoke, odd since the fire was cold. There was no sign of a new fire and this smoke didn't have the clean scent of charred wood. It was thick and acrid. His nose stung with it.

Taisce started into the forest, careful to keep close to their small camp. He found the source of the smoke nearby lying in the brush. The thing was barely more than a charred husk, the remains of a creature that he couldn't even identify, but the smell was horrible. Taisce cupped a hand over his nose and mouth, trying to block the stink. It did nothing to help his watering eyes. He seized upon a nearby fallen branch. The thing was burnt black, flakes breaking free and dusting the ground like snow when he used the branch to roll it to its other side. This side had been buried in the grass, insulated from some of the heat of the fire, and it still bore scraps of singed and matted fur. A single glossy yellow eye stared at him. It looked like a wolf but not any that he had ever seen before in his books. The body was larger, bulkier. Instead of rounded paws, its forelegs ended in something like curved fingers tipped with claws. Taisce stared into the glazed eye in horror. Why was this thing lying half burnt beside their camp? What had happened while he slept?

Taisce threw down the stick in his hand, skirting the carcass of the beast in a wide circle, and moved deeper into the woods.

"Sef?" he called. Taisce called out a second time. When there was no answer, Taisce felt panic squeeze at his chest. Sef's earlier barbs rang in his head. He couldn't have run off in the night. Sef had left his pack, his horse. No matter how much the man disliked Taisce, surely he wouldn't leave his only belongings behind. "Sef?"

There was no sound of movement, no answer of any kind.

Taisce shook his head, trying to clear the sudden buzzing from it. Perhaps Sef had gone off in search of food. Or his morning relief. There were a number of perfectly reasonable explanations. Taisce pressed on. The farther he walked the more he noticed the slashes of bark scraped from the trees, the black marks of recent fire. Broken branches littered the ground under foot, cracking loudly as he passed. Taisce followed the trail. It was impossible to miss a path so obvious. Along the way, he found two more shapes lying farther out under the trees. He didn't go near. One glimpse had been enough. At the end of the trail he found Sef lying on his side beside a crooked tree. Taisce fell to the ground beside him and immediately began to search for wounds or patches of dried blood. His hands ran over his chest, his arms. There was nothing.

Sef groaned.

So he was alive at least. That was a relief. Taisce barely caught the thought before it could translate itself into speech. He got to his feet again. Now that he'd established that Sef was in no danger it occurred to him to be angry. He'd woken up alone, with strange creatures lying dead about him, and here was Sef sleeping peacefully in the middle of the woods, not even in view of their camp. He'd been so adamant about the danger and yet he'd wandered off without even waking his companion. He didn't look so very concerned now. He looked like an oblivious drunkard. Taisce drew back a foot and kicked Sef squarely in the back.

Sef jerked, arms flying out as he rolled over onto his face. "*Na*? *Vui*--?" Sef sat up on his knees, head whipping this way and that as he tried to regain his bearings. "Where'm I?"

Taisce glared down at him, hands on his hips. "You're beneath a tree. What are you doing beneath a tree? You couldn't possibly have rolled this far in your sleep. Our camp is that way." He pointed in case Sef had forgotten that too.

"A tree? *Vu'es* tree?" Sef asked, a slur leaking into his voice as he did another full circle inspection of his resting place. "Where is he?"

"Where is who?" If he hadn't already been annoyed, Taisce would have lost his patience then. The man wasn't making any sense at all. "You're drunk."

"That'd be better," Sef said. He staggered to his feet, brushing as much dirt from his clothes as he could manage. His cuff was stained an ugly black that no amount of rubbing would clean. He squinted at the sky as if it personally offended him before covering his eyes with one hand. His lips pulled back in a wince.

"If we don't leave soon we'll never make it to Clotsfield," Taisce said, turning on his heel and marching back to collect his things from their camp. He carefully avoided where he'd found the burnt carcasses. He'd still gotten no explanation for them but at the moment all he wanted was to get away from the foul stink they created. "I could have been there already if I hadn't had to waste time looking for you."

Behind him Sef made a sound like a wounded bear. "Oh, my head."

Taisce was repacked and sitting astride his horse before Sef even made it back to camp. There was no reason to delay any longer but Taisce derived such petty pleasure from watching Sef stumbling over exposed roots and fumbling with the simple closure on his sack. He kept one long fingered hand pressed to his temple throughout, as though concerned his head might topple from his shoulders if left unattended. And when Sef ended up on his backside instead of in the saddle, Taisce couldn't contain his smile any longer.

"Come on then," Taisce called. He could almost feel the glare that followed him as he rode into the trees.

Away from the clearing the smell of rancid smoke was greatly lessened. Taisce took a deep breath to ease his burning lungs. He wished he could ask Sef what that *thing* had been but now was certainly not the time. Even if Sef had been halfway lucid Taisce doubted he would have provided a sensible answer. Not in the mood he was in. Taisce could hear him swearing and muttering gibberish to himself as he attempted to catch up. If Taisce asked him about the beast, he would probably answer the question with another of his own, or worse yet, more of the mockery which he seemed to favor. It always left Taisce baffled and incensed. Did Sef hate him or was he being intentionally difficult? Eventually he would force the man into a proper answer.

Taisce was so lost in thought that he nearly missed the thing lying on the ground. He barely caught sight of it before his horse reared in fright. There was a brief moment of clarity, a feeling of being suspended in time, watching the ground shy away. Then he crashed into a wave of fear, knees gripping tight as he tried to keep his seat. Taisce hadn't even known he was so afraid until that moment. He imagined himself falling and then broken, again. Long after his horse had settled, dancing sideways to avoid the obstruction, Taisce's heart continued to pound. He was locked in place, so stiff that he couldn't have unwound the reins from his fists if he tried. The tight muscles in his leg throbbed with pain.

"What's the matter?" Sef asked, halting his horse alongside Taisce's.

Taisce slid from the saddle. Having solid earth beneath his feet had never felt so wonderful as it did right then. He left the reins to Sef, grateful to be rid of them.

The shape on the ground was obviously a person once Taisce got closer. He didn't know which part should have been most shocking: the fact that she was unclothed or that she was lying face down and unconscious in the middle of the forest. A series of puckered pink scars marred her back but he was most concerned with the angry red trail of a fresh burn behind her left shoulder blade. He dared not touch the blistered skin, not without being given leave to, but it would need treatment, more than he could provide. At least she was alive. He didn't need to look hard to see the rise and fall of breath filling her lungs.

"Hello?" Taisce said, tentatively reaching out to touch the woman's uninjured shoulder.

"Leave her."

Taisce jumped at the sound of Sef's voice. "She's hurt. She needs a doctor." Her skin felt cool to the touch, shockingly so when the summer sun was already bearing down on them through the trees. "So cold."

Without thinking, Taisce tugged his shirt over his head and laid it on her as a makeshift blanket. It was barely long enough to cover her properly but it was better than nothing at all. "Can you hear me?" he whispered. Perhaps she'd run into the same horrible beasts that he'd found dead in the woods. But whatever the case, they couldn't leave her in her current state.

The woman shifted, a hiss escaping from her lips as she shifted onto her injured side.

"You're badly burned." His hands fluttered over her like nervous butterflies. He didn't know how to help her without causing undue pain. "What happened to you? Do you remember?"

The shirt slipped from her shoulders as she sat up, making no effort to cover herself. Her eyes slid from Taisce to Sef and back again. They were a translucent brown, like watered down tea. Her dark hair settled around her shoulders but it was hardly sufficient cover. Taisce flushed and turned his gaze away. The girl was barely older than his sister Adeline and so badly scarred. He felt an immediate surge of concern.

"Who are you?" Her voice was huskier than he might have expected, deep and surprisingly even considering the amount of pain she must have been in.

Taisce rescued his shirt from the ground and settled it over her shoulders again. "You have nothing to fear from us. Are you in very much pain? We'll take you to a doctor."

~~*

Sef stayed mounted, the better to watch over the fool trying to save a woman who would have him dead in an instant if she could. No doubt the only thing keeping her from attempting to rip out Taisce's throat was the sun glaring down at her. A few hours more and she would not show so much restraint. Sef had wondered where the last wounded wolf had gotten to last night. Now he knew. She wore his mark on her shoulder; the blistered red burn was a match to the one he'd given the wolf. There was no doubt about her identity. She even stank of dog.

"Are you able to stand?" Taisce fretted over the little beast like a nursemaid, dressing her in the shirt off his back before offering her an arm to lean on.

The boy was maddeningly naive. He had no idea what it was that he was helping. But for the moment, Sef kept silent and consoled himself with the expanse of flesh that Taisce was showing now that he'd removed his shirt. His back and shoulders showed a pleasant amount of definition though he was compactly built, not roped with the thick gnarled muscle of a laborer. The sun starved skin looked even lighter against the sweep of his deep bronze hair. He'd forgotten to tie back his hair this morning and it fell around him in a tangle. Sef sank his teeth into his lip. The boy's hair was positively indecent. At the sight of it, all kinds of filthy things sprang to mind. Sef would have to do something about the situation quite soon. Perhaps Clotsfield would be able to offer him a much needed distraction.

"What *are* you doing?" Sef asked, rousing himself from his lascivious reverie in time to stop Taisce from lifting the girl-shaped thing onto his waiting horse. The horse danced in agitation and gave a nervous whinny.

"She can't very well walk like this. She's wounded." He frowned at Sef. Ever the gentlemen.

When Taisce turned back to his chivalrous efforts Sef stopped him once more. "Wait." He sighed before dismounting. "You won't make it three miles with that leg of yours acting up. She can take my horse."

Taisce managed to look offended and pleased at the same time, frowning even as his eyes lit up like candles. Before he knew it, Sef was smiling back at him like an even greater fool and surrendering his horse to the thing dressed in female skin.

As she passed him, she smirked and her tongue poked out to lick her full lips. The look was for Sef and Sef alone. Her meaning was clear. Sef's eyes narrowed in response to the silent challenge.

"Do you need help mounting?" Taisce asked.

"I'll help her," Sef said. He reached out to boost her into the saddle but she pulled away.

"I can manage," said the girl, one foot already in the stirrups. She swung herself up the rest of the way without any trouble or embarrassment at her near nudity.

Sef slipped up beside Taisce. "She seems quite well enough to return to her own people. Is it really necessary to go out of our way? You had important business to attend to in Clotsfield," Sef reminded him in a low voice. Not that the girl couldn't hear him just fine. Sef suspected her ears were more than up to the task of deciphering his whispers.

"She's a girl alone in the woods and she's badly injured. Of course we have to help her," Taisce insisted. He favored Sef with another disapproving frown.

"You don't think her nudity a little strange?"

"Obviously some terrible misfortune has befallen

her. We can't abandon her here."

Sef drooped. Before he could say more, Taisce had returned to his own horse. "She wasn't so injured that she couldn't get into the saddle just fine," Sef grumbled, but that too was ignored.

Their pace through the woods slowed now that Sef was on foot. He did his best to keep alongside Taisce's chestnut horse. The girl should be manageable until the sun dipped to the horizon but he had no desire to test the theory by leaving them alone together.

She rode in silence, bringing up the rear of their tense trio. Sef cast her another searching look, which she openly returned. In her own way she was quite beautiful. The wild cloud of her hair was as black as a moonless night. She had the tanned skin of most of the locals, the sturdy build of the wolf she was. Even injured, she moved like a predator, with ease and silent grace. He had known other wolves like her in the past. They were a tight knit clan of hunters, usually keeping to their own company and spurning outsiders. Enthusiastic lovers though. And ruthless when they felt they'd been slighted. He'd learned that the hard way. There was a beautiful vitality to them. But nearly having his throat ripped out had left him less than enamored with their beauty however great it might be. He would not trust this girl to be any different from the rest of her kind.

"You should not have helped her."

Taisce said nothing.

"You don't know what you're getting yourself

into, milord."

"I don't recall asking for your opinion."

"It is freely given," Sef said with a hint of amusement tugging at his lips.

"Was it not also your opinion that I was unfit for traveling companions?" Taisce asked stiffly.

Sef chuckled, glancing back at the girl riding his stolen horse. At least if anything happened to it, he would not be terribly inconvenienced. "Perhaps if you had better taste in traveling companions. That girl..." He paused.

"Do you think me a fool?" Taisce snapped.

"Yes." Sef answered the question without hesitation. He wouldn't have wanted to miss the sudden redness that came into Taisce's face. Perhaps if Sef made him angry enough he would flare once more. "But you knew that already."

Taisce's jaw clenched tight but his eyes remained stubbornly gold. If anything, they darkened a touch before he turned away again.

"I think you need someone to tell you what a fool you're being," Sef mused quietly, speaking more to himself than Taisce.

"Pray tell, whatever could have led you to that conclusion?" Taisce asked after a long, cold pause.

"Has anyone ever dared call you a fool?"

Immediately something softened in Taisce's expression. An openness came into his features before he hid it away again. "That's none of your business."

"So you have a girl stashed away somewhere, do

you? Or a lad?" Sef pried. He smiled tightly. "Are they pretty? Have you bedded them?"

"I would thank you not to speak of my sister so disrespectfully," Taisce snapped.

It was nearly impossible to hold in a whoop of joy. Sef cleared his throat and schooled his features. "No lover then?"

"No."

He'd expected it to be harder to secure an answer to the question that had been plaguing him. It was almost disappointing to have it come to him so easily. Almost.

Silence fell between the three of them again, not that the girl had had much to say from the very beginning. She remained a constant annoying presence in the air, like the screeching of the cicadas in the distance. Sef couldn't wait to be rid of her. He kept his eyes trained on what little he could see of the horizon through the thinning trees. They would be out of the woods soon, breaking onto the plains before they reached Clotsfield. Sef hoped they would make it well before night fell again. The girl would probably not be any problem to fight off, even as a wolf. She was already injured and young besides. But by bringing her with them, Taisce had unknowingly provided a beacon to call the rest of the pack to them.

How many wolves had Sef killed the night before? Three? Four? They would be out in force tonight seeking vengeance for their fallen kin. Sef felt nothing in the woods surrounding them but that didn't mean they weren't there.

Their best chance was to be safely within the walls of Clotsfield before darkness crept up on them. The wolves would never venture there. Clotsfield was a peculiarly genteel little town, caught somewhere between the wilderness that surrounded it and the scholarly city it once aspired to be, but the people were well accustomed to defending themselves. Even a grandfather wolf would have trouble healing a bullet to the face.

"Those berries are edible," Taisce said without warning. He slid to the ground and began rooting around in the plants surrounding them. The berries of which he'd spoken were clustered low to the ground in a particularly dense and thorny bush. Taisce stooped to pick through the leaves before producing a handkerchief to bundle his findings into.

Sef slipped a hand around his pack. He still had most of the food that Sirena had given him but he had no desire to share it with the wolf girl. He had saved a decent portion for Taisce, hoping to draw more information out of the boy with the promise of a meal. But that would be impossible like this. "Milord, we'll reach Clotsfield much faster if you don't keep stopping."

"Suddenly you're in such a hurry," Taisce mocked. "I see more further along. Wait here." He straightened, holding the handkerchief around the berries in his hand and wandering off into the trees.

"Damn these woods," Sef grumbled.

"You care for him a great deal," said the girl. It was the first words she'd spoken in hours.

Sef's first impulse was to laugh. His second was to slit her throat before Taisce could return from berry picking and interrupt him. He did neither.

He spoke without turning to her, eyes instead searching for Taisce's shape through the obscuring leaves. "You won't have him."

"Do you take us for cannibals, fool? I have no desire to feast on your lover."

"I have no idea what a wolf desires. I only know you attacked our camp last night."

"You trespassed on our land. Had you run away properly, as you were meant to, we would have let you flee in peace. And now you're a murderer."

"I was a murderer *long* before last night, my dear," said Sef with a cold chuckle.

"You speak so callously," she mused but Sef could feel the intensity in her stare. "No matter your excuses you won't be forgiven for what you've done."

The laughter bubbled forth from deep within him, loud, overwhelming. He pressed a hand to the pain in his chest before he looked up at her again. "And I suppose you would like to be the one to carry out my execution." The look she gave him was laced with all the venom she'd been suppressing. He laughed again. "Oh, if only you could. I would be in your debt."

Her hands tightened on the reins and he waited for what she would do next. He suspected she was too smart, too careful, to attack him so blatantly when the odds were unsure. She had been weighing him against her experience this whole time. At length she chose her wisest option and did nothing at all.

"What's your name?" Sef asked.

She shifted in the saddle, favoring her injured side and fiddling with the overly long cuffs of Taisce's shirt. It was the most nervousness she had shown since they found her.

"Your name costs you nothing," Sef said. He looked around for a spot to rest while he awaited Taisce's return. How many berries did the boy intend to pick? The summer sun was quickly turning the forest into a sauna. Sef fanned himself with one hand, ruffling the hair at the back of his neck in an effort to better cool himself.

"Erin."

"Hmm?" Sef glanced up.

"My name is Erin," she said, a little louder this time.

"Ah. It's a pretty name. It suits you."

He took a moment to consider the earth beneath him. It was much too mossy to stretch out upon. He would end up stained and smudged with greenish blotches if he did. Perhaps if he spread out a blanket he could escape unscathed. But Taisce really was taking much too long.

"Aren't you going to tell me your name?" Erin asked with a huff.

"Sef." He rooted around in his bag, seeking the extra burlap sack he'd stashed there to use as a temporary cushion, until the silence finally drew his attention. Erin had gone pale, eyes widening so much they seemed to fill her face. Like that she looked much younger than her years, more like a frightened child than a young woman. The expression was one he'd seen many times before, though not recently. He'd almost started to suspect that the tales had withered away and died for good. Maybe it would be better that way after all. "I see they still tell stories about me," he said, returning to his search. He palmed a crust of bread to eat in secret. Taisce would have his berries. He could keep them.

"It isn't possible."

"And yet." Sef swept a hand along his length.

Rider and horse danced backwards a half dozen steps and for one moment Sef thought she intended to make off with his stolen horse. If she did, he certainly wouldn't chase her. Then she reined in the nervous animal, her unblinking eyes still on him. "You're lying."

Sef paused in his search to pin her with a look of his own. He knew the effect it would have. He had gotten so good at hiding his truth, wrapping it in smiles and foolishness, but with that stripped away he was little more than a husk, tired and gray as a tree coated in winter ice. He saw his expression mirrored in her horrified eyes.

"Whatever stories they tell, they're all true. I'm the one. Do you doubt me?"

She had no words for him, though he gave her credit for how quickly she pulled herself together again. People would call her and her people monsters but she had never been in the presence of a real monster, not until now.

"Leave us be. I have no desire to kill you," Sef said. But he would if he had to.

Out of the corner of his eye, he saw her nod. Her bare feet hardly made a sound as she slipped from the horse, hesitating only a second before she darted into the forest.

No sooner had she disappeared than Taisce returned, shuffling through the brush so noisily it would have been impossible to miss him even in the midst of battle. He came laden with a berry stained handkerchief and a cluster of something small and pale in his other hand.

"What in blazes took you so long?" Sef asked wearily. He lay back, bread crust hanging from the corner of his mouth as he spoke. The loaf had gone stale and almost inedibly hard but it felt good to have something to gnaw on.

Taisce stopped. "Where did she go? What did you do to her?"

"I did nothing." It was too much effort to feign astonishment. He felt impossibly tired. He wished he could blame the midday heat for his lethargy.

"If it's as you say, then where did she go?" Taisce tried to glare at him but the effect was rather lessened by his overburdened hands. He held them cupped together in front of him like a child displaying a pebble collection.

"What have you there?" Sef nodded at his hands.

"I found mushrooms. What did you say to her? Why did she leave?"

Obviously he wouldn't be turned away from the

unwelcome topic of the girl so easily. "After a rest, she felt much recovered. Nothing more. I didn't lay a hand on her, if that's what you're indelicately implying." Sef sat up part way and cast a wary eye at the bundle of mushrooms. He knew nothing about plants and the beastly looking fungi of the forest. "Are you sure those are edible or have you decided to poison yourself now?"

Taisce fidgeted, eyes darting away and back again. "They're perfectly safe. I... I'm a student of botany," he said eventually as if it were a great secret.

"Botany?"

"Yes," he hissed. Taisce threw himself onto a nearby log and set to work pulling the bits of stem and leaf from the berries. His stained fingertips grew darker with his efforts. "Aren't you going to tell me that flowers and berries have no place in a businessman's mind?" he asked after a time.

"I haven't the faintest idea of what does or does not belong in a businessman's mind," Sef said. He glanced away. Then finally the slender wire frames winking at him from atop Taisce's nose registered and he looked back. "You're wearing glasses."

Taisce blushed, swiping berry juice over his cheek as he yanked his glasses off and hid them. "Only sometimes." He scrubbed at his pink face but whether it was to remove the hot blush or the staining juice from his cheeks it was hard to say. Sef found this sudden awkwardness unspeakably amusing. And more than a little attractive. More and more, he longed to take Taisce into his arms. If he did it now he would taste of sweet berries. The idea was a pleasant one. He was still lost in thought when Taisce stood again. "I should go and find her. Surely she hasn't gone far yet and she's injured. She needs a doctor."

"She'll be fine. She's in no danger here," Sef said with another wave of his hand. "Her family is nearby. She'll go to them."

"She told you that?"

"She did."

Taisce stared into the trees, shifting from foot to foot as he thought.

"And you would be wise to get to Clotsfield as soon as possible. Your man will be worrying until you're reunited," Sef added casually, though that thought was furthest from his mind. In fact, he would rather have continued to steer the boy clear of his faithful dog. It would make his plans so much easier later on.

Slowly Taisce nodded his agreement and sat back down, though he cast many a glance into the woods around them.

CHAPTER SEVEN
IN WHICH THEY ARRIVE IN CLOTSFIELD AT LONG LAST

The sun hovered just above the distant tree tops when they finally reached the outer wall of Clotsfield. It was one of many low stone barriers that ringed the city at a distance, meant more to warn travelers of their arrival than to keep anything in or out. They had better walls for that.

Clotsfield was large and sprawling but lacking in charm of any kind, like a man passed out face down in the dirt. Where Ciaran was compact and bleached to apparent cleanliness, Clotsfield's years had turned it a weathered and well-used grayish brown. Clotsfield had been cobbled together over time, collecting travelers and farmers and anyone else too weary to move on to more comfortably situated cities, and it showed in the mishmash of buildings that crawled up the mountain's side. Most of the buildings were short and squat, the better to withstand the summer heat, but some wore bright colors and peaked roofs or were packed together out of mud and old greenery. There was no logic to any of it.

Just inside the first wall sat a number of small farms. It was clear from their looks that they barely produced enough to feed the people who worked them. As Sef and Taisce passed, the villagers looked up from their hoes and rakes. The suspicion in their eyes sparkled like cut glass. Sef tipped his hat to each in turn. None returned the greeting. He hadn't expected them to.

"What are you doing?" Taisce hissed, spurring his horse into a quicker pace to catch up to Sef.

"I'm being friendly of course."

The look Taisce shot him was just as displeased as the grubby villagers' had been.

Sef sighed. "Where would your man go? The inn I suppose?"

"If anyone has seen him it would be Brannigan or Felix."

"And they would be...?"

"They're my father's men."

"Right. That explains so much," Sef said. "Tell me, milord, what exactly does your family *do*?"

Taisce blinked at him in innocent confusion. "Whatever do you mean? It's business of course."

"Pray tell why your father has men so far from home? Clotsfield is no trade route I've ever heard of," Sef said, leaning forward in the saddle to get a better view of the boy's face.

"And you're so well versed in trade routes, are you?" Taisce asked with an arch of his eyebrows. He shook off whatever discomfort Sef's interrogation had caused and straightened in the saddle. When he spoke again he'd fallen back into the haughty tones Sef remembered from their first meeting. "Come along. We're nearly out of daylight. Brannigan and Felix can't be far."

Sef shook his head but followed without comment.

~~*

The velvet blue sky of twilight brought with it a pleasant coolness. Taisce was grateful for it. He felt as if he were coated in a layer of grit from their ride into town and drying sweat slicked his back and shoulders. He longed for a bath but that was impossible until they found Brannigan. Taisce was reduced almost to rags, yet somehow Sef had managed to keep his shirt and trousers impeccably clean. He'd even returned the infernal hat to the top of his head, setting it at an angle as they rode into town. Taisce didn't know why it irked him so.

His stomach turned over. The berries and mushrooms had made for a rather sparse meal. Between that and the heat he felt almost dizzy with nausea. Again. Unperturbed, the cicadas and crickets chirped out their shrill songs.

"There's an inn not far from here," Sef suggested.

He'd nearly forgotten his lack of coin while they were traveling through the wilderness, but now it came back to Taisce in such a rush that he froze. And Sef was still looking at him, waiting for his response.

"We must locate Brannigan and Felix first," Taisce insisted.

"Would it not be better to ask after them then? The inn—"

"I would rather not waste time wandering around this horrid city in the dark."

Sef raised an eyebrow at his tone. "Are you in such a frenzy over your lost companion? Or perhaps it's something else that concerns you so."

"What are you suggesting?"

"You're a terrible liar, milord." Sef leaned forward in the saddle the better to gaze at him head on. He smirked. "You forget, I already know you have no money. It's no great secret."

An undignified sputter left Taisce's lips before he could catch it. He wanted to deny the accusations just on principle. But denying the first would only damn him further. And denying the latter would be pointless. Even if he couldn't deny it, he didn't have to acknowledge it either. "If you're concerned for your payment..."

Sef waved away the half formed question. "There are other ways for you to repay me. Now. How do you intend to find your destination when you refuse to stop and inquire? Have you a map at least?"

"No," Taisce said and he cursed himself for being so ill prepared once again.

Beside him, Sef reined in his horse and slid to the ground with a sigh. Taisce glanced about in surprise. An inn stood beside them, windows already bright with lantern light. He hadn't even noticed in what direction Sef had been leading them.

"Wait for me here. Don't wander on alone," Sef said.

Taisce stiffened at the stern instructions—he wasn't a child that needed to be led about by the hand—but there was no chance for a reply before Sef had disappeared through the rough wooden door of the inn.

He could feel control drifting from his grasp like sand. It had begun as far back as Blume, the day that Rupert disappeared, but since Ciaran Taisce could feel it spilling away faster and faster. At home, he would have known whom to contact, for money, for information, for anything he might ever conceivably need in this life or the next. He was out of his depth here. These places were no longer points on a map in his study. Now they were real and they were full of cracks and crevices for Rupert and Norland to slip through. Taisce had bounced from one bout of bad luck to another. Though it pained him to admit it, even to himself, without Sef's aid Taisce might not have made it this far.

The door to the inn opened with a bang and a rush of boisterous conversation as Sef stepped out onto the cobbled street. It seemed rather early in the evening for such drunkenness, Taisce thought.

Sef clapped his hands together. "Well then. That was rather simpler than I had expected. Your destination is at the top of the hill."

Slowly, Taisce turned to look in the direction Sef indicated. The lamp lighters had made lazy progress up the sloping road ahead but much of it was still swathed in deepening shadow. It felt as if Sef had just told him to ride off the edge of the world. "Up there?"

"Yes."

Taisce blinked but the way became no clearer.

"Lead the way," Taisce murmured, waiting for Sef to nudge his horse on before doing the same.

Clotsfield was a curious place made even more so by the dying light. It had the look of an older time. Many of the streets were unpaved and slanting as if the entire city was intent on scaling the mountain it abutted. In the distance, Taisce could make out faint stretches of the plains and forest they'd left behind. It spread beneath the city for miles before fading off into the moonlit darkness. It felt a bit like standing upon a map drawn to enormous scale. Unreal. Disconnected. Only two days ago things had made so much more sense. Now he was a ship lost at sea with nothing but an untrustworthy compass to guide him. If one could even call Sef a compass at all. Taisce glanced at the man riding beside him. Sef had offered no additional assistance beyond this particular branch of Taisce's journey and there was no reason to suspect that he would. The man was horrid and inscrutable but his potential loss tugged at Taisce in a way he wasn't prepared for.

Taisce shook his head. It made no sense.

"You're quiet, milord. Still agonizing over your poverty?" Sef asked.

Taisce gritted his teeth, all sentiment forgotten in an instant. "I think I shall celebrate when I'm free of my debt to you," Taisce said. "The weight of it is a nuisance."

"I haven't asked anything of you yet."

"And why haven't you?" Taisce asked, suspicion burning in his throat at the mere mention. "How grossly do you intend to overcharge me? I would prefer you tell me now."

"I never said I wanted money."

"Then what is it that you *do* want?"

Sef chuckled and slanted a look at him. "If you thought a moment, perhaps you would chance upon something." And with that he rode on ahead.

The suddenness of the comment took Taisce by surprise, the meaning too blatant to misunderstand. Taisce closed the distance between them again. "I'm not some whore," he hissed, leaning in close for discretion.

"I didn't ask you to be."

"You talk in riddles but we both know what you meant."

"I should hope so. You're an attractive man and I've been incredibly unsubtle about how much I'd like to take you to bed, but I'd prefer to have you there by choice."

It was such a curiously backhanded compliment that it took Taisce a moment to come up with an appropriate retort. This was not the kind of flirtation he was used to. He was used to coy proposals and sidelong glances in need of deciphering. Subtlety. He thought he could grow used to such forthright treatment if given enough time. Not that he would ever share that discovery with Sef. And still Taisce had made no answer.

He studied the backs of his hands, still loosely looped through the reins, and could think of nothing to say. He couldn't speak of what he was thinking just then, the decision that had started to transform like a butterfly in a chrysalis.

Sef held out a hand, pulling both of their horses to a standstill. "It seems we've arrived." He jerked his head towards the narrow house beside them. It bore a simple brass sign beside the door: *Brannigan & Felix, Business.* "Well, that's certainly specific."

Even in the dark, Taisce could see that the shutters were painted the garish yellow of false sunshine. The rest of the house was unremarkable. It was narrow framed with equally narrow windows, making up for its overwhelming narrowness by stretching up three long stories. The weak light of the nearby street lamps was hardly able to reach the top floor. It could almost have ceased to exist. Perhaps there was no roof up there at all. Taisce found himself imagining the half formed third floor, roofed with nothing but the purple night sky and stars. He wouldn't mind that at all.

He dismounted and hitched his horse to the post, keenly aware of Sef's stillness. He hadn't made any move to follow. "You're not coming?"

"I have no business here."

Taisce frowned. "Will you be here when I return?" He was glad that the darkness hid the color in his face but it did nothing to ease the blood thundering in his ears. At least the damnable man couldn't hear it.

Sef raised an eyebrow but he nodded once. "I'm in no hurry." He lounged over his horse's neck, giving it a pat.

There was nothing left to dawdle over so Taisce climbed the stairs and knocked on the door. The hour was late, but not obscenely so, and this was business after all. Some of the windows still flickered with a feeble light. Surely someone was home and awake. He raised his fist to knock again when the door creaked inward.

"Yeah?" The person at the door was tall and thin, head crowned with an impressive top hat trimmed in blue silk ribbon. It took Taisce another moment to make out the blue and black flounced skirt and long coat. In the dim light, he was unsure who he was looking at. Their short hair and hat suggested one thing but the ample skirts said another.

"I'm looking for Brannigan," Taisce said.

"Then you've found her," she said, "but I have business to attend to. You'll have to deal with Felix instead." She called inside to announce him. Taisce hoped the mysterious Felix was in less of a hurry than Miss Brannigan.

Leaving the door ajar, she stepped out onto the narrow stoop beside Taisce, buttoning her coat over her breast and pulling up her collar as if against the cold. "Sorry 'bout that," she said, sounding anything but. She tipped her hat and set off down the street, tipping her hat again, more leisurely this time, as she passed Sef. He returned it with a nod and the kind of smile he probably thought was charming.

Taisce was left staring at the vacated door. She hadn't actually invited him inside, but when no one came to welcome him, he ventured into the foyer, closing the door gently behind him. "Hello? Felix?"

The inside of the place was different from what he would have expected based on the exterior and his brief meeting with Miss Brannigan. The walls were painted a cheerful, deep cherry pink, faded in places but no less bright for it. A set of steep stairs led almost straight up from the door, disappearing into the shadows of the second floor. At his left was a small sitting room carpeted with a queasily patterned rug and cluttered with so many trinkets that Taisce didn't know where to turn his eyes. It felt like a bustling circus though nothing in the room had moved an inch.

From the doorway at the back of the sitting room, a short, round man appeared. He wiped his glasses on a cloth and set them atop his nose again. "Yes. Yes, hello," he said. His mustache twitched as he spoke, the gray in it catching the light.

"You're Felix?" Taisce asked, already full of misgivings. What kind of business office was this?

"That's what they call me," smiled the man. "John Rhys Felix, at your service."

With his half dozen inches of superior height, Taisce felt like a giant beside the little nesting doll shaped man. He brushed the thought aside, straightening his shoulders. "Good. I am Taisce

Brenton. I trust you know me." Taisce kept his expression cool but it was hard to still the wild beating of his heart. Thus far everything that could go wrong had. What if Finn had mistaken the names and there was no help to be found here?

Taisce's fears only lived for a moment.

Felix's eyes widened behind his glasses and he dropped into a repeated bow like a buoy bobbing in stormy waters. "Of course. Of course." He paused to squint up at Taisce. "But what are you doing *here*? We weren't due for a review for quite some time, my lord." He glanced around suddenly as if wishing he'd had time to hide the knick knacks. Which perhaps was exactly what he'd been thinking.

"I'm in need of assistance," Taisce said, steeling himself for the rest of his admission. It was easier to make to Felix. He behaved as he should, with respect. Not like Sef who was probably outside laughing at Taisce that very instant. "My purse was stolen and I'm without funds. I need you to provide me with more. My father will reimburse you for your troubles, of course."

Felix nodded, looking only a little pale at the mention of money.

"And my man Finn, has he been to see you yet?"

"Could be. Could be. I wouldn't know much about that though. Mae is the one who handled him. Said he was a frightful mess. Showed up yesterday 'round midnight. Believe she sent him off to the Saints' to get bandaged up proper."

Taisce slumped, relief flooding him though the

news wasn't quite what he'd hoped. "He was injured?"

"His nose was a mushy mess," Felix said. He'd continued to nod throughout their exchange as if he'd forgotten that he was doing it. "No permanent damage though I suspect." *Nod. Nod.* "He'll be good as new after a bit of rest."

"But it was Finn?"

Felix finally stopped his incessant nodding to scratch a hand through his thinning brown hair. Then he held the hand up nearly as far as it would go. "Big fella, about so high? Couldn't tell much about him because of the state he was in like I said. Not too many Brenton types around these parts though."

It wasn't much to go on but it would have to suffice. "Can you take me to this Saints' where you sent him?"

"Afraid I can't. But I can tell you how to get there."

Taisce frowned. "That's all?"

"Ain't far at all. You could see it from here if you squint." Before Taisce could attempt to persuade him again, Felix put a hand to his shoulder and ushered him to the front door. "The Saints' is just up the street. Turn left at Fisker and you can't possibly miss it even in this gloom. Damn lamp lighters, slacking again. The whole street for the Saints' is lit up like it's feast days all year long though. You check on your man and I'll have the rest of your request put together upon your return, my lord," Felix promised with a squinty eyed smile.

"Thank you," Taisce said, shying away from

Felix's guiding hand at his back. The man smelled faintly of fish. It wafted around him like an invisible cloud.

At the door, Sef spotted them and touched a hand to his brim in greeting. "Oh. I didn't know you had another man with you," Felix said, eyes never leaving Sef.

Taisce forced a chuckle. "No. He's not one of my father's. He's... a friend." It pained him to utter the words out loud where Sef was in danger of hearing them, but there was no other expedient way to end the discussion. Felix had broken out in a sudden and extremely fishy sweat at the sight of Sef waiting in the dark.

The answer seemed to suit Felix or, if it didn't, he didn't seem inclined to question it. "Oh. Yes. Of course. Yes." He nodded to them both in greeting and farewell. "I'll have everything you need in an hour or so, my lord," he said before dashing back into the house and slamming the door behind him.

"Odd," Taisce said, staring at the closed door for a full minute before turning and collecting his horse from the hitching post.

"Have you found your answers then?" Sef asked with a stretch and a yawn as though he'd been napping. His tone made it clear just how little he cared for the answer. One wondered why he asked at all.

"Yes. Thank you," Taisce said stiffly. He mounted and turned up the road. "It's this way."

"What is 'this way'?"

"Finn has been taken to the Saints'. It seems he's come to some harm," Taisce said carefully, burying the sudden rush of guilt. He had nothing to do with whatever had happened to Finn. They'd been separated. It could have been anything. But somehow, that didn't comfort Taisce at all.

Just as Felix had said, the Saints' was impossible to miss. The street dead-ended in a large paved circle and brightly glowing lanterns ran around the perimeter, painting the cobbles in shivering gold. Taisce half expected to find a great tree in the center of the place, something high enough to see from all the surrounding streets and strung with paper decorations and glittering foil. He forgot the oppressive warm breath of the summer air when they rode up to the Saints'. It seemed almost magical. Bright and inviting. He hadn't seen so many lights since he'd left Blume. The circle shone almost as brilliantly as day, with slips of shadow outlining every bit of glass and metal, but it was nothing compared to the building at the end of the street. The walls of the Saints' had been set with a million tiny tiles of glass, both clear and multicolored. In the lantern light it twinkled like the stars on the clearest night he'd ever seen.

"It's beautiful," Taisce whispered.

He longed to reach out and run his hands over the tiny mirrors, the chips of blue and green and yellow glass. He knew it couldn't possibly feel as beautiful as it looked but he wanted to do it all the same.

For once, Sef remained silent, but Taisce could feel

his eyes. He'd almost developed an innate sense where Sef was concerned. He ignored it in favor of the glittering display in front of them. "Such an odd beauty for a place like this," he murmured.

"This used to be a library. Scholars would come from all over the kingdom to study within these walls," Sef commented.

"What? How do you know all that?" Taisce asked, scrambling to catch up before Sef reached the broad double doors of the Saints'. He'd dismounted so quietly that Taisce hadn't even heard his feet touch the pavement. The arched doors of the Saints' were just as impressive as everything else, easily ten feet tall, cut from fine-grained wood, and carved with scrolled leaves and vines. The wood had been buffed to smoothness from so many years of use. Taisce pressed a hand to one of the doors. It felt as soft as silk.

Sef grabbed the ring on the opposite door and pushed it inward without waiting. He swept inside and, after another look about him, Taisce did too.

The lanterns were fewer here, set more sparsely throughout the room, and their light barely made it to the outer walls let alone the vaulted rafters of the main chamber. It was cavernous. The center of the room had been set with heavy wooden benches for services and curtains and screens had been erected in a maze-like tangle to partition off the rest of the vast room. Somewhere among these, Finn could be waiting. Taisce hesitated to begin his search. If what Felix said was true, Finn would be in a very sorry state indeed.

The decision was taken from his hands. A woman stopped before them. Her hair was hidden beneath the draped veil that marked her as a priest and there was quiet kindness in her eyes. "Are you in need of shelter?" she asked.

"I'm looking for someone. A large, stocky man. Alone. He would have arrived very late last night, badly wounded."

She nodded in recognition. "The wolf attack." She smiled wanly and held out a hand to direct them. "He's resting now. I'll take you to him."

They weaved their way between the makeshift beds, most little more than sacks stuffed with straw, scattered over the hard stone floor. Many of the beds were filled already, though their occupants were awake. Their eyes were like a hundred tiny pinpricks against his skin. He knew he would not have been welcomed even if he had sought shelter there.

The priest led them to a cluster of beds beside the far wall. A colored glass window stretched into the darkness above them. It might have been a Saint adorning the glass but Taisce was unable to tell. Age and weathering had darkened it and the lanterns' light barely crept past the bottom of the high-set window frame. He could just make out the curled yellow scroll set into the bottom of the panel but the words on it were in no language he had ever seen. He glanced at Sef. He was looking at the window too, face unreadable. His lips moved soundlessly.

Taisce tore his eyes away from the window. He

wasn't there for sightseeing.

While he'd been distracted, the priest had roused a large hulk of a man sleeping on one of the straw mattresses. She gave his shoulder another shake and nodded towards Taisce.

He barely dared to breathe as the man turned. His face was indeed a mess. His nose had been plastered with a thick layer of bandages and his forearm was wrapped with even more of the white gauze but there was no mistaking him.

"Finn." Taisce had the unthinkable urge to throw himself on the man and hug him but he fought it down. "Thank goodness," he said instead.

"My lord!" Finn had no such qualms. He attempted to rush forward, tangling in his sack mattress and falling to one knee before he managed to make it to Taisce's side. Finn cradled his chest with his unbandaged arm. "My lord! I feared you were lost forever." He smiled so brightly that Taisce could have counted each of his teeth.

He blushed, glancing around to see who might be listening. "I was fine," Taisce said weakly.

"I swear I'll kill those nasty little wretches the next time!" Finn spat, unable to contain his sudden rage. "They surprised me, my lord. Snuck up on me. There was naught I could do but I heard the evil things they said. About your honorable self too." His face turned an alarming shade of purple, which only served to highlight the bruises and cuts on his face. He sputtered another string of obscenities before he recalled to whom he was speaking. "How did you escape, my lord? I chased them when I heard... but they'd already scattered like the plague rats they are. Did they hurt you? Are you well?" he demanded, reaching out as if he planned to inspect him personally.

Taisce shook his head. "I'm fine. Did they do this to you?"

"Not them. The wolves. I was more than a match for those little vixens when they didn't cheat."

"The wolves?"

Sef snorted but when Taisce turned to scold him, he'd already wandered off again, trailing a hand along the chalky, white stone of the wall.

"What wolves?" Taisce asked, turning back to Finn.

Finn spread his hands as if molding his attackers from the air in front of him. "They were massive beasts, like the monsters out of a storybook. They pulled me from my horse but I fought them off. Seems they didn't like the taste of my blade." One fist waved before him as if repeating his attacks. He smiled, puffing up with pride.

"What kind of wolf would attack you without provocation?" Finn was covered in scratches and seeping cuts. Obviously *something* had attacked him.

"It's a wonder he wasn't killed," Sef said, making Taisce jump. He hadn't noticed Sef's return nor the fact that he was standing directly behind him.

"Who is this?" Finn asked, eyebrows drawing down into a glower at the newcomer.

Sef leaned around Taisce's shoulder like some

kind of grinning gargoyle, as he waited for his introduction. It wasn't necessary. Finn's eyes widened in sudden recognition. "You!"

"Me," agreed Sef.

"You sneaky devil," Finn accused. "I remember you. You were in Ciaran. What do you want with my lord?"

"A great many things."

They stared at each other, Finn's glower greatly hindered by his bandaged nose and the scabbed scratches on his forehead.

Taisce sighed. "Enough. Sef was assisting me through the forest. Now, it's been a very long day and I require rest. I've spoken with Felix and he has offered to provide supplies for the rest of our journey. Are you fit to travel, Finn?"

"I'll be good as gold tomorrow, my lord. The Saints bandaged me up well. These wounds are nothing." He beamed, wide jaw protruding.

Taisce cast him a doubtful look before nodding. "Have you your horse?"

Finn's smile vanished. "No, my lord. It was... taken. The wolves." He looked at his toes.

"Then we'll have to secure you another before we move on." Taisce nodded and turned towards the door.

His gaze swept the interior of the place again. It really was quite lovely. Under different circumstances he might have liked to explore it more thoroughly. Sef's words came back to him again. He'd said it had been a great library once. Taisce wished he could ask him what he knew of it.

Chapter Eight
IN WHICH THEY COME TO AN UNDERSTANDING

True to his word, Felix welcomed them back with an anxious smile and an offer of cold coffee. "I've gathered what you asked." He led them through the sitting room and into the cramped office that Taisce had spied on his earlier visit. A thin-legged desk and an enormous bookshelf filled most of the already small room, barely leaving space for Felix, let alone his guests, but the four of them found spaces for themselves before the door was closed to discourage interruption. Taisce looked around, noting the peeling wallpaper in the corner behind Felix's desk. At least there were no trinkets littering the shelves and staring at him with their vacant little eyes.

On the desk sat a pouch, presumably full of the requested money, and beside it a rolled map. Beside that was a ledger bound in dark green leather. Taisce surveyed each item in turn while Felix settled into the chair behind his desk. It was no easy task with the room filled almost to bursting.

First Felix slid the pouch closer to Taisce. "I was

only able to collect a small amount of money so late at night. If that's unsuitable, my lord, I can arrange for more tomorrow." He smiled, eyes slipping between Finn and Sef who had settled at the far corners of the room so they could glare at each other undisturbed.

Taisce worked open the tie on the pouch and peered inside. It was as small an amount as Felix had implied. Taisce's stolen purse had contained three times the number of coins that Felix was now offering him. He closed it back up, retying the leather cord with more care than it necessitated. "Our journey is sure to be quite a long one. I would be glad of as much assistance as you can manage," Taisce said.

"More?"

"Yes. More."

Felix ran a finger along his collar. "Very well, my lord." He cleared his throat before picking up the rolled parchment. "I took the liberty of locating a map of the area as well. In case you were without." He unrolled the heavy parchment himself, spreading it over the blotter and pinning down the corner with an oddly shaped paperweight that Taisce had initially taken for some kind of strange sculpture. Felix smoothed the paper to keep it from curling up again. "I didn't know your destination, but this map was drawn quite recently. It stretches almost to the south deserts."

Taisce gave it only a cursory examination. All the lines blurred together the harder he tried to focus on them. Without his glasses, it looked like nothing more than a child's scribbling. "Yes. Very good. That will be quite helpful," Taisce said. He pressed a thumb to his temple.

"This is the ledger for the last year's business. You'll see that everything is absolutely in order, my lord." Felix held the leather bound book before him like a shield.

Taisce waved it away. Even if he'd had any interest in their affairs at present, an attempt to read the tiny columns of facts and figures right now would only strain his eyes. "I'm not here to make a review of your ledgers. What I do need is a bed. Can you spare one?"

Felix's look was brimming with nervous curiosity. "Only one?"

"More if you have them."

"Yes. Yes of course," Felix agreed quickly. "Right this way." He bustled from his office and collected an oil lamp from a side table before leading them on to the steep stairs. "It's not as fine as you're used to I'm afraid, my lord, but I hope you'll forgive the meager accommodations and think kindly on us all the same."

"I'm sure it will be fine," Taisce said without much hope. At least it would be an improvement over sleeping on the hard ground for another night.

The rooms Felix led them to were at the top of the house, on the mysterious third floor, which Taisce was strangely disappointed to see did possess an actual roof. Each room was as cramped as everything else in the narrow little house. Taisce felt more and more as if he were clay being squeezed by a great hand. By the time he left, perhaps he would be seven feet tall and thin as a string bean after being pressed between the brocade-papered walls of Felix's house. He'd ceased thinking of it as a business altogether. One office hardly seemed enough to qualify it as such.

"I hope this room will suit you, my lord." Felix threw open the final door on the hall to present the largest room yet, though that was a shallow accomplishment. The most impressive feature of the room was the slant wall filled with dormer windows. Perhaps in the morning he would wake to a lovely view of the town, but Taisce doubted it.

"This will do nicely." Taisce hoped that would be enough to appease the man's obsequious hospitality. His headache was growing by leaps and bounds now that it had taken root.

"There is a bath just downstairs if you'd like it. Or I'll have a maid bring wash water immediately so you can be to bed, my lord." Felix looked in danger of fainting with the pressure of keeping up his attentions and the sweat gathering at his temples only increased with his agitation.

Taisce smiled tightly. "Thank you. You are a dedicated host, but you needn't trouble yourself."

After a few additional offers of refreshment and other services, Felix finally withdrew. Taisce wanted nothing more than to throw himself into the bed and sleep undisturbed for the first time in weeks, but Finn was still loitering in the hallway, as was Sef.

Catching Taisce's eye, Finn scuttled closer and leaned in conspiratorially. "Will you be all right on your own, my lord?" There was no missing his meaning, or the way he turned to glare in Sef's direction.

"Quite," Taisce said, sending Finn on his way before he could protest. He'd had more than enough helpfulness for one night. When he looked up again, Sef had disappeared into his own room, though the door had been left conspicuously ajar.

True to his word, Felix sent a maid up with a basin of wash water and a threadbare towel. The girl was just as round as her master, hair hidden beneath a simple cotton bonnet and apron askew over her dark dress. She set the things she'd brought onto the side table and withdrew with the silent tread of a cat.

Once she had gone, Taisce allowed himself to slump onto the bed. The room was small, but the bed was soft enough. The wallpaper pattern was a mix of vines and tiny flowers, better suited to a nursery than a proper guest room and, in the lamp light, it seemed to writhe around him. He longed for his own room, the high ceiling, the mahogany paneling, everything illuminated by great shafts of light from the many windows. His room had never felt as dark and claustrophobic as this even in the dead of night. Or perhaps it was the weeks of sleeping beneath the stars that made him feel so boxed in. He'd hardly had a roof over his head since he left Blume. He had almost forgotten what it felt like to look up and see plaster.

Weeks of travel had left dirt beneath his nails and he'd accumulated yet another day's growth of beard. Taisce scratched at his chin. No one would think to call him a gentleman now. Not that Sef or Finn were in much better condition. They were just as travel worn as him but, while they had retreated quietly to their rooms, Taisce found himself pacing.

It was the first promise of restful sleep he'd had in days. Despite its other flaws, Felix's house was as silent as a church. Nothing disturbed the peace in Taisce's room, not the ticking of a clock or the call of an owl. He should have enjoyed it. He pondered it as he made another loop around the room. He and Finn would continue on their way tomorrow. But what of Sef? Taisce had grown used to having the infuriating man around. He wasn't good for much, surely, but Taisce didn't know if he could survive another month of nothing but Finn's company either.

He sighed. Surely he'd been bewitched to even consider it. And yet he was.

Taisce put aside his thoughts, gaze falling on the bowl of wash water. Shaving would have to wait until later—he couldn't manage that without a mirror at least—but the cool water felt good on his skin. He splashed it over his face before stripping out of his shirt and picking up the towel to clean away the film of dirt coating his body.

Taisce had hoped that washing would take the tension out of his muscles and ease his soul so he could sleep. It did neither. If anything he felt more awake.

He stalked out into the hall again.

When he checked, Finn was fast asleep, so Taisce left the sack of his washing beside his door and moved on. Finn could attend to it in the morning when he woke. There was no need to wake him over it now.

In the house below, Taisce heard quiet voices. He crept to the stairs, inching down them in a crouch as if he were a child again spying on his father's business. It wasn't difficult to make out the louder tones of Miss Brannigan. She was doing an excellent job of cutting off most of Felix's stuttering comments. Taisce settled himself on the step at the top of the first floor, in the shadows where they'd be unlikely to catch him.

"How could you give them the upper floor?" Miss Brannigan cried. Her voice carried neatly from further in the house. Probably Felix's office.

"But, Mae—"

"You should have packed them off to the Saints'."

"You know very well that I couldn't do that. They'll be gone tomorrow. And I feared—"

"Yes, I know." She sighed loudly. "I saw the one he had outside. There's something of the devil in him." She paused again, even her pacing growing silent. "Did they see the books?"

Whatever his answer was Taisce couldn't hear it. He could barely even make out the sound of the little round man's voice when he strained.

"Then what could they possibly want here if not the books? You haven't been fixing them again, have you?" Miss Brannigan asked, voicing rising sharply.

"I wouldn't, Mae."

"Oh don't pretend to be offended. We both know you're a swindler when you care to be."

"Not in a long time. In ages. Everything is perfectly right."

"That's all well then," she said. "We wouldn't want his highness to send his demons after you." Her words trailed off into a low drone, but he had already heard more than enough to satisfy any curiosity he might have. Brannigan and Felix argued with the familiarity of a married couple.

They'd been talking about him, of course, but at least they seemed ignorant of the true reason for his visit. It was best to keep the matter of Rupert's disappearance as discreet as possible. This far south it was unlikely that anyone would recognize him, just as it was unlikely that any gossip would make its way back home, but he liked to be sure. Rupert's reputation might be saved after all. The knowledge did little to soothe Taisce's nerves. Still so far to go and no word or direction to lead him. If Rupert hadn't passed through Ciaran, he must have gone somewhere else. There were only so many paths through the mountains and plains. Taisce only hoped that he found the right one soon.

He sat in thought until he heard footsteps below him again. If he didn't move, they would find him still eavesdropping. Taisce slipped back up the stairs to the third floor. Sef's open door let a trickle of lamp light spill across the rug and onto Taisce's toes. He pushed the door open without knocking.

He'd expected to find Sef asleep already, forgotten lamp burning away on his bedside table, or perhaps nosing around the room in that nefarious way he had. Instead Sef stood with his back to the door. The small window beside his bed hung open. It was set high up the wall, just high enough for him to rest an arm on as he peered out at the darkness.

"What are you looking at?" Taisce asked.

Sef barely glanced at him. "Nothing in particular."

"Are you from the area? You seem to know it well."

There was a puff of dry laughter as Sef turned away from the window, pulling it closed behind him. In the dim light, his eyes looked like bottomless pits. Maybe the man really was a friend to demons, given the strange power he seemed to possess. "No. I'm not from here."

"Then where?"

Sef glanced down. His smile sharpened into something like a grimace. "A place that doesn't exist anymore. But that's not what you've come for, is it? Come to repay your debt instead, milord?" His eyes slipped back up to Taisce's, taking their time as they moved over him.

The brazenness with which Sef spoke never failed to leave him speechless. Taisce was tempted to deny it, but there was no point. They both knew why he'd come. Taisce pushed the door closed behind him. "If you wish to think of it that way I cannot stop you."

Sef's eyes widened. For once, Taisce had managed

to surprise him. It felt good, better than he would have expected. Then the man's expression twisted into one of hunger. It was as frightening as it was invigorating. The feral gleam in his eyes. No one had ever looked at Taisce that way, as if they could devour him completely. Sef turned down the lamp. "Really now." He crooked a finger at Taisce. "Come here then."

Taisce hesitated, anticipation curling in his stomach. He could leave. Nothing would stop him if he decided to end everything there and walk out of the room after all.

Sef waited.

As an afterthought, Taisce checked the door again, but there was no key in the lock. A closed door would have to suffice.

Sef's hands were almost shockingly cool as they slipped up Taisce's spine. "I've been waiting for you."

He didn't give Taisce a chance to respond before their lips met in a teasing kiss. The brush of his lips was gentle, like a breath. It didn't suit him. Taisce arched up, seeking the satisfaction of warm skin against his, and his tongue swiped over Sef's lower lip. He wanted something more, something to remember. Morning always came so soon and he wouldn't see it wasted, not when all they had between them and the rest of the world was an unlocked door. With greedy hands he tugged at Sef's loose shirt, wanting the flesh beneath.

Sef chuckled into his neck. The vibration set off a riot of delicious shivers. "Take off your clothes, milord."

"And yours," Taisce hissed. He pulled away only far enough to tear off his shirt and toss it aside. Sef's gaze caressed every inch of skin as he exposed it. Taisce was slower to let his trousers drop. Not with shyness. It was easier to be anything he wanted here in this room, in this city where no one knew him. It was a freedom he'd never realized before and he wanted to savor each moment. But again, Sef had other ideas. He reached for Taisce and pulled him close, fist in his hair, lips covering his, kissing a trail from his mouth and along his jaw. His teeth grazed Taisce's ear. Cool fingers slid down his chest and over his stomach, drawing desire like lines on his skin.

Sef's shirt was lost to the floor, but his trousers hung low on his hips. Taisce tugged at the fastening until it finally came free. That was as far as he got before his attention was taken with the scar on Sef's chest. It ran at an angle from below Sef's left shoulder nearly down to his stomach. Taisce pressed a hand to either side of it before dropping a line of open mouthed kisses along the raised skin. He tasted it with his tongue. The salty tang of sweat. The tremor of the rapidly beating heart encased within. So Sef was flesh and blood after all. It brought a smile to Taisce's lips. "How did you get this scar?" Sef's skin was otherwise unblemished, not a scratch or bruise marred it.

"That's a story for another day, I think," Sef said.

"Oh?" Taisce raised an eyebrow, but he was quite

content to let the enigma last a little longer.

He shoved Sef backwards until he toppled over the bed and then climbed on after him. Having Sef beneath him was all he could have wanted. Sef's hands circled his thighs, fingers digging into the muscle, massaging, and Taisce groaned. Each kneaded circle reduced him to a quivering mass of nerves. He could almost have come from that alone, but the careless graze of knuckles along his prick had him shouting in surprise. Sef cupped a hand over his mouth. "Careful, milord. You'll wake the house," he said with that infuriating grin.

Taisce glared at him. "Shut up." He settled lower over Sef's body. It was as interested as his own. He could feel him, already risen to attention, already eager for more. He wrapped his arms around Sef. He would have wrapped his entire body around him if he could, anything to keep him so close. Sef pressed a kiss to his temple, another to his lips, before rolling Taisce beneath him. The darkness in his eyes was captivating. Like looking into a starless sky.

~~*

Taisce woke aching and lethargic. Rolling over was too difficult a task when his body seemed to have gained twice its usual weight during the night so he stayed face down on the bed and tried to stretch life back into his limbs. His hand brushed bare skin.

A surprised "oh" popped from his lips before he could catch it. Sef was already awake, watching him with an amused smirk. Sef's bed. Sef's bed he'd been sleeping in. Taisce nearly fell off the edge of the mattress in his scramble to sit up.

"Good morning," Sef said.

"What are you still doing here?" Taisce tugged the wrinkled sheet closer around him, hoping it might hide him from the consequences of last night's impetuousness. He glanced around the room but the light from the window gave him no clues as to the time of day.

"You may recall this is my room."

"I thought..." Taisce trailed off. Had he really expected that Sef would disappear into the night like a phantom? It seemed silly now in the light of day.

"Regretting it already?" Sef asked, eyebrow rising in question. Or perhaps it was challenge that Taisce saw on his face.

"No." He wasn't in the habit of regretting his choices. There was no reason to start doing so now. All the same, he couldn't laze about in a borrowed bed all day no matter how much the option appealed. Taisce twisted, searching the floor for his discarded clothing.

Sef pulled him back, laying Taisce out beneath him. "Stay."

It was tempting. In the morning light, the intensity had drained from Sef's face leaving him looking pale but no less handsome. Taisce reached up, tracing the line of his cheek. Then he pushed him away. He slipped from the bed before Sef could stop him again. "Finn will be looking for me before long."

He rummaged about on the floor, finally dragging his rumpled trousers from the pile and tugging them on.

Sef stretched, arching his back like a cat and giving a pleased groan. He made no effort to cover himself as the sheet slipped down to his hips. "It's quite pleasant to have a bed. A shame it's only temporary."

Taisce was momentarily taken with the pull of muscle in Sef's abdomen, the thin line of hair leading lower. There'd hardly been time to enjoy the view last night. He tore his eyes away but not quickly enough. Sef's smile twisted into a familiar leer. He scrubbed a hand through his hair, setting his waves in even greater disorder. "Surely there's no hurry."

Taisce turned away. He had to find the rest of his clothes before he changed his mind. "This is a matter of great importance. I haven't the time to waste." Silently he added, *No matter how much I might prefer it.*

But letting Sef tempt him into one day's rest wouldn't be the end of it. It would be too easy to give in. Again and again until he'd truly lost any chance of finding Rupert. He couldn't abandon his duty because of one night's pleasure.

Sef rolled to face him. "Really now?" For the first time he looked honestly interested but Taisce wouldn't indulge him. Not yet. He had too much to consider. Alone.

~~*

Sef frowned as Taisce disappeared, closing the

door behind him. Back to tiptoeing around, no doubt. It was unfortunate after all the progress they'd made last night. He couldn't remember the last time he'd had such a spirited lover. Taking his pleasure with the boy had been better than he would have dared expect, without any of the chilly formality of Taisce's usual demeanor. Beneath him, Taisce had shown his true nature. It was a transformation that Sef would have been happy to repeat this morning.

He scratched lazily at his bare stomach, too comfortable to bother with being aggravated. He would learn all the boy's secrets soon enough. No sense rushing things.

"I think I would like a bath," Sef decided.

It didn't take long to find the cute little maid from the night before and charm her into filling a bath for him. No doubt the others in the house would like one as well but that wasn't his problem. If they wished it so badly, they should have secured the bath for themselves first.

While he waited, he prowled the house. It felt more like a tree than a dwelling for people. The upper floor he'd already seen and the second floor was much like it, just a narrow hall surrounded by doors. Behind one sat the bath. He'd found that last night while Taisce slept. He suspected the rest merely hid bedrooms but their doors were locked and he couldn't be bothered to persuade them to open. With all his other sources of entertainment evaporating, he wandered back down to the first floor and the overly decorated front room. The trinkets on every shelf made him feel as if he'd wandered into some kind of bazaar. He rearranged a few of the little figures, grimacing at a porcelain prince in fine robes edged in gilt. He turned that one to face the wall just as someone came into the room.

"Oh."

It was the woman he'd seen at the door the night before. She wore no hat and coat today, only a simple, pinstriped shirtwaist and full skirt. A string tie hung at her neck in the place of a necklace. It made her look more the school mistress than the business woman she purported to be. When she saw him, she pressed a hand to her chest, drawing Sef's eyes. The jeweled ring on her middle finger was much too elaborate for the rest of her attire even if it was only paste. He suspected that it wasn't.

"You gave me a fright. What are you doing in here?" Her tone swung between astonishment and reproach so neatly it was hard to keep from imagining her in front of a collection of school children.

Sef smiled. "I came to express my gratitude for your hospitality, Miss...?"

"Ah yes. My manners. Of course." She held out her hand, all reluctance forgotten and cheeks tinged pink from his smile. "Mae Brannigan."

He cradled her hand in his, lips brushing over her knuckles before he returned it to her.

She pressed her hand to her chest again though her surprise had disappeared. "Please let me know if you need anything else."

"Thank you." His lips formed another smile before he excused himself and slipped back up the stairs. She'd been easier to charm than he'd thought.

The maid left the bath just as he reached the second floor. "It's ready," she said in her meek whisper before scurrying away like the mouse she resembled.

The room had filled with steam, no doubt helped along by the mounting heat from outside. By midday, it would be an inferno. Sef wasted little time climbing into the metal tub. The water caressed his skin as he slipped deeper and he exhaled on a sigh. Such a luxury was this. It was almost as good as Taisce's ministrations. Almost, but not quite.

He slipped lower, letting the water lap at his chin before finally taking a breath and submerging himself to the top of his head. The water pressed in on him, filling his ears with a warbling like voices speaking all at once. Like screaming. The ghosts of hands weighed him down, settling on his chest like rocks. Sef gasped, arms flying out to catch himself as he slipped down the metal side of the tub. Water rushed into his mouth. It stung his nose. He came up, coughing and frantic, sloshing water onto the floor.

Too much like drowning. Too much like memories that should know to keep themselves buried.

Water dribbled from his mouth as he hung over the side of the tub, gasping for more air though his lungs were already filled to bursting. He pushed the lank hair from his face and squeezed his head tight.

He wished he could squeeze all the unpleasantness out too. Perhaps a bath had been a bad idea after all.

The door swung open suddenly and Sef jumped, sending another wave of water over the turned edge of the tub.

Taisce stood framed in the doorway. He'd neatened his hair and redressed properly. His linen shirt was starched and crisp, despite the wilting heat of the bath. As his eyes fell on the tub, he took a step back. "I didn't realize."

Sef painted on a look of ease. The thin smile was the most difficult part to get right. "Come in, milord. Join me."

Taisce hesitated before he asked, "Is there something the matter?"

"Nothing at all." Sef sat back, stretching his arms around the sides of the tub to brace himself. "What is it that you require?"

Another curious look passed over his features before Taisce closed the door. His attitude had changed so much from the night before. The action was the same but it had lost all its assurance. A pity. Sef wouldn't have minded another go. He could have laid them out on the floor while it was still slick from the spilled bathwater. Taisce's body would have been a welcome distraction from his pounding heart.

When Taisce turned around again, face set, Sef cocked his head. "Have you suddenly lost your voice? What is it?"

"It seems that Finn was able to gather some information while we were separated. You said before that you knew this area. How well do you know the country to the south?" Taisce seemed to be holding his breath but Sef couldn't begin to guess why.

He leaned his head back, a sudden weariness taking hold. "I know every inch of this godsforsaken country better than I would care to. What is it that you're asking?"

Taisce fidgeted. "I want to hire you. As our guide."

The silence stretched on the steamy air. There was nothing but the sound of water sloshing round the tub, the beating of Sef's heart, the gentle rasp of his breath. And then he began to laugh. He laughed until his sides ached and he gasped, sending more water onto the floor. It bubbled across the tile and Taisce stepped back to avoid it.

"Is that a no?" he asked. His tone bordered on defiance.

Ah, yes, that was the arrogant little git Sef had first met. He knew the boy wouldn't stay docile for long. He never did.

"And what is my payment to be?"

Taisce swallowed hard. They both knew which direction his thoughts had gone. But then the arrogance was back along with the haughty lift of his chin. Even travel-wearied he looked every inch the spoiled noble just then. And how beautiful it was. "One hundred croy. Payable upon completion of the task."

"The task?" Sef suspected he knew what the task

would be but there was no harm in playing at ignorance in the hopes of more information. Sef grabbed up the cake of soap, busying himself with it while he waited to hear the rest of the proposition. He could feel Taisce's eyes following the progress of his washing, could practically feel the hungry curl of his tongue over his lips as Sef spread a thick lather over his chest and down beneath the surface of the water. "What is this task?"

The answer was a moment in coming and Sef glanced up. As expected, a flush had crept into Taisce's face. His mouth hung slightly open and hungry. "As you know, I'm seeking my brother. Finn's information indicates he's moved farther south and I intend to follow. When he's been found, you'll get your money."

Sef knew he would accept. They were bound together already, though Taisce didn't yet know it, and this was indeed an interesting proposal. If nothing else, it would alleviate his boredom for a few more days, keep him from hating the rising of the sun any more than he already did. Perhaps it would also finally shed light on why Taisce felt so much like the key. Still, Sef hummed a little and pretended to mull it over. His gaze crept over the wallpaper around him. Such busy patterns in every room. He didn't like it.

"Will this be a dangerous journey then?"

Taisce's mouth snapped shut. He frowned at him. "No more dangerous than it needs to be."

"You've made it plenty dangerous for yourself

already, milord. How many times is it that I've saved you since we met?"

Sef hadn't thought it was possible for Taisce's frown to darken any further but somehow he managed it. "Don't make me regret my offer so soon after I've made it." He folded his arms over his chest. "I'll have your answer."

"Very well. I accept your gracious offer. I hope your purse is big enough to satisfy me." He scrubbed soap through his hair, massaging a thumb over the throbbing pulse in his temples, trying to ease the ache away. He felt so very old today. Strange that he would after last night had been so entertaining. "Would you assist me, milord?" He nodded towards the waiting pitcher of rinse water.

Taisce had been idly fidgeting as if he had more to say but he froze at the question. By the look on the boy's face, anyone would think Sef had suggested they screw on the floor in full view of the household. Which—to be fair—had crossed his mind before being rejected. Milord didn't seem inclined to any such fun in the daylight hours. But at night... oh, that was a different matter entirely.

Finally Taisce nodded. With both hands, he took up the pitcher and tipped it over Sef's head. Sef smiled, head dropping back to allow the water to run off down his back. Perhaps he didn't mind keeping certain parts of the boy to himself.

Sef finished rinsing the soapy lather from his body and stepped from the bath. The maid had thoughtfully left a towel for him and he took it up, rubbing the excess water from his hair. All the while, Taisce stood waiting patiently. Not looking away though. It seemed Taisce had given up the pretense of being uninterested in him. "Is there something else on your mind, milord?"

Taisce shook himself out of whatever trance he'd fallen into. "You've shaved."

"So I have."

He ran his fingers down his throat and frowned at the drag of bristling hair. "I haven't had a proper shave in weeks."

There seemed no point in answering what hadn't been a question. Sef waited for the boy to make whatever point he was aiming at. Finally Taisce's eyes met his. "Shave me."

Sef's eyebrows leapt in surprise. "Is that an order, milord?"

~~*

The boy really was too trusting.

Sef examined the gleaming straight razor in his hand. It was impeccably cared for, the metal bright and untarnished, and it had obviously been sharpened to a keen edge. And the boy had handed it to Sef as if it were nothing. The razor could probably slice a man open before he'd even realized what was happening. Or it could slit Taisce's throat from ear to ear. Sef tested the blade against his thumb and hissed when he found it as sharp as he'd expected. He licked the blood away.

"Hold very still," Sef whispered, startling the boy when his words brushed over his ear. "We wouldn't want you getting cut."

Taisce turned to glare at him but he didn't pull away. Such trust. The fact that he didn't even realize it, just showed how innocent he truly was.

Sef set to work quickly, tilting the boy's head to get a good angle at the throat, feeling like a sculptor coaxing fine marble into art. His fingers grazed along Taisce's ear, down the side of his neck, and over his jaw, the razor following. They crested the high curve of a cheek. Sef swiped his thumb over the pink lips he'd kissed last night, wiping away a trace of lather. The tiny bump at the bridge of his nose drew Sef's attention higher. He'd expected to find freckles dusting the boy's cheeks but they were a creamy unmarked tan from his recent travels. His eyes were laced with gold and chocolate brown, his eyelashes tipped with copper from the sun.

No, he decided. Instead of marble, Taisce would be sculpted from metal. Hard, unbending, but so pliant when warmed. Sef liked that image much better. He ran a hand along Taisce's neck, moving up to cup the back of his head.

"What are you doing?" Taisce asked suddenly. It was the first sign of anxiety he had shown since they began. This boy and his misguided caution. Of course he worried now that the danger was gone.

Sef chuckled. With the hand at the back of Taisce's neck, he tipped his head to the opposite side under the pretense of surveying his work. "You're the proper gentleman once more," Sef said. He stepped back quickly before he was tempted to take the boy on the floor of the bath like he'd imagined. Not that any distance could truly be called safe when he kept remembering the way Taisce arched in pleasure.

There was a mirror on the stand beside Taisce. He cast another curious glance at Sef before he picked it up, examining his face in the yellow light from the window. "You did much better than I expected."

"Thank you for that confidence, milord," Sef said dryly.

His sarcasm was left unchallenged. "I think I'd like a bath as well," Taisce mused, still running a hand along his smooth jaw. Then he turned back to Sef. "Alone. We leave in three hours time. If you have any business in this town, I suggest you finish it quickly."

The dismissal was absolute. Sef grinned at him, sweeping into a bow so low his fingers brushed the floor. "Of course. Milord.

CHAPTER NINE
IN WHICH THE WEATHER PLAYS A PART

The ride out of Clotsfield was much the same as the ride in. Boring. Humorless. It was also marred by the addition of Finn, who glared daggers at Sef whenever he was able.

Felix had sent them on their way with an enlarged purse and a generous gift of bread and other provisions for their journey. At Sef's suggestion, he had also added some jerky—beef this time—to the bundle before he tied it closed with shaking hands.

"You're too kind," Sef had told him with the bright smile he knew had the tendency to unnerve people.

Felix nodded, eyes following the bundle wistfully as Sef carried it away to Taisce. It didn't seem necessary to inform him that Sef had also relieved the house of two jars of preserves from the cellar. It had been a good decade since he'd had any to speak of and it didn't seem likely that Felix would mind. The cloth wrapped jars sat at the bottom of his saddle bags now, hidden from prying eyes.

"And where is it that we're headed again?" Sef

asked with boredom that he didn't even have to fake.

"We must go south. To Mission," Taisce said.

"Right. That's at least a half week's ride in good weather. Why are we going there?"

Taisce sighed. They'd gone over this before in vague terms. Prying information from the boy was no easier now than it had been before. "Finn heard tell of a man matching my brother's description and that of his... companions," Taisce bit out, voice going sharp on the final word as it always did when they fell into that particular subject. Sef still had no idea who or what these 'companions' consisted of. It could have been a pack of dogs for all he knew. Taisce would tell him nothing about them. "They were headed to Mission."

"In search of some legend," added Finn.

"A legend?" Sef frowned. He disliked legends as a general rule; so many of them had an unfortunate habit of being true. But there were none centered around Mission that he had ever heard of. Further south... that was another matter entirely. "What legend could they be chasing in Mission? Perhaps he misheard," Sef said, smiling at Finn. When he saw the scowl still pointed at him, Sef was tempted to blow a kiss at the puckered and ugly face. The reaction would have been well worth it.

"Ciaran offered nothing and this is the only new information we have. Unless you've uncovered something of use," Taisce said, "we will assume that they *did* continue to the south. And we will follow."

Sef leaned forward in the saddle, taking the lead

as they left Clotsfield behind. The terrain would be rougher from here, rocky and coarse. He found that he missed the endless green forests already. "And *why* are we following this brother of yours over half the country? Does he not know the way home on his own?" He chuckled.

His question was met with silence. Finn looked away into the distance and Taisce had succumbed to more angry-faced redness at the question. "It is none of your concern," he said finally, blurting it so suddenly that Sef wondered if he'd been holding his breath in along with the words.

"I would be of more use to you if I knew what it was I was hunting."

Taisce chewed prettily at his lip. "He has been misled," he said. His lower lip was berry red from his worrying at it. "He travels with a man who calls himself Norland and with a woman. I don't know her name. I assume they're the ones who have spirited my brother away. They were abnormally close, always whispering together and making wicked plans. They're sorcerers. You see now why we must get him back. Quickly. He must see reason," Taisce declared, brows drawing together in a tight frown.

"Really now?" Sef couldn't resist jabbing at the wound with just one more question. "And if he does not want to be reasoned with?" He suspected he already knew the answer.

As expected it wasn't Taisce who answered. It was Finn. "Then we will make him." The idea seemed to give Finn a particular kind of pleasure. He grinned as if imagining a plan he'd nursed for years. That at least was something Sef could understand.

"I see." It was hard to contain his amusement with the two of them. The reluctant bounty hunters. Taisce especially was ill suited to the task. Everything about him was soft and fine. Even his anger came wrapped in gauze most of the time. "Well, you've done an excellent job on your search so far," Sef chirped.

He could almost feel the moment that Taisce turned to glare at him. Suddenly the sun felt hotter, the breeze drier. It was invigorating. All around him the plants sang. The sky howled. His blood pumped in time with the world around him. Expectation sat lightly in his bones. With Taisce riding beside him, a mystery locked within him, Sef felt alive once more. And soon, he hoped that he would finally be dead.

~~*

They made it as far as the Kanton River before they stopped. The trees had become sparser and they offered little shelter from the elements. Despite the heat of the sun, the brisk wind cut through Taisce's flesh and straight to the bone. Sef had offered the option of diverting further east to a nearby town, but Taisce had refused the potential delay. That didn't mean he had to like it. Resting the night in another inn would have been preferable to a night spent with the wind trying to tear him to pieces.

Taisce dismounted, grateful to have his feet on solid ground again. Slightly less solid ground would have been better. The rocky terrain and hard packed clay didn't look like it would offer the most comfortable sleeping arrangements. He surveyed the open plains around them with a sigh. "I miss my bed," he mumbled.

"It was your choice, milord," said Sef from beside his own horse.

When he checked, it seemed Finn had finally found something to agree with Sef upon. He nodded silently. One hand rubbed at his bandaged wounds.

Taisce glanced around again. Compared to the forest, the terrain here was almost unbearably dismal. The looming gray clouds overhead weren't helping either. "How far to the next town?" Taisce asked, trying to keep the hope from his voice.

"From here?" Sef frowned. He squinted up at the sky as if the information were suspended there on a scroll. Then he turned to look west. "If we head on to Sutherland? We would make it there with a bit of time to spare before midnight."

"So far? What about back the way we came? There must be something closer."

Sef rubbed the back of his neck and squinted harder into the west. "It *was* closer. When we passed it two hours ago. To make it back there now would take at least four. We would never make it before the rain."

"What rain? I see nothing," said Finn.

Sef didn't even bother favoring him with a glance. He spoke only to Taisce. "The rain is coming from the west though we may miss it if we keep south. But the choice is, once again, yours, milord," Sef said with a cheeky grin. He pointed at the approaching clouds.

"And you didn't think it was necessary to mention this earlier?" Taisce frowned at the sky. He hadn't even noticed the clouds until Sef mentioned them. They swirled through the sky, heavy and deep blue. Not just rain but a storm.

"You didn't ask." Sef's smile widened.

"Next time, don't wait for me to ask," Taisce snapped. He sighed again. As he studied the clouds, a brisk wind sprang up around them. It whipped his hair into his face and tugged at his coat. "Very well. We ride on." As he swung back into the saddle he took a moment to glare at Sef. "And you best hope that you're right."

"And if I'm not?"

"I'm sure I can think of something," Taisce said, tight lipped as he nudged his horse on.

Sef led them along the river at a steady pace, but he paused more and more frequently to glance at the approaching storm clouds.

"Will you stop doing that!" Taisce cried after two hours of his paranoia. "What are you looking at?"

"The storm has shifted."

Taisce frowned at his back. Sef had been acting strangely ever since they left Clotsfield. No matter where he looked, his face wore a troubled scowl. Taisce might have suspected it had something to do with him, but if he was the cause of this unease, Sef would have told him. He was always more than happy to alert Taisce to any problems he had caused.

Sef's preparations before leaving Clotsfield had apparently consisted mainly of securing a waistcoat, a new shirt, and riding pants. Taisce couldn't help wondering where he had found them on such short notice. Surely no tailor could construct a wardrobe so quickly. The pants were well fitted, the leather hugging his hips as if they'd been made for him. His waistcoat was functional, without unnecessary adornments aside from the large gold buttons that secured it in the front and the black on cobalt jacquard fabric. Despite Sef's height, everything fit beautifully. He looked, in a word, perfect.

His reappearance, dressed in fresh clothing, even new boots, had taken Taisce aback. It was the first time he'd ever seen the man so composed. His blond hair was combed into loose waves at his temples and his green eyes seemed to twinkle. For a moment, Taisce stared helplessly. Ensnared. His eyes raked over the cream linen of Sef's shirt, the dark fabric of the waistcoat, the long legs, shining boots. Dressed like that, he could imagine Sef on his arm at any function back home. Could imagine dragging him to his bedroom after and peeling away all those pretty layers until he found the secret beneath.

But then Sef went and ruined any fantasy Taisce might have had. He smiled and the insolence leaked right back in. It felt like he was doing it on purpose. "Is something amiss, milord?"

"No. Everything is perfectly fine." Taisce had hardly dared to breathe for fear of giving himself away. He'd turned away instead. "Make sure you've collected your things. We leave presently."

Taisce had never met a man who so infuriated him. He was acid poured over the orderly flow of Taisce's life. If he were at home, Sef would have been turned out immediately for his rudeness, for his disdain, for his... everything. But Taisce's familiar rules did not apply here. Everything that he knew was buried beneath this new landscape. He looked at the dry tangle of brush passing around them, the gathering darkness of storm clouds. He missed his crowded cities where people knew their place. He missed knowing *his* place.

~~*

The rain found them first.

It came in a howl of icy wind better suited to winter than early summer.

Taisce shrugged off the first sprinkles. They were surprisingly cold after the warmth of the day but easy to ignore if he focused on the pinpricks of distant light. As if angry at being ignored, the rain grew more intense, splattering them all with large soaking drops. Taisce's hair was heavy and saturated. Rain ran down his face.

"How much farther?" he yelled. The wind tore his voice away the second he spoke.

Sef simply pointed ahead.

They rode hard, not slowing until Taisce saw the battered wooden sign of an inn.

The place was as shabby as he'd been expecting,

but Taisce couldn't be bothered to care. He was sopping wet and the chill had already wormed its way deep into his muscles. They secured their horses, dragging saddlebags free, and hurrying to the shelter of a roof and four walls. As they pushed in the door a young woman startled. The broom she'd been using to sweep the bare wood floor slipped from her fingers. An older man hurried to his feet and came forward to greet them.

"We require rooms for the night," Taisce said. He palmed the water from his face. The cold droplets snaking down into his collar made him shiver even harder.

"All of you?" The man looked between them. He tugged at his beard. "We have beds if you have the coin."

Taisce glanced at the two men flanking him. It was a pity he now had to pay for one more bed. His purse would be empty in no time at this rate. "Three beds."

He slipped a hand into his purse, prodding the collection of coins there. It would be a pity to see them go but he couldn't very well ask Finn to sleep in the stables when he was wounded, and Sef would never go whether Taisce asked or not.

The room the innkeeper led them to was dark no matter how high he turned the lamp and it smelled vaguely of wet hound. Throwing open the windows was no help with the smell. It only let the rain in. Taisce slammed the windows closed and wrinkled his nose. Sef laughed. "Not to your liking, milord?"

He stripped out of his sodden waistcoat, hanging it on the window latch and setting to work freeing himself from his equally wet shirt. The material clung to his skin, outlining the bridge of his collarbone.

"What are you doing?" Taisce gasped.

Sef's hands stilled. "I'm relieving myself of these wet things. I have no intention of suffering a chill when I can stop it." Then he yanked his shirt over his head. He turned away, shaking the water from his hair. Taisce's eyes stayed glued to the curve of his spine, the sensitive dip at the small of his back.

"Have some decency, man!" cried Finn, but his voice held little power. Taisce could tell how exhausted he was.

"Rest yourself, Finn," he said, biting back a wince. Whether from the rain or from exertion, Finn's bandages were again streaked with pinkish blood. His arm and chest needed to be tended. Hopefully they could find someone in the morning who was fit to do it.

Finn grumbled, retreating to a bed beside the door to wring out his clothes in peace.

"I'll just go see if they have anything to take this chill off." Taisce hesitated. Sef and Finn had called a truce for the moment and seemed unlikely to start any more arguments in his absence. Sef was mumbling about proper maintenance while he tried to press the water from the heavy fabric of his waistcoat. Finn shifted about aimlessly, casting anxious glances at Taisce and clearly embarrassed to disrobe around him. He'd already made plenty of protests against the impropriety of the three of them sharing a single room. He was becoming quite the matronly chaperon. Perhaps Father would be pleased he'd sent such a capable nursemaid along on the journey. Taisce sighed. "I'll return soon."

The inn was quiet. He had no idea if it was due to the late hour or if it was empty save for them but stillness was welcome after the howling rain and the drumming of hooves.

The innkeeper had vanished from the parlor and so had the girl. Taisce turned in a circle. There were a few doors at the side of the room. The first proved to be a closet when he tested it.

"Excuse me," said a tiny voice from behind him.

Taisce spun, slamming the closet door as he did.

The girl bit her lip. She looked at her own toes more than at him. A laugh, just as dainty as the rest of her, slipped out between her bitten lips. "Did you need something, sir?"

Her hair was long and almost as dark as her skin. She'd barely managed to contain the mass of it with a blue satin ribbon. The rest of her clothing was rough and worn almost to gray. It made him wonder where she'd gotten the ribbon.

"Yes. I was..." He hesitated. What had he been looking for? Warmth? A moment's privacy? Those were hardly things he could ask her for. "Have you any wine?" he asked instead.

She bobbed a curtsy and scurried away.

"Odd girl," Taisce murmured. A low fire crackled away in the parlor's hearth. It drew him like a magnet. The deep orange glow of the flames promised the warmth he craved. He perched on a low stool he found in the corner, holding his hands out to the flames. Even banked, the fire felt blazing hot. His skin dried in an instant, the warmth traveling from his palms up into his arms. He pulled the stool closer to the fire. If he could have done so while escaping notice, he would have curled up on the hearth instead. Anything to get closer to the fire. He was so very cold.

"Planning to leap into the flames?" Sef asked.

Taisce jumped. He hadn't even heard the infernal man's approach. Good then that he hadn't settled on the hearth as he'd imagined. Taisce slid the stool back, immediately mourning the loss of the fire's heat. "I was considering our course."

"An impressive feat, milord, since you don't know where we're going." Sef shot him a searching look. He seemed to grow straight out of the shadows left by the dimmed lamplight. Taisce noted that he'd dressed in a fresh shirt, though his hair still hung on his forehead in damp waves. "Your dog is already snoring away in his bed."

"He's much more gravely wounded than he let on," Taisce said, eyes on the fire. The remaining logs were charred white and glowing. They wouldn't last much longer.

Sef made no comment.

"Perhaps you're right. I seem to be making a mess of this entire affair." Taisce wrapped his arms more tightly around himself, trying to hold in his shaking.

"I was ill suited to the task from the very beginning."

A quiet step announced the girl's return. She held a tray laden with an earthenware pitcher and cup. "Your wine, sir," she said, darting a look at Sef. She blushed.

"Ah. Yes, thank you," Taisce said, eyes already back on the smoldering fire.

She set it on the room's only table, hesitating a moment before saying "If there's nothing else..." and disappearing.

Sef took up the pitcher. He gave it an audible sniff and frowned. "It smells almost of vinegar, but I'm sure it will relieve one of their faculties just fine," he commented. He poured a full cup, swallowing it down like water.

"That's mine," Taisce said.

"Then stop sulking over there like a child. It's insufferable." Sef poured another cup, swirling the wine around and around. The wind battered the windows in their frames.

"I find your *candor* insufferable," Taisce said, finally rising from the stool and turning to face him. "You have no right to speak to me in this way. You are no one. I am a noble son and I demand your respect!" His hands curled into fists at his sides.

Sef drained the second cup of wine more leisurely, eyes never leaving Taisce's. "So you are. But that means nothing to me."

"I am your employer."

"Only because I wish it." Sef lowered his gaze to refill the cup. Without thinking, Taisce slapped it from his hand. He'd expected it to break against the floorboards but it hit with a quiet thud and rolled away trailing spilt wine. It was the blankness of Sef's expression that shook him.

"Why do you do that?" Taisce cried. "One moment you're almost kind and I think you may even like me. Just a bit. But then the next moment you're mocking me again. So which is it?"

"You really want to know?"

"Yes. I do."

Sef set the pitcher aside, moving with aching slowness while Taisce waited. He watched every breath that rose in Sef's chest, the tug of his shirt as he moved, the way the dying fire glowed in his eyes like a coal. The space between them disappeared as Sef stepped around the table. Taisce fought the urge to back away. Sef's face was unreadable, cold as marble.

"How can I love your *or* hate you, milord? I'm not even here." He smiled as sharp as daggers. One hand curled around Taisce's arm. It ran up, caressing his bicep before traveling still higher to his throat. Sef's thumb settled over his pulse, stroking along the wildly beating flow.

Taisce searched his eyes for something. A glimmer of warmth or desire. He found nothing. "I don't understand you."

"The feeling is entirely mutual." Sef pulled him in roughly, pressing a wine-laced kiss on his mouth. Taisce would have gladly taken it. Despite his harsh words, he could have sought solace in the man's arms for another night. But Sef pushed him away just as abruptly as he'd pulled him in. "Goodnight, milord." Then he turned to retrieve the cup from where it had fallen.

~~*

Sef fell back in the lumpy armchair to listen to the unhappy serenade of the wind outside the inn. Like ghostly fingers it snuck in through the cracks in the walls, poking at him, prodding him when all he wished for was oblivion. But sleep never came so easily to him no matter the weather. He felt pulled in so many directions.

The boy's face played through his mind over and over again. The stricken look. Strena help him, Sef had almost caved at that look. Luckily now he was too drunk to make it up the stairs to the tiny room where Taisce was sleeping. Were he able, Sef would have given in to the urge to claim the boy again, to rouse him from sleep and smother him with open mouthed kisses. He would touch every inch of him, bury himself in warm flesh until they were both nothing but sensation. Glorious, immediate sensation. Sef closed his eyes on that thought. The memory of Taisce's hoarse cries rang in his ears as he drifted towards sleep.

But it wasn't sleep that found him. It was memories. All of them unwelcome.

CHAPTER TEN
IN WHICH ALL THINGS ARE UNWELCOME

There had been dancing almost every night for a month.

It bored him.

Weeks of festivals and feasts to commemorate his brother's birthday and the beginning of the Rites of Succession. It had been a long time coming and it took just as long to celebrate. As usual, his brother Éthys was radiant with pride. He'd never had any reason to be anything *but* proud. It made Sef feel sick to see him seated at the head of a table decked with boughs cut from the garden's many fruit trees. The branches were so fresh the leaves hadn't yet wilted.

Sef should have stayed at the feast. If he'd stayed, he could have withered with the rest of them.

Why hadn't he stayed?

Why...?

Sef hit the floor hard.

"Drunkard," barked Taisce.

Sef's eyes felt lined with broken glass when he opened them. He was eye to toe with Taisce's boots.

If his head hadn't been pounding he would have pulled the boy straight off his feet for disturbing him. Just one sharp tug on his ankle was all it would take.

"Wake up." Taisce nudged him roughly in the shoulder. When he did it again, Sef summoned the energy to grab his ankle and pin the offending foot to the floor. His shoulder already felt bruised where it had slammed into the floor.

"You could have had a bright future as a barker," Sef mumbled. "You certainly have the voice for it."

"Remove yourself from my boot. We're leaving."

Sef blinked up at him.

The morning light set a halo around Taisce's head. His hair was barely held in check today and flew wild about his shoulders in defiance of the tie he'd used to restrain it. Purple smudges beneath the boy's eyes said he'd slept about as well as Sef had. At his side, Finn glowered, pristinely grim with his fresh white bandages. How early had they risen without Sef's noticing?

The dog was a scabbed-over eyesore but Sef wouldn't waste magic on healing him unbidden. They'd found someone else to tend to him. So much the better.

Sef grimaced, face compressing with concentration as he tried to sit up. It took much longer to achieve than he had expected and when he'd managed it his head throbbed even worse.

His gaze flew to the window. It was aggravatingly clear out this morning. The sky was painted clear blue. Not a cloud to be had anywhere.

Nothing to delay them further. And so much *sun*.

Sef slanted another look up at Taisce. He was back to his standard scowl, which suited him so much better anyway. That pitiful mewling kitten from last night hadn't been right for him at all. It was best if he stuck to what he knew, and Sef wouldn't apologize for reminding him of that. His words had all been true. The world was cruel. It owed none of them favors. Clinging to Sef for reassurance would only bring the boy pain.

"Then let us away!" Sef cried, catapulting himself upright and almost toppling onto his face again.

His head.

Oh, his head.

He put a hand to his temple and wished his head really would roll off of his shoulders. It would save him so much misery.

~~*

With the storm past, the sky was cloudless and radiant with golden sun. It stabbed at Sef's eyes. And the heat—the heat made his head spin. He was usually better able to handle it but not today. It would have been a relief to let himself slip from the saddle and onto the hard packed ground. If he was truly lucky, perhaps he would knock himself out. Dreamless unconsciousness sounded like bliss.

His misery seemed to improve Taisce's mood tenfold. The boy was humming to himself, some song that Sef was sure he should remember but couldn't place for the ache in his skull. It felt like a team of coach horses rode through his head in an endless circle, their hooves beating in time with his pulse. Around and around and around without stopping. And the boy wouldn't stop *humming*. Sef curled his hands into the reins to keep from reaching out and strangling the good humored song right out of his throat. His glares had done no good when he tried them.

Throughout the morning, Sef clung to his horse and imagined tying Taisce to a rock and leaving him baking in the summer sun. The boy's song could no longer torment him if he'd been abandoned to the vultures.

At dusk, they made camp beneath the sky. They were still some miles distant from any towns and riding further would have made little difference in the scenery. The land was sparse and scrubby, the trees dwindled to little more than twisted green sticks. Sef advised the boy and his dog to get used to it. There would be more of the same in every direction from here on. And worse.

"Tomorrow will be Mission if we set off early," Sef said tightly. He dismounted and poked around until he found a convenient spot to call his bed.

"Are you sure?" Taisce shielded his eyes from the setting sun. He squinted into the distance.

Sef made no effort to answer. With his eyes already closed, he fished through his things until he touched upon his water skin. The water inside tasted foul but that was no fault of the skin. It was that horrid wine. It soured everything. He took a swallow of water anyway and forced it down his throat.

"What are you doing?" Taisce stood over him, his long shadow draping Sef like a shroud. "We have to set up camp. Start a fire. It will be dark soon."

Sef barely raised his head. He aimed a hand at the patch of dry grass not far from Taisce's feet. "*Inse*," he hissed. The grass sprang into a vigorous column of flame and Taisce leapt back with a startled squawk. Sef dropped his head back to the ground. "You have your fire."

"I've told you how I feel about magic—"

"And I've told you I don't care. You have your fire, now leave me be."

"Insufferable," Taisce muttered as he stormed away. "Finn, find stones to ring the fire with before it sets the entire plain on ablaze."

The two busied themselves scrambling after stones and some kindling to build up the fire. Sef laughed watching them. Like mice. He was tempted to start more fires and watch them scurry, but starting the one had only made his head ache worse.

The song Taisce had hummed ran through his mind again. He'd heard it somewhere before, but it was lost in the tangles of his too long memory. It was hard to keep anything straight anymore. Names. Faces. They all blurred after a while. Even his own. His brothers'. Hard as he tried he couldn't remember what they'd looked like with their eyes open and their mouths smiling. When he pictured them they were corpses, gray skinned and half rotten. They were all corpses. All but him.

He should be a corpse too.

He held up a hand and tried to picture his tanned skin gone sickly gray and peeling with decay. Or perhaps he would turn into one of those delightful desiccated corpses, leathery as dried fruit. He wouldn't have to see it if he did. He wouldn't have to see anything anymore. He could close his eyes and never have to worry about waking again. It was something he couldn't even begin to imagine.

Sef fell asleep like that, dreaming of hearts stopping and time slowing as everything finally, wonderfully, turned to dust.

It seemed like mere moments later he was awake again. He stared up into the dark sky. The fire had gone out, dwindling to cold ash while he'd slept. Both Taisce and Finn were wrapped in their blankets. Neither had thought to keep watch over their sleeping camp. If this was how little care they took in their travels it really was a wonder that Taisce had made it far enough to find Sef. He tempted Fate at every turn and Fate was known for slitting the throats of the unwary.

But not tonight.

Sef could feel movement out on the plains where the moon couldn't catch them. They'd probably been drawn by the spark of magic earlier, or maybe not. The wolves were a persistent lot. He'd thought—hoped—that he'd imagined their pursuit but it wasn't hard to believe that they'd followed them this far waiting for an unguarded moment. This was certainly it if they had. Miles from any town worth naming on a plain as flat as a platter.

Sef studied the sky. The moon was still high. Morning would not save them. Not that he had expected that bit of luck. That left them with only two options: fight or flee. Of those he greatly preferred the latter.

~~*

Taisce woke, jerked upright and straight out of sleep. His shout was cut off by Sef's hand slipping over his mouth. "Quiet." The words were barely a hiss.

He blinked. It was nowhere near dawn. The moon offered the only light, barely enough to see by. It made of Sef a bewitching apparition. He was nothing but a pair of glittering eyes and an angular face cut from gray stone. Finn slept on undisturbed with his back to them. Taisce pulled away from Sef's grip. He couldn't concentrate with Sef's hands on him.

"What's the meaning of this?"

Sef's eyes almost glowed in the darkness, reflecting the moonlight and seeming to increase it. "They're coming. We must go."

"What? Who's coming?" Taisce peered into the darkness but it all looked the same to him. "I see nothing."

"They'll be here soon enough. If we don't hurry, you'll see more of them than you'll like."

"What are you talking about? Are you still

drunk?"

"Sadly no," Sef said with a wry smile twisting his lips. "But I thank you for asking." His gaze shifted away and his smile evaporated. "Wake your dog. There may be too many of them for me to kill this time."

"To what? I don't understand any of this," Taisce said, but he scuttled over to where Finn was still snoring and shook him awake. "Why won't you explain what you're saying for once?"

"What's it? What's going on?" Finn grumbled. The words slurred together.

"You'll have to ask him that," Taisce said with a nod towards Sef.

That was all it took to rouse Finn. He sat up, already glaring at Sef. "What's this about?"

"As I *just* finished saying, collect your things. I would rather we were gone before they got here," Sef snapped. He was on his feet, throwing their things about in his haste. He stopped so suddenly that Taisce almost tripped over him. "Get to the horses." His face had taken on that cast that turned Taisce's blood to ice and his hard-edged smile did nothing to soften it. There was a scrape of metal as he unsheathed a thin bladed stiletto.

Taisce opened his mouth to ask Sef where he'd gotten the knife but the man was already gone. Something had knocked him sideways, hardly more than a shadow laid on top of the night sky, something that growled so low Taisce could feel the rumble of it deep in his chest. Sef cried out. The thing—whatever it was—covered Sef almost from head to toe with its bulk. If not for the sounds of struggle he might have missed them completely. Taisce scrambled after, barely remembering to pull his own dagger.

"Stay back!" Sef yelled.

Taisce skidded to a halt, stumbling to his knees in the dusty soil. There were more sounds in the dark. The pounding of many feet. The snarling of dogs followed by a howl. No. Not dogs. *Wolves.*

Suddenly Taisce recalled what Finn had said.

Attacked by wolves.

Were these the same creatures?

Finn had barely escaped with his life the last time and here they were again. Surrounded by them. He could see the wolves, like ghosts flitting about the edge of their camp in a wide circle. Waiting. Watching. The moon reflected in their eyes.

One of them leapt at Finn and knocked him sprawling onto the ground before retreating again. It paced around him, joined by two others, fencing in their already wounded prey. Finn's face was grim.

There were so many. They came in droves of black fur and flashing fangs, buffeting Taisce with their passing. His attacks went unnoticed. Only a few of the beasts had chosen Taisce and Finn as their targets. The rest had thrown themselves into the fight surrounding Sef. He'd been swallowed into the center of their writhing mass until nothing of him was visible.

But Taisce could hear him.

Sef roared just like the wolves, dragging high pitched howls from the animals he struck. Every moment seemed to bring more until it was impossible to number them in the dark. Taisce lost sight of him, spinning around to meet his own attacker. It snapped at him, ducking his swinging blade, and butted against his weak leg. Taisce cried out at the jolt of pain that dropped him to his knees. He was covered in sticky blood, not his own he thought, but so far not a single wolf had fallen. They were toying with him. Wearing him down with feints and almost playful nips.

Something brushed his arm and Taisce nearly leapt out of his skin. "It's only me, my lord." Finn had drawn his own knife. Taisce knew it by the dark and mottled metal of the blade. It reflected the light in uneven shards. He put out a hand to haul Taisce back to his feet and held on when he wobbled and nearly fell again.

"Sef. We must help him." Taisce looked at his bodyguard, waiting for him to agree. He could see Finn's eyes turn towards where Sef still fought against the sea of wolves. He was shocked when Finn shook his head and pointed in the opposite direction. "The horses, my lord. We must get you away from here."

There was no time to put the plan into action even if he'd agreed with it. The circling wolves had slowly started to close in.

Taisce kicked a wolf that came too close and another quickly replaced it, snapping at his leg. He stabbed at its yellow eyes, pleased by the pained yip the move elicited. Dodge. Slash. A wolf swiped at him with one large paw and Taisce barely leapt away in time. Another dodge. Another kick. His muscles screamed for rest but every time he sagged Finn was quick to right him.

They had to get free. Collect Sef. Escape.

Sef was screaming somewhere in the dark but Taisce couldn't find him. He turned, seeking the source.

Taisce didn't see the next wolf's lunge and he took Finn down with him as he fell beneath it. The thing was huge, larger than any wolf that Taisce had ever seen. He hadn't quite appreciated their size until he was pinned beneath one. Now that it stood with both paws on his chest, bearing down on him with its full weight, he realized how terrifying they truly were. It slavered over him, close enough that Taisce could have counted every one of its teeth before it ripped his throat out. When they'd fallen, Finn had disappeared, split off from him by more of the wolves. Taisce was alone. Unarmed. His dagger had fallen just out of arm's reach. He felt like an insect pinned under glass and the wolf seemed to sense it, wide mouth almost smiling down at him.

Another howl broke through the noise of fighting, this one higher but not in pain.

The wolf over Taisce raised its head. It let out a thin, confused whine. While it was distracted, Taisce clawed backwards over the ground, pulling up clumps of dirt and grass as he dragged himself out from beneath the wolf. It snapped at him in warning. A scrap of his collar came away in its teeth, hanging from its jaws like a streamer. Then it fell back with an almost human scream. Another wolf had caught it by the leg. The new wolf was smaller, its black fur marked with a patch of silvery scarring. It looked at Taisce, blinking once, then with another fierce tug it pulled the other wolf off its feet. Taisce sat, frozen, as they snapped at each other, biting and snarling. The smaller wolf had saved him. As he watched, the first wolf knocked it down, teeth going for its throat. Taisce grabbed up his knife. The larger wolf's fur was rough and bristling beneath his palms but he wrapped his arms tight around it, holding on as his dagger sank deep into its side. Blood ran out over his hands. When he pulled away they were stained with so much blood they almost disappeared into the surrounding darkness. Beside him the beast fell to its side with a faint whine. Its legs twitched. After a moment it lay still.

Taisce held his bloodstained hands out before him. He'd done it. This hadn't been like those long ago hunting trips where he was merely tangential to the killing. This time the death was all over his palms, running into the fine lines and beneath his nails. He felt sick.

The second wolf had gotten back to its feet. It limped closer, pausing a few steps away. Taisce tensed but it didn't move on him as he'd expected. It only blinked large eyes at him and cocked its head. Then the wolf bolted. Taisce was still staring after it when Finn reappeared at his side with a groan. He looked down at Taisce's bloodied hands and pulled the dagger from his fingers before helping him to his feet.

The bodies of injured wolves lay scattered over the ground but most of the fighting still focused around Sef. It was a mass of snarling and flashing silver like some kind of nightmare creature. There was no way Sef could survive that alone. Taisce had hardly taken a step when Finn pulled him back. "You mustn't."

Sef screamed from the center of the fight. There were words to it but they were nothing Taisce had ever heard before. They hung in the air, seeming to crackle, before they caught. The plain lit with blue fire. It raced between the wolves, jagged and brilliant, leaping from one to the next. Wherever it passed a terrible howling grew as the wolves fell one by one in a smoldering heap. And last, in the center of them all, Sef wobbled and then toppled too.

The air stank of char and seared meat. Taisce put a hand to his mouth to keep from retching. Finn still held his arm but he pulled away, charging towards where Sef's body had fallen. There was no way to tell how gravely injured he was in the dark. His body was spattered with blackish blood but whether it was his or the wolves' Taisce didn't know. A streak of the stuff ran down one of Sef's cheeks and into his hair. His shirt hung in tatters, baring his chest to the night air, and his hands were crusted with dark charcoal smudges as if he'd thrust them into the heart of a fire.

Taisce raised Sef's head gently and set it atop his thigh. He was afraid to try and rouse the man, afraid that he would find it to be impossible.

"Sef?" he whispered.

There was an answering groan. "Still not dead," Sef rasped. "For a moment, I hoped..." He rolled off Taisce's lap. He pressed his forehead into the dust and coughed brokenly, as if something jagged was caught in his throat. When he sat up there was a streak of fresh blood on his lower lip. He smiled blearily and reached out, barely grazing Taisce's cheek before the touch fell away. "I expected you would run and leave me for them."

"What nonsense are you speaking?" Taisce asked, but it was hard to keep the relief from his voice.

"Don't look at me like that, milord. They couldn't have killed me. You haven't even paid me what you owe me yet." Sef paused to cough into a curled hand. "We need to move on. Someone will have noticed what I've done. It's not safe to stay here."

Taisce looked at the empty plains around them. There wasn't much to see. It was all darkness without a glimmer of light from a nearby dwelling. Close around them were the humped bodies of the fallen wolves, some of them still sending up thin twists of smoke. He had no objection to getting away from them as quickly as possible but he wondered what had happened to the few wolves that had run at the end of the fight. Were they lying dead out there somewhere or had they gone back to wherever they'd come from? "There's no one here."

"Magic travels far, milord. And it travels very fast. Someone will feel it. Best we're not around in case they're unfriendly."

"You talk in so many riddles." Taisce sighed but he stood and offered a hand to Sef.

Sef looked at it, smile flashing in the darkness, before he took it. "You have no sense at all, milord." He didn't release Taisce's hand once he was upright. Instead he turned it over in his grasp until the palm was exposed. "You have blood on your hands." He studied Taisce's face. "How does it feel?"

Taisce snatched his hand away, hiding it behind his back.

"That's what I thought." Sef stumbled away, wading through the mass of burnt animals back towards the remains of their camp.

Taisce hurried after him. He was careful to keep his gaze level, only dropping low enough to keep from stumbling. "Are you going to explain what just happened?"

Sef paused. He glanced at Taisce sidelong. "No. I hadn't planned on it." Then he continued on undeterred until he'd found his tattered bag.

That wasn't the answer Taisce wanted. He had expected it from Sef but for once he refused to accept it. He planted himself beside Sef, blocking the scarce moonlight and throwing shadows over his attempt to gather what looked strangely like jam jars. "Explain."

"I liked it much better when you weren't speaking to me," Sef grumbled under his breath. There was a clink as he shoved the jars into his bag, shoving them into the bottom and throwing everything else on top. "Very well, milord. But I would prefer to explain while we're moving. Away. Quickly."

~~*

They rode into the darkness, Finn taking the lead for once while Taisce and Sef trailed after. It didn't stop Finn from turning in his saddle with annoying frequency to glare at them. If he wasn't careful he would lead them straight off the nearest cliff. The lantern hardly threw enough light to see five feet in front of them.

Their camp had been collected, what they could find of it after the wolves had trampled over it, and tossed into saddlebags. Taisce was glad to find his bottle of red ink was still intact, though his pen had been snapped in two. The horses had also gotten free during the attack but they hadn't gotten far and were easily caught. "Perhaps they were saving the horses for their supper," Sef commented.

Taisce rather wished he hadn't.

The night was silent, almost deafeningly so after the rage of the attack. The piercing howl of the dying wolves, like the wailing of a child, still echoed in his ears. Even the insects had stopped singing. Taisce shuddered. In the dark with nothing before them and nothing behind them, he could imagine that they were riding off the end of the world. This was unknown territory for him. He had never imagined he would be there, in the wilderness with blood on his hands and fear tearing at him like a living thing. It was horrible and wonderful all at once. Adrenaline thrummed through his veins.

"Werewolves," Sef said so suddenly that Taisce gasped. He'd been so lost to his own thoughts that he'd almost forgotten he was there riding beside him.

"What?"

"They were werewolves, milord. The two-natured. I trust you've heard of them. They came to recoup their losses by gathering more."

"I don't understand you," Taisce sighed.

"Back in the woods of Avy while you were sleeping so peacefully, they attacked. And I killed them. To protect you." He said the words as if they were nothing, no different than discussing what wine he would have with dinner. "That girl, Erin, she was one of them. It was her pack that attacked us then and it was the same pack again tonight. I do collect enemies quickly while I'm around you."

Taisce stiffened, head coming up at the mention of the girl. "Then you *did* do something to her."

"I did nothing to her, as I said. There was no need."

"But that was days ago. Miles away. Why would they attack us here?"

"You would rather they waited to ambush you on the return instead?" Sef grinned. "Her people are not known for their forgiveness and they can travel just as easily as we can. Perhaps even easier. They came for their revenge where it was convenient to do so."

Taisce glanced back again. There was no way to

know if anyone gave chase. The moon touched the long grasses and low brush with delicate fingers leaving everything a blue-tinted impression. Anything could lurk in the shadows between. Though he couldn't see them any longer, he was still horrified by what they'd left behind. "You killed them all," Taisce murmured. His mouth felt dry as the ground over which they traveled.

"Not all. Their pack numbers in the hundreds. That was a hunting party, nothing more."

"Then there could be more coming," Taisce said.

"Not now. This attack failed. They'll bide their time for now."

"Then what?"

Sef's shrug was barely visible in the moonlight.

"I've never seen a true Were before," Taisce breathed. "I thought the lines had died out."

Every child had heard the stories, full of sensationalism and horror, about the human wolves, the two natured as Sef called them, but Taisce had never thought to be faced with a real one. The clumsily drawn illustrations in his books had done nothing to prepare him for the reality of their powerful jaws and burning yellow eyes. Knowing that they were human inside of all that made it even more unsettling. He'd killed someone tonight. It hardly seemed to matter that he'd thought it was only a wolf at the time or that he'd been defending himself. The argument was weak. His gaze dropped to his hands upon the reins. If only he could say with some level of assurance that knowing what the creature was would have changed anything.

"They keep to themselves," Sef said dismissively. "Usually. And they don't care for cities, milord. When would you have met them?"

It was true of course. Taisce had spent much of his life wrapped in business deals and city life, traveling no farther south than L'Engle and then only briefly, but it stung to hear the words pass Sef's lips. It felt like a rebuke. Taisce said no more but he made sure to keep close to Sef in case anything lurked in the darkness around them.

CHAPTER ELEVEN
IN WHICH TROUBLE HAS A HABIT OF RETURNING

Mission sprawled at their feet like a glorious mirage. Just after dawn, they'd crested a ridge and Sef had called them to a halt with a sweep of his hand.

"I have delivered you to Mission. As requested."

It looked small, a handful of crisscrossing streets like a child's discarded game of pickup sticks, lined with rows of similarly shaped buildings and the taller, thinner shape of a clock tower near the center. The sun inched over the horizon, painting the land in orange and yellow, such a welcome change after their night flight. Mission resembled nothing so much as a golden treasure to Taisce. His object, his prize. Rupert could be within those streets somewhere. It felt as if Taisce could seize the whole city with one outstretched hand.

Finn grumbled, horse dancing beneath him. "Doesn't look like a proper city at all."

"It's the best you'll find for quite some distance," Sef said.

They rode on, a new sense of purpose bubbling through Taisce.

By midmorning, his spirits had dwindled. Mission was larger than it had looked from a distance, full of back alleys and secretive people. Ciaran had hidden its corruption beneath a layer of whitewash and forced civility. Mission made no effort to hide at all. The people here wore their weapons openly, knives and swords and, increasingly common, pistols, all on display. Taisce eyed them warily, noting every face that turned his way and tugging at his buttoned coat to be sure all of his belongings were where they should be. He'd already been robbed once. No need to go making a habit of it.

As the sky lost the blush of dawn, the heat increased, becoming stifling. Taisce had never wished to leave any place as quickly as he did Mission.

"You're sure you've not seen him?" Taisce insisted, forcing the small watercolor portrait of Rupert into a man's hands a second time. He'd been stopping everyone he dared as they passed on the dusty unpaved streets and his patience was wearing thin. It didn't help that this man hadn't stopped frowning since Taisce had addressed him. "He would have been traveling with two others, a man and a woman. The man has a suspicious charisma about him and wears a tacky hat with a green band."

The man frowned beneath his bushy mustache and shoved the picture back at Taisce. "Told you already. Never heard of him." He thundered on down the boardwalk without a backwards glance before disappearing into a nearby shop. The cheerful tinkle of the bell over the door seemed to be mocking Taisce.

"It's no use, my lord," Finn said, returning from the opposite direction where Taisce had dispatched him to search. "I've asked everyone I could find. No one will speak to me."

It was no wonder, really. Taisce looked Finn up and down. With his imposing stoutness of frame and now the stark white of his bandaged wounds, Finn looked more like a common criminal than an upstanding gentleman. His hands looked capable of crushing bone. The tiny portrait pinched between his fingers only served to emphasize the problem.

Taisce sighed, gaze touching the cloudless white sky. The sky seemed so very big and far away in this place, as far away as everything else. "We shan't give up hope just yet. We'll search once the midday heat has dissipated and perhaps we will find these people to be more helpful then." He fanned himself absently. The heat here was even worse than it had been in Ciaran. Pity he couldn't remove his coat.

Finn nodded. When he thought Taisce wasn't looking, he wiped the sweat from his brow with his cuff. At times like this, Taisce envied the man. Finn had little need for the rules of propriety, the rules that smothered Taisce as effectively as his coat was doing right now.

They walked back to the inn together, though Finn trailed behind as if he really were the faithful dog Sef kept accusing him of being.

"We can complete our journey alone, my lord. We don't need... that man," Finn said, startling Taisce. It was as if Finn had known the direction of his thoughts.

"He has seen us this far. With a bit of luck, Rupert may reveal himself and we'll be turned towards home by week's end." If only that were true, it would be a mixed blessing.

"But..." Finn hesitated. "But if we don't find your honorable brother here, I think it would be best if you find a different guide, my lord."

Taisce cast a sidelong glance at him. He was fidgeting and sweating in an uncharacteristic way. "Why do you say that?"

Finn looked away. He seemed in desperate need of a hat to wring, anything to keep his hands busy while he struggled for words. "I don't trust him." And there he faltered into silence once more, face turning red and lips clamping shut. Taisce had seen that face in the past, though only rarely.

"Out with it," he demanded.

Finn turned his eyes to the heavens, grimacing as if he were in pain. "He's taken advantage of your kindness, my lord. I've seen the way he looks at you. It's not proper. He's a vile rodent. He's not suited to you," he cried, in a rush now that he'd started speaking his mind.

Taisce stumbled to a halt.

He hadn't been trying specifically to keep their relations from Finn. He'd barely even considered it at the time. But the thought that Finn was so violently opposed... It shouldn't have surprised him. Taisce was of much the same mind. He knew, logically, that it was scandalous. A noble son did not consort with... whatever sort of man Sef was. And a sorcerer on top of that. The very word made Taisce's skin crawl. He didn't know what had come over him in Clotsfield. Or before... Or since.

No.

That was a lie.

He knew. He understood it, but speaking the truth aloud, and to Finn of all people, would be worse than just thinking it. Because the truth was Taisce hadn't cared where the man came from or what he was. He had wanted him. He had wanted and, for the first time in his life, he had taken that which he desired and damn the consequences. He still wanted him. The reasons for that were more complicated, something he couldn't even explain to himself or anyone else. They were miles from Blume, far from prying eyes that watched and weighed his every action. Much as Taisce longed for the safety and comfort of home, that was one thing that he did not miss. Unfortunately it couldn't last forever. Eventually they would return home. Propriety would again surround him like the slippery, unclimbable walls of a well and there would end this moment of indescribable, fierce freedom.

Taisce clenched his fists, steeling himself for the question he had still to ask. "You won't tell my father?"

Finn gaped, but he immediately shook his head. "No. No, of course not, my lord."

Taisce nodded. "Very good. Then this discussion is concluded."

"But, my lord."

"Sef has been invaluable already and he will remain in my employ until I decide otherwise. Leave his handling to me."

Finn sputtered beside him and finally fell silent though the troubled look didn't leave his face. It closely matched the feeling in the pit of Taisce's stomach. He hoped that his decision had been the right one.

~~*

Sef wasn't in their rooms at the inn.

Taisce tried not to panic, first noting that the sack Sef carried with him everywhere was still resting in the corner of the room. But Sef himself was nowhere to be found and there was no sign of where he had gone. Instead of locating his brother, Taisce had now lost a second person in the space of three hours. At his back, Finn was trying his best not to look hopeful as he said, "Perhaps he's left."

"The young fella you were with?" asked the innkeeper when they returned to the parlor. The old man was hunched over his eagle headed cane as if that were the only thing keeping him off the floor. It very likely was. His arms wobbled with the weight of his frail body but his eyes were bright and clever.

"Yeah. I recall him. Left just after you. Said something about"—and here he lowered his voice—"Burke."

"Burke?" Taisce asked, looking at Finn for assistance but he was similarly baffled. "I have no idea what that is."

The old man laughed. The sound was like the high screech of birds. "Not a what. It's a *he*. And you'd stay clear of him if you know what's good for you. No good, that one."

Finn nodded along with the innkeeper.

"Where would I find this Burke?" Taisce asked. The innkeeper's pale eyes widened and he waved his hands as if the pronouncing of the name would summon demons from the very air.

"You don't wanna find him, good kid like you. Fact is, if you see him, you turn and go the other way."

"How can I be expected to avoid a man I don't recognize?"

"Exactly," cackled the old man.

Taisce drew in a slow breath through his nose before he tried again. "I need to find him. Where is he?"

The innkeeper shook his head.

Taisce sighed. This was getting them nowhere. "What would it take to persuade you?"

The innkeeper's eyes widened again but this time in interest. His face brightened in a smile that Taisce was becoming all too familiar with during his travels. "Well, I never dislike the sight of a few croy."

Taisce fished for his purse, dipping inside to find

a suitably small number of coins with which to tempt the old man, and found his purse quite a bit lighter than it had been. He frowned.

Sef.

He would have to deal with the man later. First he would have to find him. Taisce laid out a short stack of coins on the ledge beside him, looking from them to the innkeeper. "I trust this will suffice."

~~*

"Come now, Burke. It seems you've lost your touch." Sef smiled as he set his cards down one at a time on the table between them. "That's fifty you owe me now."

Sef leaned back in his chair. With his free hand, he gave the velvet cushion an appreciative stroke. Burke certainly knew how to welcome a guest; nothing had changed there. A serving girl had brought a bottle of good wine and a tray of sliced fruits and cheese. All told it probably cost more than Sef's current wardrobe. The apples alone must have traveled over half the country before finding their way to Burke's table. They would never have grown this far south, not without a hefty gift of magic. Sef tugged a grape from its stem and closed his eyes as the sweet-tart taste filled his mouth. After living off of little more than bread, Burke's table was better than a banquet. Sef was so tired of living like a scavenging rat but there were risks involved with staying in place too long.

Burke scowled good-naturedly, coins slipping through his thick fingers to scatter across the table. When one rolled too close to the edge, Sef slapped a hand over it to stop it.

Burke had aged in the few years since Sef had seen him last. Gray had bloomed at his temples. On anyone else it might have looked stately but Burke had the kind of smile that wouldn't be disguised so easily. He looked as much the crafty weasel as he ever had, just older now. He might wear jeweled rings on almost every finger, a sign of his years of steady wealth, but they both knew what kind of methods he'd used to secure it.

"You surprised me, showing up on my doorstep like that without a word. Didn't think you'd come back. At least not so soon," Burke said. He gathered the cards and began shuffling them with a snap. His eyes dropped, forehead creased in concentration. No doubt he was scheming, plotting how to cheat his way to victory in the next hand of cards. Sef smiled. He didn't mind. It was only fair if they both intended to cheat.

"I hadn't planned on it." Sef dropped his head back to stare at the cracks in the ceiling. "I'm in the employ of a rather insistent little git. It was his decision to come here."

Burke let out a choked sound of surprise, halfway between a laugh and a gasp. "That's not like you. What did he promise you to make that happen?"

Sef tilted his head, eyes rolling to touch on Burke again. He didn't answer and the look in his eyes made it clear that he didn't intend to.

The silence was broken by the snap and purr of shuffling cards. "Another hand?"

Sef nodded.

From the corner a caged bird chirped, renewing the song they'd interrupted with their talking earlier. Sef watched it flapping its cheerful yellow wings and hopping about its perch. It was the brightest thing in the room. Burke's taste had always run towards the dark and ominous. Even the walls were the color of spilled wine.

"We've known each other a long time," Sef commented after a while.

Burke collected his cards, tapping them into order on the table in front of him. "That we have."

"Perhaps I should have taken your offer instead. I could have lived comfortably for the cost of a few more corpses."

"Better that you didn't. You don't look good covered in blood," Burke chuckled. His rings clinked as he laid down a card and took a new one.

"No. I don't," Sef said without the same humor.

"Anyway, I've gotten out of that whole nasty business. Too much mess."

Sef raised an eyebrow at him. "Really?" He threw a coin into the center of the table and dropped his chin into his hand to wait for Burke to take his turn.

"The King's Guard finally found their way down here, stopped up most of the open trade. I got out before then. You know me. I'm too old to dick around with secrecy and cleaning up bodies. Making examples of people. Building empires. It's buggered exhausting."

Sef nodded.

"Most of the traffickers and the dealers ended up hanged or fled to compounds in the wastes. Only thing left were the users and the magic addled. No offense," he added.

"None taken."

"There's no money in killing them either. They've spent it all on their powders." Burke's lip curled up in a sneer.

Sef didn't fault his attitude even if it stung. They both knew of the powders and the barbed pleasures they offered, but Sef had taken it further than that. The wonderful floating feeling of happiness had ensnared him immediately. Such a welcome respite from the truth of his life, a life he was grateful to forget. But inevitably it had dissolved like spun sugar and left him with an ever-growing emptiness. An ache. And it wasn't until later that he realized the other gifts the powders offered. Hallucinations, mostly. He was used to those. The lucky lapsed into hallucinations that lasted hours but many died, vomiting and bleeding from the nose while they writhed like some terrible monster.

Sef had always had a limited supply of luck. He never went back to the dens after that. Wine was so much less painful to recover from.

But even now, the mention of the powders was enough to set Sef twitching, hands scrabbling like anxious spiders. He'd stopped using them but the craving remained. His saving was the fact that Burke would never use the stuff and he would beat Sef bloody before he let him touch them again in his presence. Burke didn't know all—not all the time spent in the dens, smoking and plying himself with all manner of things, coming out pale and closer to death than he'd ever been before—but he knew enough. Sef couldn't remember what he'd looked like then. Probably much like the corpse he longed to be. But still a living corpse. That was the problem.

"What business are you in now?" Sef asked, changing the subject for his own comfort as much as for curiosity.

Burke chuckled. "You ask as though you haven't seen my place. Sex is always lucrative." Burke spoke without a flicker in his expression. He never had had any shame, no matter what he did. Neither of them did really. "I can arrange you a companion later if you have a need." He cast a look at Sef when he didn't immediately accept. "What's this? You can't have sworn off, have you?"

Sef tossed his bet onto the table, covering his hesitation with the jingling of coins. "Mind your own business, old friend."

"A body never knows where it's safe to step around you. Don't recall our conversations ever being this hazardous before. But tell me." Burke leaned forward, resting his elbows heavily on the table between them. "Man? Woman? Neither?"

Sef's frown broke into a smile again when he met Burke's gaze. "I won't be inviting you to watch again if that's what you're after. This one is mine."

"That's not like you either." Burke set his cards face down and heaved himself out of his chair, wandering to the far corner of the room. He returned a moment later with a metal box of tobacco and rolling papers which he offered to Sef. He turned it down without raising his eyes from his cards. Sef had hardly been paying attention to the game at hand. He feared Burke might actually win this time and take all the money he had spent two hours earning himself. Cigarette rolled and lit, Burke quickly disappeared behind a cloud of fragrant smoke. Sef inhaled deeply. The blend was surely different but the scent was familiar, a memory that went back many years, more than Burke had been alive. Sef's father had favored something similar. He'd forgotten his father's face but the smell of his tobacco lingered in Sef's mind, persistent as always. Sef had always loved the smell. He wasn't sure the same could be said about his father.

"If you didn't come to talk, what did you come here for?" Burke asked finally.

"A respite."

"You know I expect better answers than that. Old man," Burke finished with a smirk.

Sef growled at him. "Don't remind me."

"You do a fine job reminding yourself. I can see you brooding. My eyes still work quite well despite my advancing age."

"I can assist you with that."

Burke chuckled. "You wouldn't kill me and you

know it. You like that I know all your secrets."

"Not quite all." Sef smiled, though he knew it wouldn't intimidate Burke in the slightest. He could snap the man's neck, and Burke still wouldn't believe Sef was capable of it. More misguided trust.

"I know the largest of them though it still sounds like madness. I wouldn't have believed it if I hadn't seen it with my two eyes," Burke admitted. The man blew a cloud of smoke towards the ceiling where it curled in on itself. "And I win this hand," he declared as he laid down his cards.

"Bugger." He threw his cards in Burke's face. He also added a few more colorful epithets under his breath but Burke just laughed. Sef threw one leg over the arm of his chair, slipping sideways to get more comfortable. He undid another button at his neck. The room was steadily becoming hotter. "Take your winnings, you bastard. They won't be yours long." He closed his eyes, drowsy with relaxation. "Can't you get that girl to open the windows in here? It's positively stifling."

Burke stubbed out his cigarette on the side of the tray. "Rose!" he called, voice rising to a controlled roar. Sef had seen more than one person cower at that tone but the servant girl had seemed unfazed by it earlier. She'd even seemed to be smiling beneath her quiet civility. Sef would bet a hefty sum that Burke had taken her to his bed on more than one occasion.

Burke called again.

When she didn't appear, Sef turned towards the door. "Odd."

Burke joined him in staring. "Very odd."

When a third attempt at summoning her yielded nothing, Burke finally rose to go search for the girl himself. Before he'd made it halfway there, the door burst open. Of the five faces on the other side, none were Rose but one face at the back was familiar enough to make Sef scramble out of his chair. It tipped over but he hardly noticed, too busy staring at the intruders. He'd thought never to see Xavier again. Or more precisely, had *hoped* never to see the man again. His dark hair was oiled and swept back from his forehead in a style that only added to his boyish looks now. He still looked far too young for the kind of life he led. "You're supposed to be in Palina," Sef said weakly.

Xavier showed his teeth in a smile. "Surprise."

"We don't accept vermin here," Burke said.

He made a better showing than Sef would have expected of a man at his age. Without a moment's hesitation, he pulled a cudgel from its hiding spot in one of his bookshelves and swung it on the first man who forced himself through the door. It connected with a resounding crack, the victim dropping to his knees as Burke moved on. He swung on the next man but he'd already lost the element of surprise. A second later, he'd also lost his cudgel.

Sef didn't wait to see how Burke fared after that. He bolted for the floor length windows on the far wall. Jumping and risking a broken leg would be better than whatever Xavier had planned for him.

The glass exploded outward with one good kick

and he slipped out onto the narrow balcony beyond. That was as far as he got before one of Xavier's men caught him by the hair. Another latched onto his arm. They yanked him back. Tossed him into the wall so hard the mirror crashed to the floor. The silvery shards bit into his palms when he fell after it. His ears were ringing.

Xavier stripped off his narrow glasses, depositing them in a pocket before turning to look down at Sef. "You shouldn't have come here."

"I wouldn't have if I'd known you were here. What's the matter? Bored with Palina already?" Sef grasped at an easy incantation but nothing came. Even if it had, that meant letting Xavier see. Xavier, who knew so well how to use things against him. So Sef stayed silent.

Xavier hadn't stopped smiling yet but it didn't go anywhere near his eyes. In fact it seemed to pull all traces of humor from the rest of his face. "Get him up." He glanced at Burke's unconscious mass in the corner. "And get rid of the other one. We'll need privacy."

At a nod from Xavier, one of the remaining three men, hired muscle from the looks of them, pulled Sef upright with an arm tight around his throat. Behind him, he could hear the sounds of Burke being dragged from the room. A heavy thudding filled the air followed by a bitten off scream from one of Burke's girls. They'd thrown him down the stairs.

"I must have been blessed by the Saints," Xavier said. His eyes sparked with contained anger. He'd hardly changed at all, still round cheeked despite being in his thirties and an almost gaunt thinness everywhere else. His punch snapped Sef's head back and filled his mouth with blood. Sef only wished it would have knocked him out. He would rather be unconscious for whatever happened next. Xavier flexed his hands, leather gloves creaking faintly. There was only one reason for wearing gloves like those in this heat. Sef couldn't take his eyes off them.

"I wasn't even supposed to be here. Rather stay in the mountains where things are civilized. Less dusty. But business is business," Xavier went on. "I think perhaps you were right. Fate *has* taken a dislike to you, hasn't she?" He put a finger under Sef's chin, tilting his head up for inspection. "You don't look so good." He swung again and Sef would've crumpled if he was able.

"I have money," Sef gasped when he could breathe again.

With the next punch, blood flowed from his nose and ran over his lips, mixing with the blood already in his mouth.

"We'll get to that. But first: a little lesson about what happens to liars and thieves. Do you know what they used to do to thieves?"

Unfortunately he did. Instinctively, Sef's hands curled into fists. If he could have hidden them behind his back he would have. "Wait." Xavier ignored him. It took two men to hold up Sef after a few more punches.

Xavier stepped back to survey his work. "Put him

on the table." He eyed the forgotten game of cards. The tray had fallen, scattering its contents over the floor along with the handful of coins from their last bet.

"Wait," Sef panted. He fought against the hands dragging him forward but his heels slid over the carpet undeterred.

One of Xavier's men pulled a knife from his belt. The blade was wide and heavy, the kind of thing used for clearing tough stalks in the field, but the rusty stain on the metal said it had been used for more unpleasant things. It glinted wickedly, drawing and holding his gaze.

"Let's talk about this. I can get you your money back. All of it. Everyone will be happy. You get what you want. I get to keep all my pieces."

"That's where you're wrong. Mounting your hands on my wall will make me plenty happy," Xavier said. "Do you know how long I spent looking for you? Months. I spent months. I was a laughingstock. Betrayed by my own people. Betrayed by *you* of all people, they said." He nodded at the men holding Sef. "Get him down."

They slammed Sef against the polished wood so hard that stars burst in his eyes. The fist at his collar dug into the nape of his neck. Almost choking. He couldn't concentrate on forming a proper spell. The only thing that came out was a pitiful fizzle of energy, hardly enough to raise the hair on their arms, let alone loosen their grip. "No. Don't." He pushed back but three sets of hands held him in place.

"You don't want to do this," Sef said. "We were friends."

"Shall we start with the right or the left?" Xavier mused, but it was clear he'd already made his decision. One of the men twisted Sef's left arm behind his back. Another pulled his right across the center of the table.

Sef shook his head wildly. Helpless laughter bubbled up in his throat. It tore at him, more painful than a scream. "I don't think I can fix a hand."

The knife flashed in the corner of his vision. He squeezed his eyes shut, still shaking his head.

CHAPTER TWELVE
IN WHICH TAISCE PLAYS THE HERO

It took less prodding than Taisce had expected to convince the innkeeper to divulge Burke's whereabouts and within minutes they were back out into the street in search of the man. He never should have left Sef alone at the inn. They'd been in town only a few hours and he'd already relieved Taisce's purse of half its contents. Who knew what kind of mischief he would get up to if left to his own devices longer?

"That man is trouble," Finn grumbled barely two steps behind Taisce.

"We have already discussed this. The matter is closed."

That didn't keep Finn from muttering his many other opinions as they made the trip to Burke's building.

The establishment was not that dissimilar to the other buildings on the street. They were all the same hastily constructed wooden boxes with warped wood plank walks fronting them but, where the other businesses were painted in subdued shades of brown and beige, or simply left bare to weather the elements, Burke's was painted a garish orange. The sun had faded it almost to peach but around the shutters the original color was as brilliant as ever.

Taking in the exterior, Taisce frowned. It definitely looked as disreputable as he'd been led to believe. It was no surprise at all that Sef would frequent this place. The building was as shady looking as he was.

There was a crunch underfoot at the same moment Taisce noticed the broken window on the upper floor. He looked down. Glass lay scattered in the street. It sat atop the dirt, still clean and obviously freshly broken.

Finn toed at a large shard of glass, stepping over the rest and tilting his head back to look at where it had originated. Whatever he made of the matter, he kept it to himself.

Then Sef's voice rang out. His words were muffled but the tone was clear.

Taisce charged inside.

The interior was dark and so lushly over decorated that it took a long time for Taisce to get his bearings. At his entrance, two women started. Between them on the burgundy cushioned settee a man groaned and tried to sit up.

"The stairs?" Taisce demanded.

One of the women flinched but she pointed to the far wall.

The upper hallway was lined with doors, all of

them closed, but it wasn't hard to locate the right one. Sef's voice emanated from the door at the end, every word he said underscored with hysterical laughter. Taisce shoved the door in.

The room was cramped with people but his attention went immediately to the two in the center. They held Sef prone on the table, one arm out, an evil looking knife poised over him.

"Let him go," Taisce barked.

Sef hardly seemed to hear. His whole body quivered with his struggles.

A dark haired man watching from the side of the table put up a gloved hand, stilling whatever they'd been planning. Taisce immediately disliked him. He might have been handsome if not for the coldness in his expression. His mouth sat in an unwaveringly straight line, neither pleased nor frowning. From the blandness of his demeanor he could have been anywhere instead of presiding over an attack. "If you have business with the thief, you're welcome to him once we're done," he said reasonably. As if Sef were cattle, something to be haggled over.

"Let him go," Taisce repeated. "He's in my employ and I'll not see him harmed."

Finally Sef turned to face him. Blood was smudged over his lips and his eyes were round with panic. Taisce had never seen such a look from him. He'd turned into a stranger wearing Sef's face. "Yes. He'll give you your money, Xavier. Ask him. Ask him."

The man, Xavier, raked Taisce with a look,

seeming to take in everything about him in the space of seconds. "Is this true? Would you settle his debt?"

The answer came forth without a moment's thought. "Of course." He stiffened at the challenge in the man's eyes. Xavier spoke as if he knew something Taisce didn't. It was probably true.

"He means so much to you, this piece of trash?" Xavier shot him a questioning look. He gestured to his men and the one who held Sef pulled him upright by the arm twisted behind his back. The fight seemed to have left Sef's body. He sagged and a jittery, unnatural smile stretched his lips. "You agreed awful quick. Tell me. What's he worth to you? What will you give me for his safe return?"

Instead of answering, Taisce straightened his coat and checked that it was buttoned properly. He studied Xavier through his lashes, trying to ignore the pitiful figure Sef cut. Xavier's expression had changed little, but the talk of bargains had added a certain sharpness to his features. There was no doubt that he intended to come out the victor. Taisce planned to keep that from happening. This was a situation he was familiar with at least. Granted, he usually negotiated over contracts, not flesh and blood, but at the root these matters were the same.

Taisce glanced back as Finn came into the room behind him. He'd certainly taken long enough, but his presence gave Taisce an extra confidence. He wasn't outnumbered so terribly anymore. He had a man of his own. Finn was at least as large as any of Xavier's men.

"What does Sef owe you?" Taisce asked finally.

Xavier whistled. "It's not just money he stole. How does one put a value on the great damage he did to my reputation?"

"I can't make reparations for anything so vague," Taisce said, waving a hand as if to swat the comment aside. "I deal only in facts and figures. Tell me your demands now or forfeit your claim."

There was silence between them while Xavier's smile gradually thinned and died away. "Who are you?"

"Is my name a part of the negotiation? If that's the case, I ask to be repaid for my identity with yours. Exactly who are you?"

"You're crafty. And you speak with a serpent's tongue," Xavier said. He considered another moment. "If I don't know with whom I'm speaking, how can I know that you have the means to fulfill my demands?"

"If I'm unable to meet them, you may have Sef back with my blessing. Though I doubt that will be the case." It took all his willpower not to look at Sef as he began to struggle anew.

Xavier nodded at him. "You're not from around here. I'd know you if you were. Where do you conduct business? Lowry? North? What are you doing in my territory without introduction? A man would think you're plotting something, coming here in secret."

"My business is my own but you may rest assured that it has no connection with yours," Taisce said with a haughty lift of his chin. He had no idea what Xavier might be engaged in, but if his treatment of Sef was any indication, it was even more unsavory than Burke's business. Being in the same room with the man was almost unbearable. "Make your demands if you will."

"This one will have you wrapped in pretty chains if you're not careful," Xavier said, leaning over to address Sef for the first time. "He's slick as a devil, isn't he?" He turned back to Taisce, setting his hip against the table and crossing his arms. "You give away nothing, just like a true villain. Very well. He's stolen three hundred croy from me. Add another two hundred to that and I'll return your pet."

Taisce swallowed. So much money. He had never imagined the sum would be so great but there was no time to agonize over it while Xavier was awaiting his answer with a smug look of satisfaction on his face that said he thought he'd won. Even if the prize hadn't been so great, Taisce's pride would never have let him be beaten by such a man. Taisce swallowed again in an attempt to soothe his dry throat. It had gone painfully tight after he'd heard the final sum.

"Very well," he said, reaching into the inner pocket of his coat. The ring had fallen to the bottom of his pocket but it was easily found. He pulled it out, holding up the signet ring for Xavier's eyes but keeping the etched crest obscured. The emerald cut gems that bracketed it were easy enough to spot even at a distance. "This is worth twice that. Release him and it's yours."

Behind him, Finn stammered, one hand flying out as if he would take the ring himself. "You can't," he whispered. Even Sef raised his gaze to the ring in Taisce's hand.

Xavier's eyes narrowed. The style of the ring was unmistakable. "You're noble." His tone went wintery.

Taisce said nothing. It wasn't necessary to confirm what was already obvious.

"And what's to keep my head on my shoulders once I've taken that ring?"

"I'm a gentleman," Taisce said, bristling at the insult. "I've given my word."

Xavier snorted but he reached for the ring all the same. He rolled it between his fingers, holding it up to the light before he turned back to Taisce. "I want something else."

"The bargain is already more than fair."

"Not quite yet, *your lordship.* But almost." Xavier smiled at him, all teeth. "I'll take a favor of yours as well."

"I haven't agreed to that," Taisce said, but he knew that he would. His eyes flicked to Sef. He'd regained some of his fight but his struggles were hampered by the arm wrenched behind him and he was still white with panic. Taisce turned his attention back to Xavier and folded his arms in feigned impatience. "What favor would you have?"

"No, no. Not yet. I won't need the favor just yet, milord," he added after a pause. Taisce's title had passed Sef's lips with the same taste of mockery but he found it nearly unbearable from Xavier. His jaw clenched. "I want the promise of one. I think a noble's favor is something I would very much like to have in my pocket."

"There are limits to what my favors can accomplish," Taisce warned.

"You're a resourceful man, I think, milord. When the time comes, you'll think of something." Xavier squeezed the signet ring in his fist. Taisce felt as if that hand might also be closing around him. He would have to see to it that Xavier's favor never came due.

"We have struck a bargain. I don't suppose you're in the habit of shaking hands?" He grinned crookedly at Taisce but didn't wait for an answer. "Let the thief go." The men obliged immediately and, suddenly unsupported, Sef stumbled and fell to the floor. Xavier nodded to the both of them as he made his way to the door. "It was a true pleasure meeting you, your lordship."

Finn stared at the door for a long time after they'd left, looking stricken. Taisce took a steadying breath. He was shaking. He didn't know when it had started but now he was helpless to stop it. He couldn't remember ever feeling so relieved. Or so furious. He was filled with such black anger. He turned on Sef. The man had found his feet again. He wobbled on them but he was already recovering quickly.

"I should have left him to do what he would with you," Taisce hissed. "You cause nothing but trouble."

"He wasn't supposed to be here. Xavier never comes so far west."

Taisce couldn't see for a moment through his rage. "So you might have escaped this time but what of the next? Do you expect never to pay for your crimes? You could have bled to death all over this garish room if I hadn't arrived in time to save you. You called me a child, but what are you? You're thoughtless and you're selfish, you stupid man. Were I wise, I would abandon you here to rot in poverty but you've stolen from that vile man and now the debt has passed to me. How do you intend to repay me for my kindness?"

Sef made no answer for once.

"Should I expect others to come forward seeking satisfaction from you?" Taisce asked finally.

"No."

Taisce gave his coat another angry tug. "And because of you, I've lost my ring," he said and his face fell a little. Then his eyes cut back to Sef. "Steal from me again and I'll take your hands myself."

Sef finally met his gaze. He nodded slowly.

"Let's go," Taisce snapped, hand already on the door knob. His breath still came in gasps and a faint tremor passed through him but the greatest part of his anger was already draining away. There was no sport in yelling at a man who looked ready to shatter. "I would have given you the money, had you asked," he added more quietly.

~~*

Taisce attempted to charge Finn with keeping

watch over Sef at the inn, but Finn would have none of it.

"My lord, that... man is still in the city somewhere. I cannot allow you to go out alone. Your honorable father would never forgive me if you came to harm. I couldn't face him."

Taisce frowned. There had already been plenty of harm done, but luckily most of it was not physical. The loss of his ring grieved him. He had kept it guarded in his pocket at all times, unable to wear it while he was abroad. Secrecy depended upon it. The finger it had adorned no longer bore the telltale line of its constant presence. His hands had tanned considerably over the last weeks. No longer fair and elegant. Despite his gloves, weeks in a saddle and fending off nature had left them calloused and rough. Finally he nodded. "Perhaps you're right. Return in four hours. No more than that."

Finn nodded before his attention drifted over to Sef, lying on a bed against the far wall. "What about him?"

"He'll cause no more trouble today." Taisce's mouth pulled into a grim line.

"I'll return soon, my lord," Finn promised.

Taisce closed the door behind him, turning the lock to assure they would be undisturbed.

"What have you to say for yourself?" Taisce asked. He approached Sef with measured steps, arms folded tightly against himself.

Sef sat up and swung his legs off the bed. Blood stained his face but it had dried and darkened to a rusty brown. No fresh blood ran from his nose now. "Nothing."

His mouth had a stubborn set as he met Taisce's gaze, but Taisce remembered the way he'd looked barely an hour before, the horrible frantic animal he'd been then.

"Perhaps I *should* turn you out then, since you care so little for being in my employ. You lie. You steal. You're horribly rude..."

"You would never reach your destination without me," Sef said with strange pride.

"Why did you let them beat you?"

Sef raised an eyebrow.

"When we were attacked—by the wolves—you fought them. I've never seen anything like that, the strange flame you used to kill them. Why didn't you do that today?" Taisce asked, pausing as he tried to make sense of it himself. The memories already seemed more fever dream than fact. "I've seen what you can do."

"Oh, I can do far worse than that. But maybe I didn't want to."

Taisce stared at him. That wasn't the answer he wanted—not the real answer—but he wouldn't repeat himself. Not now when the effort would be wasted. "And yet I seem to trust you. Why could that be?"

"Because you're a fool, milord," Sef said. His smile didn't reach his eyes but the sharpness of the look seemed to be aimed inward this time.

Taisce blew out a thin laugh. "That must be." He

stopped his pacing before Sef. "Look at me." When Sef cocked his head to meet his eyes Taisce went on. "I meant what I said. You'll cause me no more problems from now on. Is that clear?"

"You sound quite sure of that."

Taisce was glad to see the color returning to Sef's face. He had been so quiet ever since they left Burke's place.

"I am." He knew what he'd seen. Sef had been frightened for the first time since they'd met. And as the door had closed on Xavier and the threat he posed, Taisce had seen a glimmer of something in Sef's face. He was pinning his hopes on that glimmer.

Now Sef's expression had settled into something closer to his usual lazy mockery. That was better. It would do.

"You look a mess."

Taisce found the pitcher of wash water beside the basin and set it near Sef. There was no cloth for washing so he dipped his handkerchief into the water, wringing it out in silence before he raised it to Sef's face.

"Turn this way," Taisce instructed.

"There's no need to bother," Sef said but he turned obediently in the direction Taisce indicated.

The worst of the damage was around his mouth. One of the blows had split Sef's lower lip and his teeth had made another gash. Between that and his nose, half of his face was smeared with blood. Taisce started at the curve of his high cheekbones, moving slowly to avoid causing further pain, but Sef still hissed when the cloth found the scrape on his jaw.

"You seem to cause trouble only for the sake of regretting it later," Taisce said quietly. He bent to rinse his handkerchief clean. "Why would you steal from a man like that? Did you think there would be no consequences?"

"I hoped."

"Then you're a bigger fool than I am." Taisce angled Sef's head to clean the dried blood from where it had collected beneath his chin. He frowned, wringing the scarlet tinged water back into the bowl. Then he lay the cloth against Sef's cheek, letting it soothe the irritated flesh before he moved on. As the damp cloth brushed over his lips, Sef's eyes slid shut. A dark bruise had already bloomed around his eye. The shadow gave him a tired look, made him look older. It was strange on him. His impudent mirth had become so familiar.

Taisce's knuckles grazed over his lips and they parted automatically. Waiting. Taisce ducked his head. He took his time working the red stain from his handkerchief, running it through the water again and again until it came clean.

When he'd finished, Sef's eyes were open again and following his every move in silence. Most of the blood had been cleaned away, leaving behind a series of shallow pink scrapes, hardly any evidence of what had happened earlier. His split lip had healed to a dark line, a stubborn reminder in scabbed blood. Taisce worked at it with the corner of his handkerchief, trying in vain to get it clean. Sef winced but he didn't turn away. Finally Taisce gave up and dropped his handkerchief in defeat. He put a hand to Sef's cheek, turning him to the light for inspection.

"You'll do."

When Taisce made as if to pull back, Sef grabbed his wrist, holding him in place. His eyes darkened by degrees. Taisce hardly noticed him leaning forward until Sef's lips were pressed to his. Again Taisce was surprised by how cool they were. For all the heat in his gaze, his skin never seemed to warm even a little. Still, the kiss didn't disappoint. It was slower than the others they'd shared. It lingered, bordering on chaste. Sef's hand stayed braced on the bed even as Taisce's fingers slipped to his neck and up into his hair.

The kiss ended as quietly as it began. Sef drew back. His eyes stayed pinned to Taisce.

"What was that for?" Taisce asked.

Sef's smile flickered back to life, inching up higher on one side in that familiar way it had. "It was a thank you."

"You could have simply said the words," Taisce said, but he could feel his own lips curving into an answering grin.

"I could. But those are just words. Isn't this better?"

This time there was nothing chaste about his advances. Sef pressed forward, lips firm and insistent, and urged him back onto the bed. With a dark look and a line of kisses pressed to Taisce's exposed throat, Sef left him breathless. Sef's tongue trailed over his pulse before he sat up and began working Taisce free of his coat. He threw it aside. One after another he stripped away Taisce's layers with silent intent, unbuttoning his waistcoat and moving on. Then he wrapped his fingers in Taisce's cravat. He gave it an experimental tug and then tried again, harder now, pulling Taisce up and into another kiss with a wicked grin. Before it was done, he'd lost his waistcoat to the floor too.

"You're a fool," Sef whispered against his neck. He pressed the words into Taisce's leaping pulse, traced them over again with his tongue. Taisce groaned, eyes fluttering as he struggled to concentrate.

"You say... the strangest things," Taisce murmured. He slipped his hands beneath Sef's untucked shirt, fingers digging in.

Sef cringed back, but his pained wince quickly transformed into a smile. "Don't touch."

Taisce's hands retreated, fumbling against the coverlet. He'd forgotten about Sef's injuries. "I'm sorry."

"Shut up, milord." Sef gave his cravat another rough tug. Followed it with a kiss.

"I'm used to more respect than this," Taisce complained, but there was no heat in it. He knew full well he was smiling.

"I know." Sef's lips twitched with laughter. When it finally broke free it seemed like it might never stop. Taisce longed to hear more of that laugh. It was musical and honest in a way he dared not hope for Sef to be. Not yet. Seeing the look in his eyes, Sef raised an eyebrow. "You won't cry on me, will you?"

He didn't give Taisce a chance to answer. He urged their mouths together again, tongue tracing lips and dipping inside while he pulled Taisce's cravat free and discarded it. Taisce hesitated before he brought his hands up again, settling them on Sef's shoulders. He dug his fingers into the muscle there, kneading deeply, tracing the ridge of bone with his thumbs and slipping down to his back.

There was something so strange about Sef. As if he could disappear at any moment. Like a phantom. Even having his hands on the man wasn't enough to make him seem solid. He wanted to demand things, so many things, but one swipe of that clever tongue and the words dissolved. Taisce leapt beneath his touch, grip tightening, pulling. "Not yet, milord."

Sef's hands ran over him. They curled around his waist possessively, holding Taisce still as he nipped at the pale flesh of his stomach. His mouth found one hipbone then the other, kissing each in turn, while his hands slipped into Taisce trousers. They slid down his hips with aching slowness, exposing him to the warm afternoon sun.

"Such a fine body, milord." The words fanned over him like the touch of cool fingers. They ran through him. When Sef grazed him with a careless touch Taisce cried out. Surprised at himself, he pressed a hand to his mouth, heat of a different kind creeping up his neck. Sef grinned at him. "You've never had a proper lover, have you?" He crept back up, nuzzling Taisce's neck, tasting his skin with a dart of his tongue. He kissed his way back to his mouth, lacing his fingers with the hand there and pulling it aside. "I rather like that. I want to make sure you remember me."

Taisce shook his head. "I've had plenty," he said, indignantly. He scowled but it was ruined by another brush of Sef's fingers. He stroked gently over Taisce's prick from top to bottom, and Taisce arched into it, chasing the touch, seeking the rasp of friction.

"You've had courtly lovers, I'll bet. Did they send engraved requests before they kissed you?" Sef claimed his lips again. He laid Taisce flat with it, tongue tracing the roof of his mouth as Sef's hand wrapped his prick again, the stroke as rough as his mouth. "Did you make them beg to enter your noble bed? Tell me." Teeth scraped at Taisce's neck.

"No," Taisce gasped.

Sef's hand ran between his legs again, stroking him so slowly it only made him ache for more. For everything. It was all he could think of. He reached down to do it himself and found his right hand captured like his left. Taisce growled, frustrated. He dropped his head back against the bed. It took every ounce of his pride to keep from begging.

"You're a liar," Sef said but there was a smile pressed into Taisce's skin along with the accusation.

"I'm not."

"You're as much a liar as I am." He set Taisce's hands free, chasing them away with a frown. He dipped to Taisce's body again, planting delicate bites along with kisses as he shifted lower. "You're only honest when I force you to be." Sef settled between his legs, tugging Taisce along the bed with him.

"What are you doing?" Taisce tried to sit up, startled.

"Trust me."

"Never."

Sef's smile only grew. "Be careful, milord, or I'll take advantage of this weakness of yours." When his head dipped next, Taisce tensed automatically. Everything about Sef felt like an attack, a shocking assault on his senses. Another chuckle drifted up to him. Then all thought was lost beneath the onslaught of Sef's mouth. He swallowed Taisce whole, one hand stroking in matching rhythm, tongue swirling around his shaft.

Taisce cried out again, pulled into a taut line, as Sef raked his side with blunt nails and set his skin on fire. His head fell back. He could die from this. He would do so gladly if it kept Sef here, mouth covering him, sharing his heat. Taisce would shackle him to his side forever. He wanted him. He wanted all of him.

"You're mine," he growled. "Mine." He didn't even realize he'd spoken until Sef paused. He cocked his head in question, hands still playing wicked games as if they had a mind of their own.

Taisce wrapped a fist in his shirt and drew him up until they were face to face. "You're mine," he whispered. He threw an arm around Sef, gathering him closer for another kiss with the tang of blood in it.

~~*

Taisce opened one drowsy eye. "You never even removed your shirt."

"A keen observation, milord." Sef put his hands behind his head. The heat of Taisce beside him was like a furnace but not unwelcome. It flowed beneath his skin, soothing most of his aches away. Of course there was one ache it did nothing to soothe. He would attend to that later.

Taisce took a deep breath before he spoke again. He propped himself up on one arm. "I meant what I said. You belong to me now."

"And if I refuse?"

"You're welcome to try." Taisce shot him a crafty smile and his eyes crinkled at the corners, just like an imp's. Xavier had been right. Beneath all his innocence and his propriety lay a serpent's heart. It sent a thrill through Sef's veins, a surge of hunger. He tangled a hand in Taisce's hair and leaned up to kiss him.

The door rattled and they turned in unison. Sef gauged the slant of the sun in the window. The dog was early by hours yet.

"My lord!" called Finn, shaking the door on its hinges. "My lord, are you there?"

Sef glared at the plank of wood. He wished he could set it, and the man on the other side of it, alight but he was much too tired. He would be lucky to manage a weak scorch mark.

"Stop making such a racket, Finn," Taisce ordered when silence did no good. He stretched again before he climbed from the bed and stepped into his trousers. When he wobbled on his feet, he shot Sef a pointed look. Then his eyes dropped to the clothes scattered beside the bed. "Pick up this mess."

Sef scowled. The boy would pay for that later. But he swept the discarded shirt and coat from the floor, tossing them carelessly onto one of the other beds just as Finn burst in the unlocked door.

"My lord! Are you well?" he asked, but his eyes were on Sef as he spoke. Only afterward did he notice Taisce. The boy hadn't bothered with donning a shirt and he stood with his chest bare and peppered with the marks of their recent pleasure. "My lord!" Finn's face grew even redder and his hands curled into fists like fleshy boulders. Sef was amazed he didn't charge him straight off. There was no doubt about who had caused those marks and he couldn't hide his smile at Finn's outrage.

"Enough, Finn. What news have you?"

Finn cast another furious glare at Sef before he collected himself enough to shake his head. "None, my lord. I caught sight of that... person from earlier and thought it best to hurry back and assure your safety."

Taisce stared at him, suddenly every inch the noble again. Even half dressed he was elegant and proud. It made Sef want to throw him to the bed and strip every ounce of that pride from him a second time. He moaned with such beautiful abandon. "Then you've done nothing these past few hours?"

"I tried, my lord. Truly. But no one has seen your brother." Finn slumped in defeat. "They barely speak to me at all."

Sef snickered. "And it's no wonder really."

Both Taisce and Finn turned to him as if they were surprised to find him still in the room. The sudden reminder only seemed to inflame Finn anew. Sef grinned at him.

"You have no idea how to speak to people. They're probably terrified you'll crush them if they answer wrong."

Finn gaped, face turning even darker. "I would crush *you*," he growled. He had more to say, it was clearly written on his face, but Taisce stepped in front of him, cutting in.

Taisce folded his arms over his chest. "And you think you can get me the answers I seek?"

"If there are answers to be found," Sef nodded, "I can. If he's actually been this way and is as bad at discretion as you two." And here he glanced at Finn again, silently questioning.

"He came this way," Finn said, brows sinking into a deeper scowl.

Sef held up his hands. "Of course. But the day is nearly over. It might best to wait until tomorrow."

Taisce sighed but agreed. "I think we've had enough adventure for one day," he said pointedly.

Sef kept his face carefully blank. He would never speak of it again if he had his way but the boy was sure to press his advantage now that he'd found one.

The best Sef could manage was to keep still while another wave of nausea passed through him. His hands twitched, trying to curl in on themselves just like the rest of his body. The boy wouldn't trifle with such things if he understood what it was he said.

The evening passed quietly taken up with a peasant's dinner at which Sef was deprived of wine. Taisce snatched the bottle from him, pouring for himself but warding Sef off when he tried to retrieve it. He would have been glad of the wine. Perhaps it would keep his courage intact a while longer. But he was repeatedly denied.

~~*

When night fell and the dog was snoring peacefully, Sef slipped from his bed. Before he made it halfway there, Taisce's eyes opened, shining in the darkness like a beacon. Good. Sef smiled. He slid into the bed at his side, pressing a warm kiss to his lips. He brushed Taisce's unbound hair from his forehead.

Not a word passed between them. Taisce returned his kiss with one of his own, rolling Sef beneath him, holding him with his familiar weight and the rhythm of his breathing. It was musical in his ears. He pressed his nose into the crook of Taisce's neck, inhaling him, committing him to memory. The faintly salty tinge of sweat and the particular scent of his skin. He smelled of herbs and sun and the books he'd probably spent his time with instead of people. Sef ran his hands up Taisce's back, stripping away the nightshirt that would only confound him later if it remained.

"Now yours," Taisce whispered, already working it free unbidden.

Skin to skin once more, they clung to each other, Taisce grinding against him until Sef thought he would lose his mind for the final time. He grabbed for Taisce, holding him still and pressing him down, claiming his mouth in a hungry kiss, all urgency. Taisce responded eagerly. Everything else fell away but the movement of his tongue and the brush of his hair as it fell around them. There was nothing but him. The feel of him. The taste. Sef needed it all. His hands clamped to Taisce's hips, rocked up into him, biting at his lower lip, crushing him with arms that had forgotten how to be gentle. Taisce moaned so quietly when Sef would have him screaming helplessly. He smoothed a hand over Sef's cheek, thumb stroking along his lips. Sef pulled it into his mouth. He sucked hard at it, tongue running over the calloused pad, eyes locked on Taisce. He knew what the boy was thinking by the sudden jut of his hips, the stutter of his breath.

While he was distracted, Sef rolled them again, settling between his legs, fumbling with the vial of oil he'd hidden beneath his pillow. He swallowed Taisce's startled gasp with another kiss, slicked fingers questing lower. They found the spot easily, circling. He half expected Taisce to protest but he only wrapped his arms around Sef more tightly, pressing hot lips to his neck and panting in his ear.

Taisce bucked beneath him as he pressed in, a low moan escaping before he could catch it. His kisses grew more fervent, wetter, warmer, as his hands clawed for purchase. Sef smiled. His own breath came in choked gasps. His eyes drifted closed as he moved, rhythm building to a frenzy, Taisce meeting him, urging him on.

Yes. Yes, this was good. "Yes," he growled. He trailed a line of nips up Taisce's neck to the ear. "Yes."

And Taisce writhed beneath him, agreement written in every line of his body.

CHAPTER THIRTEEN
IN WHICH PROGRESS IS MADE ON ALL FRONTS

"Why are we here again?" Taisce asked, eyeing the building warily.

Burke hadn't even bothered to cover over the broken window. It still gaped like an empty eye socket, a reminder of what had happened the day before. Taisce frowned.

"Anyone who spends more than an hour in Mission, Burke would know about it," Sef said. His face flickered with a smile that darkened Taisce's spirits a little more.

"Then shouldn't he have known that that... man," Taisce fumbled, unable to say Xavier's name again, "was here?"

Sef pressed his lips together. "Yes. I plan to see about that as well."

He didn't wait for further comment before he pushed through the swinging door of Burke's place. The interior was just as dark as Taisce remembered. The damask wallpaper and the fringed curtains made him feel like he'd wandered into some kind of elaborately decorated labyrinth. Today no one lounged at the bar or on the couches scattered about the room. All the better. Taisce didn't enjoy the idea of being seen in such a place twice in as many days. He tugged at his coat, missing the small pressure of the ring in his pocket. Without it, he felt further from home than ever.

Sef was already halfway up the stairs, moving with the familiarity of long acquaintance. Taisce scowled at his rapidly retreating figure. He might have hoped that yesterday would teach him some caution, but the man seemed content to pretend it had never happened. Taisce wasn't deceived. He noticed the way Sef flinched at even the vague mention of Xavier. Taisce couldn't blame him, but he wished the infuriating man would acknowledge it. If he thought anyone had forgotten, he was a bigger fool than Taisce could ever have guessed.

By the time Taisce made it up the stairs in pursuit, Sef had already thrown open the door to Burke's office without a warning knock. As if pretending that he was untroubled would make it so. It was almost laughable.

"Wait here, Finn," Taisce said with a glance at the narrow hallway. He had no desire for a second round of surprises.

Taisce found Burke's lounge much more agreeable the second time. Now that he was able to look around at leisure he found it had a certain air of refinement, which pleased him even though the decor was much too dark for his liking. All the same, it was the closest thing to home that he'd seen in weeks. The walls were papered in deep gold and burgundy and the walls were lined with sconces and shelves of books. Carved tables stood about the fringes of the room, their clawed feet buried deeply in the plush rugs on the floor. It was not so unlike his own study. Smaller perhaps. But where Taisce favored light woods and neatly ordered botanical prints on the walls, Burke's lounge ran to... other things. Many of the framed drawings on the walls were nudes, the women in them captured in delicate lines of ink and washed into rosy life with watercolors. They hung in place of honor between the two tallest bookshelves.

"See something you like?" Burke asked, startling Taisce out of his perusal.

Taisce turned on his heel, smoothing a hand down his coat. "No."

Burke and Sef exchanged a glance.

"But what are you doing here?" Burke said even as he pulled Sef into a rough hug. "I woke from that bump on the head and you were gone. I thought you were lost for good this time."

Taisce stiffened, eyes narrowing at the way Burke patted Sef on the back. Such boisterous familiarity. Sef allowed the gesture, even returning it cheerfully, before they stepped away from each other. Then with a wry smile, "You know it's impossible." After he'd spoken he glanced at Taisce, expression clouding. He put a hand to Burke's shoulder and turned them away towards the table in the center of the room. The same one he'd been bent over only a day before, though Sef seemed to be ignoring that fact as well. They sat, again with that casual air that left Taisce at a loss. They hadn't invited him to sit and, even had they, there were only two chairs at the table. He turned his eyes back to the shelves of books. They seemed more likely to offer some sort of distraction anyway.

"Swear to me that you knew nothing of Xavier's presence in town," Sef said, voice dropping into a low growl.

"Of course I didn't! He's cut into my business plenty as it is. Ratty little bastard. Why would I ever help him?" Burke paused. "I swear it. I swear."

Sef leaned back, slinging a leg over the padded arm of the chair with a sigh. "If I find out different, you'll regret it," he warned, "but that's not why I'm here."

As they settled themselves, Taisce stepped closer to the bookshelves. Burke's library was impressive despite its small size. He seemed to favor poetry. Taisce recognized a handful of the more common poets, but the books were scattered haphazardly between volumes dealing in business, histories, and map making. He glanced up. The shelves nearly touched the high ceiling and the top shelf was taller than the rest, containing many oversized books with heavy bindings. Taisce stretched, pulling down a thin book with an oxblood cover that drew his eyes. He turned it over, looking for a title along the spine or the cover and found none. Inside, the pages were crisp and dappled brown with age. He flipped through them carefully, one after another, seeking a name. After a half dozen pages he found a faded map. It looked hand drawn, the ink splotched in places. Taisce squinted at the scrawled names, holding the book close to the window in an attempt to read them. The book smelled of age, the faint aroma of leather and the sour tang of glue underlined with the scent of mildew. Taisce fished for his glasses, turning his back to the others so he could press them onto the bridge of his nose unnoticed.

The writing in the book leapt into clarity, but it did nothing to help him solve the riddle of its contents. The lettering was familiar, but the arrangement of the letters was nothing but gibberish to him. Perhaps it had been written in some kind of code. He turned to the next page and found it covered in more of the closely packed writing. The more he stared, the more he felt he should know it.

Burke made a curious noise, waiting for Sef to explain himself.

"We're looking for a particular person. His party should have been this way quite recently. No more than a week or two."

"That's awfully vague even for you," Burke said. "You'll need to give me something better than that."

Sef pulled the rumpled watercolor portrait from his pocket and set it on the table, sliding it closer to Burke with one finger. "That's him. He was traveling with at least two others, a man and a woman, but I have no idea what they look like." He raised his eyes to Taisce. "Milord?"

Taisce hummed in answer, still poring over the book. The pages were thick, roughly textured, old paper. He couldn't help running his fingers over them. There was no trace of an impression left from the hand that had written the scrawling lines of text either.

He'd found more drawings in it, interspersed between what looked to be a history of sorts. One page held a detailed sketch of a beautiful woman, her hair long and curled. With her thin, pointed nose and narrow eyes, she had a sly look that was nevertheless elegant.

"Milord," Sef said again. He paused. "What is that you're reading?"

Taisce turned another page.

Sef came out of his chair with a clatter and the book flew from Taisce's hands before he quite realized what had happened. Sef closed it with a snap, shoving it onto the top of the highest shelf. "We have need of you, milord," he said. His jaw clenched.

"I was reading that," Taisce protested.

"You couldn't read it if you tried."

"How do you know that? You don't even know what it was." Sef's grip on his arm was tight enough to bruise. "Let me go."

Sef steered him into the chair he'd vacated, pressing Taisce down into the seat. He hovered behind him, hands still resting heavily on Taisce's shoulders as if he expected him to fly back to the bookshelf the moment he was set free. He was tempted to do just that.

Burke watched them with unreadable eyes that bounced between the two of them before finally coming to rest on Taisce. He cleared his throat. "These travelers," he prompted.

"They're little better than abductors," Taisce said. Belatedly he remembered the glasses sitting on his nose and he tucked them back into his pocket before he went on. "They left weeks ago with my brother. Our information says that they were headed this way, chasing some tale of riches." Taisce snorted. Then he gestured at the wrinkled portrait still sitting on the table. "You can see Rupert for yourself. As for the others—the man is a tall, shifty looking sort. With dark hair and a mustache. The woman is fair. Blond haired. They were part of some society together. Magical. Supposedly."

"Really?" Burke said, not a question so much as a statement of interest. "And who is this brother of yours that you're going to such lengths to recover him?"

Taisce frowned, but there was no way to avoid the question. He glanced out the window, chasing an alternative that refused to present itself. The sky was a dry, high arching blue. He missed the closeness of the smoke clouded view from his study. "The heir Brenton."

Burke whistled. "Well. That does change things, doesn't it? You left that part out, Sef."

"It makes no matter. Either you've seen them or you haven't," Sef said, prowling back to the bookshelf. He pulled down the red book, turning pages absently.

"But generally I'm compensated for my services," Burke said, steepling his fingers before him. His eyes rested on Taisce, awaiting his response.

Taisce kept his face bland despite his mounting disappointment. Money again. He rather preferred it to be changing hands in the other direction.

Before he could speak Sef interrupted him.

"You'll waive your fee this time," he said with an abrupt confidence that had Burke turning to him in surprise.

"I will?"

"Yes. You will." Their eyes met and whatever Burke saw there seemed to convince him.

He turned back to Taisce with a new smile on his face. Something in the character of it felt solicitous, as if they'd shared a secret without Taisce realizing it. The feeling irked him. If they were in each other's confidence he would prefer to know about it. Taisce hesitated to ask and admit another disadvantage. He already had a large stock of them in this conversation.

They were interrupted by a knock on the door. The woman who entered was petite with dark hair piled on her head in a loose coil, escaped tendrils spilling about her face. Her dress was modest, much more than Taisce would have expected in a brothel. The fabric was a faded plum, but it was obviously of good quality, unmended, the bodice speckled with embroidered flowers. She came bearing wine and entered without waiting for permission. When she saw Sef she stumbled to a stop. Worry clouded her features. "Sir?" she asked, turning to Burke.

"We'll need two more cups for the wine, Rose," he said. A smile flitted over his face, touching his eyes before he tamped it down.

Taisce's lips itched with a smile of their own. Love, was it? It made him like Burke a little better. Then his eyes slipped over to Sef and his smile withered. "She seems pleasant," Taisce said when Rose had left, closing the door behind her.

"Indeed," Burke said. "Yes. Quite." He cleared his throat, quashing his pride as neatly as he had the smile in his eyes. "I've seen this brother of yours and the two he traveled with, though it didn't look much like any kidnapping I've ever seen. They stayed in town only a few days. Made enough trouble to fill more. The other one, the mustache, he goes by the name Norland, yeah? No idea what the first part of his name is. He's a rude bastard, which I say as someone who is hard to offend. You've met Sef."

Taisce nodded grimly. "I'm acquainted with Norland." That night months ago came to his mind and he scowled. On the other side of the room, Sef raised his head, but he said nothing.

"Came here looking to have one of my lot. Girl, boy, didn't seem to matter to him. I turned him down of course. Not enough money in the world to convince me to turn them over to a reptile. He didn't like that at all." Burke's smile was vicious at the memory. Whatever had happened between them, it couldn't have been pleasant.

"Where did they go when they left? Did you see the direction?" Taisce asked before Burke could elaborate on their dealings.

"I didn't, but I heard of it from some others. Further on south. Word about town is that they were seeking the treasure in the canyons of Teufelis." He chuckled. "They'll end up scorched and mad from the sun before they find any treasure."

"What treasure?"

"An old legend. They won't find anything. Amateurs." He made a dismissive noise.

"But if that's where they're headed—"

Another knock at the door signaled Rose's return. She was more careful about entering this time. She moved as if she expected a brawl to break out around her. Perhaps after yesterday she did. She set the tray of cups on the table, waiting for instruction. "Sef will drink. He always does. And what of you, my lord?" He held up the cup Rose had poured for him. "Do you care for a bit of wine?"

Taisce nodded. "Tell me more of this legend. If they're chasing this foolishness I'll need to follow them to it."

Burke shrugged, nearly spilling his wine on the floor. "I'm surprised you don't know the story. But you're far from home." He tipped the cup to his lips and set it aside "According to the legend there was a monster that hid itself in the canyons. It's a dry, horrible place. Hardly more than a pile of rocks and sky that goes on forever. Story says the monster had collected a large treasure for itself. How that happened no one ever seems to bother with—that's the problem with legends. But where there's a fortune to be had, the foolish are never far behind. They came one by one to challenge the beast and steal its treasure."

"And did they succeed?" Taisce found it hard not to laugh at the story. It was a fairy tale of the silliest sort, but it seemed exactly the type of thing that would draw Rupert. He'd always been more interested in stories and easy acclaim than reality. Taisce had always hoped his brother would catch himself before he fell into ruin, but it seemed he'd done just the opposite. He'd run towards it with open arms. Taisce had envied him, his assured position, his favor in Father's eyes, but he had never wanted him to die in disgrace. And this whole venture—it was ridiculous.

"You laugh but many disappeared," Burke said. "The few that survived, they came back raving about the monster, about its eyes that glowed, and how it tore men in half." He shook his head. "But nothing was ever found. No treasure. Even the location of the cave is little more than a legend. The canyons stretch for miles. Those that came back never remembered where the cave was, barely remembered their own names, whether it was from the heat and wandering in the wilderness or something else. One or the other burned the sense right out of them."

Taisce took a moment to think over what he'd said. There was an obvious problem with it. "If no one knows where this legendary cave is, how am I supposed to follow them? If these hills stretch as far as you say, they could be anywhere."

"I heard them talking," Burke said, sly smile back in place. "Your brother and this Norland were discussing their plans. They seemed quite sure of the location."

"It's impossible," Sef said suddenly.

"I heard their plans myself."

"It's madness to go out there. You won't do it." Sef's eyes bored into Taisce.

The tone was surprising after his lengthy silence. Taisce hadn't thought Sef was listening at all. "I will go wherever I must to get Rupert back. If that's where they've gone then so shall I," Taisce said coolly. "This has been my task all along. I told you. I won't leave it half finished."

"You would die on a fool's errand." He made it sound as if there were no other options but that one. Taisce shook his head. It didn't matter. He had to go. He couldn't turn around now when he'd already come so far.

Taisce turned back to Burke. "Where? Where did they think this cave lay? I'll need a map."

"Of course." Burke's eyes lingered on Sef before he nodded.

Sef growled, hands clenching around the book in his hands. "I won't take you to Worau." He threw the book onto the table with a bang that made them both jump. He jabbed a finger at it. "And I thought I told you to burn that trash," he said before he stormed from the room. The door slammed behind him.

"Ignore him," Burke said with a dismissive wave. "More wine?"

Taisce stared at the door. "I should go. He's bound to get into more trouble if left to his own devices."

Burke refilled his cup and then Taisce's. "He won't go far while you're here."

"What do you mean?" Taisce took a small sip of his wine. He'd barely tasted it the first time, too preoccupied with the news of Rupert and the silly legend, but now as it ran over his tongue, he sighed. The taste was full and rich. Comforting. He looked into the dark depths of his cup. It was simple earthenware and heavy in his hand, without the breakable delicacy of glass or crystal. Perhaps there was something to be said for Burke's lounge and the comforts it afforded.

The silence finally drew Taisce's attention. He looked up to find Burke watching him.

"You make an interesting pair."

Taisce chuckled dryly, taking another swallow of wine before he answered. "I don't think you can call us a pair. We're barely civil."

"But you've bedded him."

Taisce choked. The wine stung his throat as he fought to swallow it down. "What?"

Burke's grin widened. Red heat flushed Taisce's cheeks, creeping down into his collar. Was it really so obvious? Or had Sef said something?

"There's no point hiding it. I deal in sex and companionship. Spotting lovers is my profession."

Burke glanced at the closed door. "I've also known him a long time. He's quite taken with you."

"He insults me," Taisce said, wincing at his petulant tone.

That drew a boisterous laugh from Burke. He laughed so long that he set his cup aside to keep from spilling it. When he'd finished he wiped the corner of his watering eyes. "Yes. He would do that. But you're good for him, I think. He's kept himself lonely too long." He looked down. "He's right about the desert though. It's a dangerous place."

"I have to find my brother. There's no possible way I can return without him. Not when I'm so close."

"Then Sef is the one to get you there." Burke put up a hand to stop Taisce interrupting. "But be careful of him. You don't know half of what you should and there's more of the legend than what I told you. You'll have to ask Sef for that; he knows it better than I do."

After a moment, he set his hands on the table, bracing himself as he stood. "Why don't I get you that map, hmm?" He headed to a door in the opposite corner of the room, unlocking it with a key from his pocket. He turned back. "I can tell you're fond of books. You're welcome to my collection while you wait. It's always a pleasure to meet a fellow scholar."

When he'd gone, Taisce was left to puzzle out his words over the dregs of his wine cup. It was no surprise to him that Sef might have more secrets. The man was nothing if not a collection of trickery and deceit made flesh.

Taisce's eyes fell on the red book. It still sat on the table where Sef had thrown it. Taisce pulled it back to him and set his glasses back atop his nose.

The writing was just as strange to him as it had been before and the longer he spent trying to read it the less it seemed to make sense. He tried a line out loud, stumbling over the vowels and accented letters. *"Ne rega famye..."* he mumbled, reading the caption beneath an illustration. The drawing was so detailed it must have taken hours to complete, full of delicately crosshatched lines. The same craftily elegant woman stood in the background. Beside her was a man, equally elegant but disapproving and stern faced. His square jaw and neatly trimmed hair had a humorless hard edged precision. Both man and woman wore crowns that marked them as some kind of royalty but from no family that Taisce had ever studied. He'd learned the lineage of Lancard's royal family and those in prominence in their surrounding countries going back centuries as part of his schooling. Despite that, the faces in this book were completely unknown to him. Taisce's eyes moved over the drawing again. So much detail. He envied the talent that had drawn such a thing.

He turned the page. It was covered in a large block of the unreadable text, confounding Taisce, so he turned to the next.

Another illustration greeted him, this one of three men. They were all tall and stately, circlets atop their heads as they stood in formal pose. The first, and presumably the oldest, had the close cropped hair and square jaw of the king. The second shared his serious eyes though his hair curled in dark disarray about his face, more reminiscent of the queen. The third... Taisce frowned. Someone had torn him almost completely from the book. The only thing that remained of him was a pair of dark boots and long, lean legs. At his side curled the barest sliver of a hand. Taisce's eyes slid to the caption neatly printed beneath the picture.

Éthys, Liam, es vi.

Taisce ran a finger along the torn edge. It hadn't been an accident. The page was hardly wrinkled and the other two men were unharmed. Only the one had been removed.

He turned more pages, searching for the missing piece of the picture. There were a number of drawings, one of a castle like something out of a fairy tale, another of a stone walled courtyard with a twisted tree growing in the center, its branches like upraised arms reaching towards the sky. Every picture had been carefully rendered in the same hand. Some of them had framed borders of stylized leaves and notes in the margin. It was as painstakingly detailed as any book he had ever seen.

Before he could look further there was a creak and Burke reappeared with a sheaf of papers and scrolls under one arm. His eyes dropped to the book in Taisce's hands. Taisce closed it quickly, feeling caught in something despite Burke's invitation.

Burke laid the maps out over the table, securing a

corner with the nearly empty wine bottle. Taisce put a hand to his glasses but thought better of removing them. Some of the maps were brown with age, others were crisp white and drawn in colorful ink. There were so many maps that Taisce wasn't sure which to look at first.

"Now this here," Burke began, pressing a thick finger to an empty stretch of one map, "is where the entrance to the caves should be." He pointed to another spot. "We're here"

Taisce rose to inspect the first spot Burke had indicated. "There's nothing there."

"Exactly. This map is quite recent. I bought it off a man just last year. But these others," and here he pulled out one of the tawny maps and laid it on top of the first, "are much older." He pointed to a series of lines, the marking of some kind of border or trail. "If my guess is right, this is the trail your brother and his friends will be taking."

It seemed to lead nowhere, the line thinning and disappearing into the same blank area as the first map Burke had shown him.

Burke's face glowed with excitement, like a child with a favorite game. He pulled out a third map. Taisce couldn't resist rubbing the corner of it between his fingers. As he'd thought, it had the coarse texture of linen instead of paper. "This is how I know your brother and his friends were on to something. They had a map much like this. Better condition even. I offered to pay very good money for it but they turned me down. The wooden scroll at the end was still attached, you see. Finest map I've encountered..." He finally noticed Taisce's expression and cleared his throat. "Yes. As I was saying, this map is much older than the others and it shows a great city in just this spot, not far from where the canyons of Teufelis are now. The city has been gone for..." He blew out a breath, "Centuries. But it's the most likely place. It's disappeared off of all the maps save these old ones. If they had a map like this one, that would be why. They're planning to look for the old city."

Taisce peered down at the last map. The hand that had drawn it was different but the language was the same as that in the red book. There was no mistaking it. Taisce leaned in closer, lips moving silently as he attempted to decipher the name on the map.

"Worau," Burke said. "It was the old capital city."

"The capital of what?" Taisce asked. He repeated the name carefully. It had a strange feel on his tongue. Heavy.

"I take it you never studied the old histories. Well... most people don't anymore." He said no more on the subject, though Taisce waited. Suddenly he'd grown tight lipped. Taisce wished it would have happened earlier while he was tossing around his maps.

"Have you a map I can actually use?" Taisce asked, looking at the aged cloth.

"You're the impatient one, aren't you?" Burke patted him hard on the shoulder. "You'll need supplies before you head into the desert. And a hat or you'll be blind from the sun before you get halfway there."

Taisce put a hand to his head. He hadn't thought of that, though it certainly explained why Sef was so fond of that horrible hat of his.

"Your brother has been missing for weeks if I'm understanding you right. One day spent gathering supplies won't delay you much and, considering how they left town, I reckon it'll help you in the long run. You're only a few days behind them."

"If what you say is true, my brother could be dead of exposure in those few days it takes to catch up to him."

Burke shook his head, rolling his maps together with great care. "Never happen. You have Sef with you. With him you'll find the place in half the time."

"I don't know what difference that's supposed to make. He's made it quite clear that he won't go."

"You'll convince him," Burke said. His lips curled into a sly smile and Taisce stiffened. Then he held up a weathered and creased roll of paper. "I'm not much of a talent but I copied this map from the original myself. It's as accurate as you'll need."

~~*

Taisce left Burke's office feeling as if he'd been spun in circles and now they would need to make preparations to head into a wasteland that was rumored to drive men mad. He couldn't say that he was looking forward to the attempt even if it *was* based off silly superstition. All logic told him to turn and run the other way. The further south he traveled the more trouble mounted, like a great wave. Eventually it would come crashing down on them.

Finn followed him down the stairs and out onto the street, so close that when Taisce stopped abruptly Finn almost fell over his shoulder. Taisce turned back to him. "We'll need supplies for the last leg of our trip."

"Yes, my lord," he said obediently but a question hovered in his eyes.

"Food, water." Taisce paused, scratching at the trickle of sweat at his temple. "Make sure we have ample supply of everything. We could be away from civilization for some time."

Finn's mouth slowly dropped open. "How long, my lord?" At Taisce's look, he hastily added, "So that I know how much we'll need."

Taisce thought back to the empty space on the map and Burke's insistence that Sef would lead them unfailingly there. The distance had not been great but the terrain would be harsh indeed. "A two weeks' supply for the four of us if you can manage it. We'll have Rupert with us on the return. I can't trust him to have anything of use. We will have to provide for him as well." Taisce reached into his purse. It had already grown so light. "This should be enough," he said as he dropped a few coins into Finn's waiting palm.

Finn stared at the money, lips moving as he counted the coins. He slipped them into an inner pocket of his coat.

Taisce waited.

Finally he waved a hand at Finn. "Get to it then."

"Now, my lord?" He looked around as if he suddenly suspected lurking danger from every shadow.

"Yes. Now. Off with you."

Finn gave him another startled look before nodding and setting off. His feet kicked up clouds of rust colored dirt. He looked back a few times until Taisce glared at him.

Taisce turned the opposite way, headed towards the post. He'd promised Adeline letters but he'd hardly provided. It had been too distressing to write letters when he had no news to share. Hopefully Sef would be in their room when he had returned; he didn't like to think of him wandering about alone after yesterday. And Taisce still had no idea how he was meant to convince the man to guide them when he seemed dead set against it. The only other option—wandering aimlessly through the desert with nothing but a fool's treasure map—wasn't something he wanted to attempt either. Instead of rescuing Rupert, it would be Taisce in need of saving if they did that. The only thing Taisce knew of deserts were the things he'd read in books. He doubted Finn was any better informed.

Taisce frowned as he stepped off the wood plank walk along Burke's building. Dust rose around his boots. He felt just as parched as the dirt beneath his feet.

He'd barely finished the thought before a hand

closed on his arm, pulling him sideways into the space between buildings. Taisce cried out but the sound was muffled as Sef's lips fell on his and he pushed Taisce against the wall. He'd lost none of his skill in the hours since they'd shared a bed and Taisce let himself return Sef's kisses with eager ones of his own. It was only too bad he couldn't let himself be swept away for long. After a moment, Taisce took hold of Sef's shoulders, pressing one more kiss to his lips before pushing him back.

"Not here."

Sef growled, using the heat of their closeness against him. His grip on Taisce's hips hadn't slipped and Sef's thumbs made distracting circles against his hipbones.

Taisce finally pried his hands away, but it was hard to say who found it more difficult. He placed a hand on Sef's chest, keeping him at a safe distance until he'd gotten control of his breathing again. "I haven't changed my mind about going. We leave tomorrow."

With a grumble, Sef dropped his forehead to Taisce's shoulder. His arms pressed into the wall, bracketing Taisce in an almost embrace. "You can't ask me to do this," he said in a strangled voice. The kiss of an accent rose in his voice again.

"I don't understand you. You've been acting so strangely..." There seemed no way to voice the many questions that had risen to his mind. He wished he could tell Sef the words he wanted to hear. But he couldn't. Or wouldn't. He wanted Sef at his side, needed it. Saying otherwise would be a lie. So he said nothing and slipped a hand up the nape of Sef's neck, running his fingers through his hair.

~~*

Sef sat in silence for the rest of the night. Barely ate. After a few hours, even Finn began expressing concern. That only irritated Sef more.

"Leave me be." His growl had the desired effect. Finn made no more efforts to speak to him.

Harder to deflect was Taisce. Sef could feel the boy's eyes watching him like silent stars. There was no avoiding them. They seemed to be everywhere, beside him, inside him, in his damned dreams.

He wished he *could* run but where would he go? There was nowhere to run that he hadn't already been twice over. And if he left Taisce now, if he let the boy die... he would never get another chance. This one might be his last—his only—chance. Where would he find another fool like him? With his innocence and his spirit and his maddening arrogance? It would have been easier if he could go back to the beginning when the boy was only a tool to him, back when that was all he wanted from him, but Sef had grown greedy. He wanted all of him. Not just the swift blow of an executioner. He wanted every bit of Taisce, every bit of him that he'd had, every piece still left untouched.

But to have it...

Could he make such a sacrifice?

He'd seen the curiosity in the boy's eyes. There was no way to keep it at bay forever, no way to slip around it like a thief in the night. Sooner or later he would ask. Perhaps when he noticed how quickly Sef's injuries faded into memory. And what then? To lie would be easy—he'd had centuries of practice at it—but to keep the lie intact would take a miracle. More than a miracle. It would take an impossibility. Sef had run from place to place, chased by the ghost of his curse all along, never staying long enough for anyone to notice his agelessness.

Not again.

He couldn't do it again.

To take Taisce as his own... how could he hope to do that when it meant giving up his past? Laying it bare, an unwelcome gift at his feet. It was unforgivable at best. And at worst...

Sef winced.

He was caged still.

His eyes slipped to Taisce. He'd fallen into a fitful sleep, curled on his side, face as open as a babe's. The journey had been wearing on the boy. He hid it well but Sef had seen the stiffness in his gait. His leg pained him. Another example of how fragile a thing he was. As easily crushed as a butterfly's wing. And just as beautiful.

Sef closed his eyes, decision made.

CHAPTER FOURTEEN
IN WHICH THE DESERT IS A LOST PLACE

Taisce woke early and agitated. The room was silent save for Finn's gentle snores. Sometime during the night Sef had also succumbed to unconsciousness but it clung to him awkwardly and he moaned, still slumped in the chair beside the window. Taisce wondered how long he'd spent staring out of it last night before he finally fell asleep. It had been well past midnight when Taisce gave up waiting for him.

Now he rose and went to stand at Sef's side. He'd never really had the chance to observe him like this; Sef had the uncanny habit of rising before Taisce no matter where they were. The only time Taisce could even remember seeing him sleep was that morning in the woods. It seemed like a lifetime ago already.

Movement outside the window drew Taisce's eyes. The street below them was sluggish with early morning activity. Sef had told him that there were ranches and small farms dotted through the countryside and it was these people who brought Mission to life this morning. Horses pulled rough wooden carts whose contents were hidden beneath dun colored tarps. Everything about the people here seemed to be colored by the encroaching desert. A steady tide of voices followed them as they went about their business. Taisce watched them. Their tanned skin and their work-wearied pace. It was strange to find that he envied them a bit.

He watched the people pass for another minute and then would have drifted away from the window if not for the familiar face looking up at him. The girl from the woods, Sef had said her name was Erin, stood in the street. Watching. When Taisce leaned out the window, she raised one hand and beckoned him down.

"I never expected to see you again," Taisce said when he joined her on the street. He'd dressed in haste, half expecting her to disappear like a ghost before he reached her, but as he rushed out of the inn she was still waiting, standing in exactly the place he had first spotted her. Today her hair was pulled back in a loose knot and she'd dressed in a long, white tunic and trousers. It suited her. He wished he could hug her but he held back. He doubted it would be welcomed.

She blinked at him as if his words were surprising. "I came to check that you were unharmed but I wasn't certain you would see me. That you would wish to." She looked away. "Where is your lover?"

Taisce started at her question. After a few attempts he gave up trying to deny it at all. Her forthright attitude was so disarming, just like Adeline's, and he smiled. They might even have been friends were things different. Maybe in another life. "That was you, wasn't it? That night when we were attacked on the plains," Taisce asked finally, grasping at the thing that had weighed on him ever since. "You saved me from that other wolf?"

Erin nodded.

"So it's true. You...?" Taisce shook his head. He felt foolish even putting voice to the question but he knew what he'd seen. "You're one of them? You're a... werewolf?"

Another nod.

"Sef told me but I didn't believe it. It seems so impossible."

At the mention of Sef's name she blanched.

"Are you all right? Your injuries, they don't still pain you, do they?" Taisce asked, immediately concerned.

"No. They're fine. But that man, you *are* still with him? You haven't left him after all? I thought maybe you had. You didn't say..."

"He's my guide," Taisce said weakly. It wasn't the whole truth but that wasn't something that had to be shared with her.

"He's... different than I expected," she said. "But you should beware."

"Different? Different how? And how do you even know him?" How did *everyone* seem to know him, he wanted to ask.

"My people, they tell stories." She shook her head.

"I tried to warn them against attacking your lover. I told them what he was but they wouldn't listen. I suppose they got what they deserved for that."

"I don't..."

She frowned but not at him, at a memory of someone else. "My uncle has a long memory and a fast temper. There's nothing I can do when he gets like this. I've tried. He doesn't like to lose. It's best if you keep away from our territory or he'll send more hunters after your lover. I'm already in trouble for helping you once. I don't think I'll be able to stop them next time even were I about."

"Then why did you?"

She paused, already half turned to leave now that she'd said her piece. "You helped me in the forest. Now I have returned the favor. Isn't that what you people do?" With that she started away.

"Thank you," Taisce called after her. And, before he could stop himself, he added, "Perhaps we'll see each other again."

"I doubt it," she said but there was a smile on her lips.

Taisce waited until she had gone, swallowed up by the growing bustle in the streets, before he made his way back inside the inn. Erin had avoided answering some of his questions, the ones about Sef mostly, but Taisce was quickly coming to the conclusion that it was best to leave his past where it was. Very little good seemed to come of dredging it up. Better it came to him on its own.

He was still lost in thought when someone called

out to him. The old innkeeper had been wiping at the narrow bar with ponderous intent but now he ducked behind it. "This was left for you last night," he said, voice muffled by his searching.

"Then why wasn't it delivered to me then?" Taisce asked with barely controlled irritation. His immediate thought was that a letter from Rupert had managed to find him here. But it wasn't a letter that the old man set before him. It was flat and rectangular, tied up in a bundle of checked fabric like a dish ready for a picnic. Taisce took it with a muttered thanks and retreated towards the stairs. He could feel the innkeeper watching him, waiting to see what it was he had delivered. Taisce had no intention of satisfying his curiosity.

He didn't need to unwrap the bundle to know what was inside. He could feel the corners of the book and through the coarse weave of the fabric he could just make out the color of the oxblood leather. He would have to hide the book somewhere that Sef wouldn't think to pry.

~~*

The desert had grown more desolate since last Sef had seen it. They'd been sitting on the edge of the thing for two days already, within easy reach of the expanse, but leaving Mission behind in a cloud of dust transformed the horrible possibility into reality. Instead of a shadow on the horizon, it was a thing made solid. This desert was as much a monster as he.

Larger and more terrible perhaps, but they were one and the same in the end.

Sef squinted in the glare of the sun and tugged his hat lower on his brow.

In his mind, he could see what it had once been. The heat had been oppressive then too—Saracque was never a haven for the lush grass and abundant plants that grew in the north—but it had been tempered with twisted trees and wiry plants. They grew from the dense, rocky ground with tenacity, clinging to every available surface, throwing their roots deep to get the water they craved. And the people had managed to tame the place in time. They had set their roots as deeply as the plants they relied on. In time Saracque had thrived.

Now all that remained was an endless stretch of gritty wind and maze-like canyons. It was a phantom that haunted him.

They rode into the desert in silence, leaving tracks scuffed into the pink parched earth as the sun sank towards the horizon. They'd left late in the day, hoping to avoid the overpowering heat of midday. As the sun dropped, Sef's eyes began to play their tricks. He had expected this but the knowledge gave him little comfort. Where nothing had been, suddenly he saw a familiar shape, the crooked silhouette of a hut, the straight line of a fence post, the curl of smoke from a chimney against the darkening horizon.

He shook his head. He knew this land like he knew himself and the change in it still ached. His home was in ruins.

"No wonder they say this place drives men mad," Taisce said quietly from behind him.

Sef didn't turn. "Yes."

No more was said as they headed down a winding canyon trail and into deeper shadows. Loose rocks scattered beneath their horses' hooves, the sound echoing off the walls that boxed them in. Eventually the path widened again, turning up towards the dusky twilight sky. Twilight always stretched forever in this place too.

There had been a great river here once. It had run dry long ago, but when it flowed it had fed into a series of smaller streams that ran through most of Saracque. It was was one of these branches that they followed. It would lead them where they needed to go.

Few maps had survived the plague that took this place. The people had fled, leaving their belongings, their former lives, as if even their memories might harbor the sickness. Those that stayed died. They burned from the inside out, succumbing one by one to a disease with no cure. At the end, there had been no hope but to burn them and their possessions to the ground, eradicating any trace of them.

It wasn't enough.

It didn't stop the spread. The funeral pyres only helped to make room for more corpses. The plague clung to his people like a leech. Few escaped it. His family certainly hadn't.

But Sef had. Only him. Cursed to live. Cursed to

watch his family fall around him. Cursed to watch his kingdom falter and finally fall to its knees.

Sef scratched absently at the mark on his hand. He'd hoped that the years would burn the tattoo away but it was as well kept as the rest of him. A constant reminder of what he was and what he had lost.

He would have been glad never to come back. It was preferable to forget that Saracque had ever existed rather than mourn its many losses all over again.

Yet here he was.

Darkness fell around them.

"How can you see where we're going in the dark?" Taisce finally asked, riding up to Sef's side when the trail allowed. He leaned forward and peered into the shadows ahead. Their lantern cut them but could do no more than that. "I feel like we're riding off the edge of the world."

"It's close," Sef said under his breath.

"What's that?"

Sef sighed. "I don't need to see to know where we're going."

Taisce fumbled in his pockets before pulling out the wrinkled map that Burke had given him. The damned fool. Sef should have let him die here years ago. This whole situation could have been avoided if Sef had had the foresight to just let the meddling bastard expire unimpeded. Taisce held the map up to the light of the moon, trying to decipher the copied scribblings. It was obvious that he couldn't read it, not without proper light and probably the use of his glasses besides.

Sef couldn't help a small laugh. "You won't need that map."

Taisce gave the paper another frustrated squint before he folded it and stuffed it back into a pocket. "But how do you know where we're going? I can barely see an inch in front of my horse and you haven't even glanced at a map. How do you know this place?"

So many questions. "You didn't ask this many questions on the way to Mission," Sef grumbled.

"We weren't riding into a wasteland then. I want to be sure you know what you're doing."

"If I knew what I was doing, milord, I would have stayed back in Clotsfield where things were comfortably boring and I had a bed." He glanced at Taisce. The boy was about to start questioning him again. He could see it in his eyes. "We'll stop here for the night," Sef said, cutting him off before he could begin his next interrogation.

"Here?" Taisce turned in the saddle as if expecting an inn to have grown straight up from the earth when he wasn't looking. "Why here?"

"It's as good a place as any." Sef dismounted. The area was flat at least. The ridge was walled on one side with steep rock to give them a bit of protection. The carcass of an emaciated tree stood nearby and he looped the horse's reins around it before he pulled the saddlebags from its back. There was nothing for Taisce to do but accept it.

"Insufferable!" The boy repeated it over and over as he and Finn set up camp.

Sef left them to it, wandering away from the small fire they coaxed into life. It drove away the chill of the rapidly cooling desert air but Sef had no use for it. Not tonight. Nothing would warm the ice wrapped around him.

The desert barely existed to him. Beneath his feet spread the rough weedy lawns of Saracque. Ahead of him stretched the roads he'd traveled in his youth. But instead of townspeople, all he could remember were burning corpses and shades. The screaming of the terrified, the wet gurgles as they choked on blood. Eyes permanently sealed by disease.

He fell to his knees in the dust.

~~*

They sheltered from the sun where they could, in the shadows of rock outcroppings or in canyon beds where the sun couldn't stretch its greedy fingers. Taisce couldn't imagine anyone so desperate for riches that they would enter the desert on their own. It looked the same in every direction but Sef led them unfailingly on. He'd never been so silent before, face an expressionless mask, eyes lifeless and dim. He was little better than a corpse astride his horse. Taisce watched his back as they rode off the end of the world. He wished he knew something to say.

Sef still came to him in the night, pale and quiet as a ghost, and Taisce welcomed Sef into his arms. But even that had changed. Sef enveloped him, pressing into him with a desperate need, kissing him like he was drowning. When they'd finished, Sef would drop into unconsciousness still collapsed atop him.

It was then that Taisce would slip back to the fire with the book Burke had given him.

He'd hidden it well, rewrapped in the fabric it had come in and then wrapped again in his clothes. Burke had sent the book to him for a reason. He only wished that Burke had given him some indication of what that might be.

The text of the book still meant nothing to Taisce though he had picked up the name of the city, Worau, with surprising frequency when he attempted to read it. What interested Taisce most were the many illustrations that littered its pages, though.

Taisce turned pages one after another, carefully, with the kind of precision usually reserved for his ledgers and plant cuttings. Glasses perched on his nose, he studied the book long into the night, trying to piece together a story made only of pictures. He found more drawings of the king and queen as well as the princes. He saw them at court, at table. Then the princes with women on their arms, looking regal yet pleased. It was there, a few pages after what Taisce assumed were the princes and their wives, that he first saw her. The woman was undeniably beautiful, with her dark hair and darker eyes, but he couldn't help finding her rather cold as well. Even drawn in such immaculate detail she seemed somehow distant. The shell of her ear, the notch at the corner of her mouth as she smiled. A whole page dedicated to the shape of her hands as she held a wine glass. And yet she remained elusive. It was strange. After a few more pages, Taisce decided he disliked her though he couldn't have said why.

A few pages after that, he had forgotten all about her, lost in the loops and swirls of the crest he found there, the same one inked into the skin on the back of Sef's hand.

Taisce woke in the morning and found Sef sitting at the edge of last night's fire. He stared into the ashes, only speaking when Taisce addressed him and then falling silent again.

It worried Taisce more than he cared to admit. Their previous travels had been peppered with idle chatter and unwanted opinions. To see him now was like watching a statue come to life. He moved and he breathed but no more than that.

The sun set and night fell again like an impenetrable curtain. Sef floated ahead of him, even more ghostly by moonlight. It was all Taisce could do to wait until they'd stopped traveling for the night. Questions buzzed in his head.

And as before, Sef wandered towards the open desert without a word.

Taisce dropped his things and hurried after him. "Start the fire, Finn," he called over his shoulder, barely stopping to be sure he was heard.

He caught Sef before he'd made it very far, following his silhouette into the darkness of another rising canyon trail. When Taisce called he made no answer. He only stopped. Taisce put a hand to his shoulder.

"Please talk to me," he begged, eyes searching Sef's face. "Please."

Silence. Then Sef shook his head. "This place is full of ghosts."

Taisce looked around, half expecting an apparition to appear beside him. With Sef around it seemed possible. "I don't believe in ghosts."

That earned him a chuckle, a pale imitation of the ones he'd heard in the past. "You wouldn't."

He bit his lip. "Can you make the trip?"

"Is this concern that I hear in your voice, milord?" Sef asked. His mouth curled up in a grin that didn't reach his eyes. "I haven't lost all my sense yet. Only some."

"It gladdens me to hear it," Taisce said, trying for the ease they'd shared before faltering and falling silent again. He took Sef by the hand and led him back to the fire. Neither said a word.

Taisce sat beside him, wondering what passed through Sef's head while he stared into the flames. His body was there but the rest of him could be anywhere. Slowly the fire dimmed. A chill crept into the air.

"I'll see myself to bed," Finn said awkwardly. He withdrew from the fireside with a wary look and shuffled off a few paces to spread out his bedroll, lying down with his back to them. It was as much privacy as he would grant. Taisce looked at him with amusement. Ever the faithful guardian. It wasn't long before quiet snores drifted towards them.

"We'll reach our destination tomorrow?" Taisce asked finally.

Sef nodded. "They're close." He closed his eyes, head drifting to the side as if he were listening to a far off sound. "I can feel them. Out there."

Taisce turned in the direction Sef indicated as if he might be able to spot his brother on the horizon if he tried hard enough. "How do you know?"

Sef's head dropped. When he looked up again he was smiling crookedly. "Would you believe me if I said the land speaks to me?"

"Yes." It was Taisce's turn to look away then. He shrugged, covering his embarrassment with a small laugh. He rubbed at the back of his neck. "That tattoo on the back of your hand. What does it mean?"

At the mention, Sef's hand curled into a fist, pulling the skin taut. They both watched as his hand flexed and relaxed. Flexed and relaxed. "I have another story for you." He shifted closer, turning to face Taisce. He dropped a kiss on his lips.

"Will I like this story?"

"I rather doubt it." He cupped Taisce's cheek with one cool hand. "Should I start with 'once upon a time' like they do in children's stories?" He leaned in again, lips brushing Taisce's forehead this time. "Tuck you into bed?"

Taisce sighed, breathing him in on the inhale. "You could." He itched to put his arms around Sef's neck and pull him close, but if he did that the story would end before it had even begun. No doubt that was exactly what Sef wanted. So he curled his hands into fists and pressed them into the ground beneath him. "Tell me this story."

"Very well, milord," Sef said. The next kiss found his jaw. Breath grazed his ear like a caress. Taisce shivered. "Once upon a time there was a beautiful kingdom called Saracque, and in that kingdom there were three princes. The first was everything a prince should be. Strong. Brave. Levelheaded in all things," he said, punctuating each word with another brush of lips. "The second was just as talented in music as he was in strategy. He too would have been a worthy successor. But the third..." Here he tugged Taisce into his arms, seating him in his lap. His hands ran beneath Taisce's opened coat. He slipped it down his arms. "The third had no interest in any of those things. He would never see a throne. He would never lead a country. And he had no use for the habits of court. The third was useless."

Taisce frowned but said nothing. Sef's hands had traveled the length of his back before sliding down to his hips. One thumb dipped into the waistband of his trousers, testing the waters. "Continue."

Sef smiled wickedly and Taisce immediately realized his mistake.

"With the story," he corrected. Taisce pulled his hand away.

"While the first and second were learning to be useful to their country, the third met a woman. Beautiful. Intelligent. A guest of the court, a scholar, the first to look at him as anything worth noticing." Sef's hands began their work again. Nimble fingers undid waistcoat buttons one after another. "Of course he would love her." He paused. A frown creased his brow. Seeing it, Taisce couldn't resist. He ducked his head and grazed Sef's cheek with a kiss. Sef gathered him closer, crushing Taisce against his chest and claiming him for a deeper kiss full of teeth and tongues and need.

He would have left the story there but Taisce finally turned his head away and pressed a finger to Sef's lips. "Finish."

"They were in love, he thought. But he was mistaken. Someone else already had her heart. When he found them together his love was transformed into grief. And rage. The third killed her lover. And for that he was cursed with eternity. Never dying. Never aging. Even though the world fell apart around him, he would remain. An insect trapped in an amber prison." He laughed bitterly. "Do you understand?" His eyes were hard.

Taisce shook his head, frozen.

Sef tipped Taisce's gaze back to his when he tried to look away. "You doubt. With your logical mind that hates magic so much." He ran a hand through Taisce's hair, freeing it from its tie. It fell around them, floating on the dry air before settling again. "You saw my book. Burke's a sneaky bastard. I know he gave it to you. Did you see them? My drawings? The first son..." Sef sighed. "Éthys. The brave and noble."

What he said was impossible. Even as fragments of the book formed themselves into order in his mind, Taisce couldn't believe it. It was too much. Taisce shook his head again. "No."

Sef held him fast when Taisce tried to pull away. "The second, Liam. The scholar. The hunter. He sang with the voice of the gods." For a moment Sef's eyes drifted closed and the corner of his mouth twitched into a smile. He swayed in a silent dance. "Oh, you should have heard him. It was beautiful."

"No."

It was too much. Taisce scrambled backwards, falling into the dirt on his back. Sef moved over him, pressed him into the ground, pinning him by the shoulders. "And the third," he said with a grimace, showing his teeth. "Me."

"You've gone mad."

"I had," Sef agreed. He settled over Taisce's shaking body, arms coming around him. "For many years. But not now."

"Why tell me this? Why now?" He stared into the darkness. It was easier than looking at the man above him. It was impossible. *He* was impossible.

"Because, milord, we're in my kingdom." Sef tossed a look at the desert around them. "And because our meeting was no accident."

"I don't want to hear any more. Let me go."

Sef chuckled. "Not yet, milord. I haven't finished my tale yet. Do you regret asking me along now?"

Taisce bit his lip. His eyes prickled but he blinked the feeling away. He wished he could say yes. He wanted to. But at last he shook his head.

"I was right about you," Sef said in his usual cryptic way. He inhaled deeply like a drowning man filling his lungs before swimming for shore. "Curses are funny things. Immortality sounds like a gift, something sought after by a thousand foolish souls. An end to suffering. But there are so *many* ways to suffer. Death is the least of them." He paused. "A plague came to the kingdom and the people fell to it one by one. The lands withered. Finally it reached its grasping fingers high enough to claim the king and queen. Then the second son. And the first. But the third son sat untouched by disease while the others rotted and fell in the streets. Even as the kingdom lay dying, it gathered the strength to rise against him. They named him as their tormentor and hunted him. Drove him out. Into the caverns hidden beneath the castle. Like a monster. So he became one." He closed his eyes. "*I* became one," he corrected after a moment. "Your brother will not find what he seeks. There are no monsters here. Only me. And I... I have no treasure left to speak of." He laughed shakily.

Taisce finally looked at Sef, properly looked at him. In the fire light, his eyes were black as pitch, his expression broken in so many pieces Taisce doubted it could ever be put back together completely. Taisce could see it in him. He could see the years etched upon him like the rings of an ancient tree, could feel their weight, their cost.

"When she cursed me, Iolan left me with one final gift. Dreams—or visions—they're so hard to tell apart. When I saw you that first time in the square in Ciaran, I knew you already. Your eyes. I'd seen them on a thousand different nights, but I never believed it. Yet there you were. Here you are," he amended. He brushed back the hair from Taisce's forehead, fingers gentle and trembling. "I think it was always meant to be you. The only man in centuries who can undo me. The man who could kill me. And the only one I want. It's rather poetic, isn't it?"

There was no air.

"No."

Sef shook his head. He was still holding Taisce, but he couldn't feel it. Taisce couldn't feel anything but the painful squeezing of his heart.

"Why me?" The words came out small and frightened so he tried them again. Tried to infuse them with the bright burst of anger only now emerging. "Why *me*? Why do I have to play this part in your twisted story? No."

"I don't know, but I've felt it from the moment I touched you. It's in you."

"I won't do it." He shoved Sef away then and stood. He needed to move before he really did explode like a flare against the night sky, white hot and scorching a path through everything. "I should hate you. Why don't I hate you?" He kept waiting for the feeling to arrive. For the betrayal to set into his bones, but instead he kept remembering the way Sef touched him. Like he was precious. Like he was everything. He wanted more of that feeling even now. "You used me. You lie. You steal. I should hate you." He looked down. Back up. Sef still hadn't moved from where he had landed when Taisce pushed him. "But I won't kill you."

"I stopped wanting you to a long time ago," Sef said quietly.

"How long?"

Sef shook his head. "Maybe since I first held you. Or earlier. In the woods... trying so hard to be brave with a knife at your throat. I don't know. It had been so long since I felt alive, since I felt anything besides weary. But I feel it now and I don't want it to stop. Not yet. Maybe it's Iolan's final blow that I would stop wanting death as soon as I found someone who could give it to me."

He fought the urge to wrap Sef in his arms again. Instead he stared up at the bright pinpricks of the stars. There were so many out here in the middle of nowhere. Nothing but stars to hear their secrets. He wanted to scream. None of this felt real. It was impossible and yet it made more sense than anything. "Is there more?" Inside he was still raging but his voice came out flat. Calm even.

"You know all. More than anyone in centuries. Every terrible thing." His smile trembled on his lips. "And now I'm yours. I've given myself over to you." He moved forward on hands and knees, creeping across the ground to him. "What will you do with me now that you have me?"

He didn't know. He really didn't know.

"How long has it been? How long since...?" Taisce asked. That seemed like the easiest question.

"Since I became a monster?" Sef finished for him. "I don't know. Centuries. Perhaps seven... I wouldn't know." He was still on his knees in the dirt, face turned up to gaze at him, expression a turmoil of expectation and fear. Maybe it was the fear that did it. The way he trembled, breath coming in ragged gasps.

"I really must be a fool," Taisce groaned. He wrapped a fist in Sef's hair and pulled until he met his eyes. "Betray me and I'll make sure you regret it for the rest of your many lives." His threat was met with a smile. Then quickly, before he could change his mind, Taisce leaned down and claimed a kiss. He nipped at Sef's lips. His tongue prodded them open, coaxed forth a hum of pleasure.

When they finally parted for air, Taisce said, "Swear to it."

"I swear."

That was all Taisce needed to hear. At least for now. There would be time for the rest later, once they'd confronted Rupert and torn him away from that horrid man and his companion. But for now, Sef had finally succeeded in distracting Taisce from any other worries. Taisce's shirt had already been tugged open to the waist, letting in the cool night air. Taisce shivered and reached to relieve Sef of his own clothing. His story had been too unreal, too much to take in so quickly. But this, the feel of his skin, the rasp of his breathing, the pounding of their pulses, this was easy. This was familiar. And it was exactly what he needed. Taisce pressed Sef back. He was already straining, eager. After days of silence he wanted to hear Sef's voice. He needed to hear the evidence of his desire, the truth of his feelings. He raked Sef's side with his nails just to hear his startled hiss.

"Have you gotten greedy, milord?" Sef asked with a twitch of his lips and an answering buck of his hips.

"I have every right. You belong to me. Isn't that what you said?"

"So I did." He let out a pleased growl as Taisce's lips marked a line down his chest.

Taisce slipped a hand down Sef's bare back, more gently this time, gliding over the curve of his spine until he met the edge of his trousers and followed the line of fabric around his waist to his buttons. He gave them a tug. "You're wearing too many clothes for my liking. Take them off."

Sef obliged. The pale light of the moon slipped over his skin, highlighting the scar on his chest, the ridge of muscle, the thin line of hair trailing down his stomach. Taisce put out one finger to trace over it, following it down to meet the line of Sef's prick. Taisce wrapped it with a hand, watching as Sef's eyes rolled and finally snapped shut with a happy rumble. The look of sudden peace on Sef's face was intoxicating. His brow smoothed, no longer pained, not worried, lips pressed together as he hummed out his pleasure at Taisce's attentions. Lips joined the clench of fingers. The weight of him, the strange lack of heat, the taste of him on his tongue, Taisce savored it all. On his knees, in the dirt, it was hard to believe that there was anything else beyond this. Beyond the stillness of the desert. Beyond the two of them. Sef's hands stroked through the length of Taisce's hair, his fingers tangling at the nape until it prickled in almost pain.

Then Taisce was on his back. There wasn't time for explanation before Sef pounced on him again, burying his head in Taisce's neck, tearing at his trousers, every movement lit with need. Sef's teeth sank into the tender flesh at the base of his neck where it met his shoulder. Taisce gasped in surprise.

This was nothing like the quiet, careful lovemaking he'd experienced before. He didn't mind. He found he craved it. Sef didn't treat him like a fragile doll. He tore Taisce apart and built him up stronger. Taisce welcomed it. Every sharp pinch of teeth. The press of fingers. There would be bruises tomorrow, a smudged map of their time together. A rock scraped at his spine, drawing another angry line as Sef buried himself in the feel of Taisce's body. They were pinned together, moving as one, breathing the same frantic breaths. Taisce saw nothing but his lover. The line of him against the sky. Sef's sharp smile as white as the crescent moon. Taisce savored him, drinking in every moment, every growling vibrato as they came together faster and faster. When he came it was like the desert itself, hot and hard and endless.

Sef collapsed on top of him as their breathing returned to normal. Taisce realized he was smiling, broadly, foolishly. As soon as he'd felt it on his lips it transformed into a laugh, spilling from him before he could press a hand to his mouth to contain it. It was a horrible time to be laughing but once he'd begun he couldn't pull it back. He couldn't wrap it into a bundle and press it back into his belly from where it had come.

Sef lifted his head. "What are you laughing at?" His tone held suspicion.

"I don't know," Taisce said because he had no words for the feeling spinning through him. He pressed one gritty hand to his eyes. "I don't want this to end." The words slipped out just as the laughter had, without intent, and just as before he wished that he could pull them from the air and hide them away again. A part of him felt weak at the admission. It was as if the ground was rushing up to meet him after a fall. There was no way to stop it from hurting him. Not now. It was too late. No matter what he did there would be pain. "Tomorrow, if we find Rupert... what will happen then? Will you return with me? Will you come to Blume?"

"If that's what you wish."

Taisce sat up all at once and Sef fell sideways off him and into the dirt. "That's not what I asked."

"Only a moment ago you were claiming me as your own." Sef rolled onto his back, hands resting placidly on his bare stomach. He was still slick with sweat and semen. Taisce's eyes followed the raised pink line of a scratch that ran the length of his left arm. He had done that. A claiming mark that would fade all too quickly.

Taisce closed his eyes. Opened them again. No answers had presented themselves in that brief moment of darkness. If anything, he'd come away from it with more questions, not fewer. "I know what I want," Taisce said. "I've known for some time. But it's pointless if you don't feel... anything for me, if you don't actually *want* me. Not as a weapon or an obligation. As myself. I won't be your new penance. If you stay, stay because you want to." He looked down.

"And what is it you feel?"

It was harder to say than Taisce would have expected after all they had done together. The words stuck in his throat, their syllables hard edged and jagged now that he was trying to set them free. Of all the things he'd said, unthinking and brazen, this was the most difficult. It was the one thing he'd wished to say for days.

He took a deep swallow of air as if it were strong drink, using it to steel himself. Just like whiskey, it burned going down. "I don't understand it but somehow... it seems I've fallen in love with you. Despite everything. Or because of it." He shook his head. "I do."

He didn't dare look at Sef, not until after the words had floated between them for a moment. When he finally did, the look on Sef's face was not what he would have expected. At worst, he had expected a mocking smile, maybe a laugh. He hadn't dared to hope for best. Not yet. Not when the future was as hazy as a mirage on the horizon. But what he found was something else entirely. Sef looked... stunned. His mouth hung open. He'd propped himself up on one arm while they were talking and now he drooped limply to one side like a discarded doll. He said not a word.

CHAPTER FIFTEEN
IN WHICH BLOOD IS SPILT

They were saddled and traveling early the next morning. Too early as far as Sef was concerned. He'd slept not a wink while the ache took root in his bones and the emptiness grew in his heart.

Taisce loved him.

Sef had seen it in his attitude. He'd felt it in his harsh caresses. But to hear it was another matter entirely. It should have given him happiness. But all he could see was what lay ahead. He'd told Taisce everything. He'd poured himself into the ground at his feet. The timing had been purely selfish, a petty attempt at... he knew not what. Had he intended to push the boy away or draw him closer with his tale? Had he managed to achieve his goal or the opposite?

Sef lowered his head the better to block the early sun from his eyes.

Taisce loved him.

Sef hadn't felt anything but cold terror at the admission. The boy loved him now but what of tomorrow when Sef's usefulness was at an end? What then?

He'd asked Sef to stay, but Sef didn't even know what that meant. Stay as what? A lover? A friend? A shameful secret? After so many years of leaving, what did it even mean to stay?

In the distance, Sef could feel the gathering of energy. It had been years since he traveled these lands and then he'd been alone. Now the desert was dotted with small spiraling points like pins in a map. Beside him hovered the ever present swirl of Taisce. His untrained magic was feeble, barely a heartbeat in the silence. It was easy to ignore most times—he'd missed it entirely at first—but the land seemed to be seeking him out now, feeding into him. The tiny thrum of his pulse only grew.

More troubling was the feeling in the distance. Two more. Or possibly three. It was hard to tell. He would have to wait until they'd drawn up closer before he could be certain. One was greater than the others. That one radiated like a lighthouse in a storm. Even blind he could have found it. It pulled at him with a child's greedy fingers. Sef would bet anything that it was the man Norland. Sef disliked him already. If his magic was so greedy, the man was probably much the same.

Which begged the question, what did Sef feel like to the others? Did his magic claw with jealous fingers or did it swirl like a mist, enveloping in an invisible cloud? He supposed he might never know.

The terrain grew rougher. Sef was the only one who heard it hiss with silent warning. This land had betrayed him once but it still knew its master.

However hard it might try to buck him, it would never succeed. They were bound together. And now the land was screaming.

Sef shivered. A wave of pain hit him, nearly toppling him from his horse, but he clung like a burr, leaning forward to keep his seat. He spurred his horse on faster.

Taisce called after him. After a moment, he matched Sef's pace. "What are you doing?" he cried. "Is something the matter? You look ill. Should we stop?"

"No more questions," Sef said through clenched teeth. He was draped over his horse, body melting into a shivering heap. It was only force of will that kept him there. "We must hurry."

Taisce squinted into the distance. There was nothing there, nothing visible anyway, but to Sef it was a piercing wail. It resounded in every muscle, every bone, like the tolling of a terrible bell.

Someone was calling him.

They'd done it imperfectly, trying to call forth the monster he'd been known as. Whatever the stories had become, they had lost that most important fact, his true identity, his true form. The storytellers had drawn him as any number of things, a great fanged beast, a serpent. Never as he really was. A broken man. Things look so different covered in blood.

He shuddered at the memories long buried, intentionally forgotten. The metallic tang of blood. The crunch of broken bone. He'd forgotten it all, locked it away in a pit where he would never happen upon it again. But now. No. This was worse than Sef had thought. This man hadn't just come for a treasure. He was calling the beast that Sef had been.

The summoning was weak. It couldn't bind him wholly without his true name, but it still sought to strangle him. Sef pressed a hand to his throat, trying to work fingers around the invisible noose of the summoning even though there was nothing there, nothing he could touch, nothing he could tear away. His mouth filled with the metallic taste of blood. He spit it into the wind.

He rode faster, prepared to exhaust his horse if it meant getting there and stopping the summoning before it gained more strength. Or, worse yet, before it was tried again with a fresh sacrifice.

Rational thought evaporated. His vision narrowed to a single point. Forward. There was the pull and nothing else. He could feel the blood running out, tangling with him, latching onto him with sticky fingers. It was as nauseating as it was irresistible.

"What's going on?" Taisce called from his side. He and Finn pushed their horses to keep pace with him but Sef was quickly pulling ahead. "Talk to me."

Sef barely spared him a glance.

"Please," Taisce cried. "What is it?"

It was the 'please' that caught him. The desperate sound of it. A single syllable laced with need. Sef didn't slow much but he turned to acknowledge the question. "They're working a spell. A blood summoning." His eyes met Taisce's and then darted quickly away. "For me."

"For... But—" Taisce sputtered, eyes going wide. Confusion and horror warred in his expression. When he spoke next it was directed behind him. "We must hurry."

There was an answering grunt from Finn. Then there was only the pounding of hooves over the parched ground.

~~*

Worau was not so different from how Sef remembered it. The once great city—crowned with a castle whose spear-like turrets could be seen for miles—had crumbled after the plague, eaten up by the harsh weather of the desert. Without anyone to revive the spellwork that had made the place livable, Worau was quickly reduced to a bleached skeleton.

Time had worn away some of the sharper edges in his mind but the loneliness of the ruins remained unchanged. It might have been better draped in vines and creeping plants, anything to detract from the starkness of death. The dry climate and years of windblown sand had chiseled down the castle walls and bored through cracks until they were as wide as windows. However, the network of tunnels that ran below had been protected from much of time's handiwork. The narrow portals, formed to look like natural caves, were surrounded by dry and scrubby bushes but were otherwise clear. Three horses waited outside, ears twitching at their arrival.

Sef slipped from the saddle and stumbled

towards the cave mouth. His legs shook beneath him.

"It's this way," Sef said in a hoarse voice. The desert air had stolen his breath. Nothing would feel so good as slipping into the cool shadow of the tunnels but he didn't want to go. He would rather go anywhere than into those dank pits running beneath the castle. He'd spent so many lost years there, more than he would ever wish to count. Spending another moment there—it was unthinkable.

The summoning pulled. His feet carried him forward.

Taisce chased after him, leaving Finn to secure their horses. He slipped Sef's arm around his shoulders and pulled his dagger with his free hand. "You look like you can barely stand. You'd be better off staying put, but I know you won't do it."

"I can't." Sef groaned. His head was split with another pain and his vision doubled, blurring into a formless, colorless world. Somewhere far off he heard laughter. It was familiar but he couldn't place it. He shook his head. He wouldn't look behind them. "Not real."

Did you draw this?

He could barely see anything as Taisce led him onward but he could tell the moment they passed into the tunnels. The sun disappeared behind a curtain of ancient stone, taking with it every ounce of warmth.

The shadows whispered in so many voices all at once.

Here. Let me show you how it's done. It's so simple

really.

He tripped, dragging against Taisce. Where was the air? He couldn't catch his breath.

It's not fitting for a man of your station to be so slovenly.

"Shut up. Shut up. Shut up."

Such a crybaby.

"What are you doing?"

You're a monster.

He thumped a fist against his temple. "It's not real. Dead. You're all dead."

He put a shaking hand out, fumbling for the cool stone and leaning into it with eyes closed. He didn't even realize he was falling until he hit the ground.

~~*

Taisce cried out as Sef crumpled like a rag doll. He leapt to catch him but Finn was faster. He grabbed Sef by the shoulders and eased him the last few inches to the stone floor of the tunnel.

He looked ahead. The passage was wide enough to let them pass with ease, slanting down and widening into a larger chamber, the end of which was lost in the darkness. He was surprised. He'd expected something different. More dirt and rocks. A treasure trove broken into a canyon wall perhaps. Nothing so formal. He'd barely had time to examine the ruins of the city before they kept on but he'd caught sight of a partially formed turret.

Sef's castle.

He still didn't know what to think about that.

And these tunnels. He didn't know where they led but he knew Rupert would be there. It was just as impossible to consider that after weeks of travel he might have reached his destination at last. It had begun to feel like an unending quest.

"We'll need the lantern."

Anticipating the request, Finn held it out, already lit.

Taisce shot him a grateful smile. It faltered when he looked down at Sef. He'd gone dreadfully pale, eyes slitted, somewhere between wakefulness and troubled unconsciousness. While he watched, Sef twitched and moaned. Taisce swept the tunnel with another wary look. "We can't leave him in this state," he said, hating the fear in his voice.

Finn grumbled but he nodded. He bent to pull Sef up and, after another grunt and some muttering that was too low to make out, he had him slung over one shoulder.

"I suppose that will do," Taisce said, only partially comforted. Sef's long legs dangled like the boneless limbs of a doll. He looked so vulnerable. Even at his most unruly there had always been some sense of control to him. Not so now.

Taisce picked his way forward carefully, lantern held high. The stone was worn into rippled smoothness from the passage of time and he felt always on the verge of sliding onto his rear. The slope did nothing to help the feeling. Before long they had reached a small chamber. From there the tunnel meandered off in two different directions. A third passage continued straight on but the opening had collapsed. There was hardly enough room for a grown man to pass. Taisce hoped that that wasn't the way Rupert had gone. "Which way?" The two open tunnels looked exactly the same.

Finn's only answer was a shrug.

"We'll go to the left then," Taisce said with confidence he didn't feel.

"Wrong. Wrong way," Sef mumbled, finally stirring. He wriggled from Finn's grasp, hitting the stone floor hard and nearly falling a second time. He put a hand to his head. "Right. Go right."

"Are you sure?" Taisce asked. He hid his relief behind a thoughtful scowl.

Sef didn't answer. He was already wobbling down the path on the right, moving more quickly than Taisce would have thought possible. He'd gone deathly pale, face glowing with sweat. After a few steps, Sef twitched and spun to look back as if someone had startled him. Finn frowned at Taisce and shook his head. Taisce didn't like the situation any better but there was no turning back now.

The tunnels had an eerie quality about them, the lantern casting jumping shadows on the sloping walls as they passed. Sef charged on ahead, seemingly unconcerned by the fact that he was outpacing the light, drawing deeper and deeper into the darkness ahead of them. Taisce sheathed his dagger and scrambled after him. His hand trailed along the walls. He had no idea how Sef could move so quickly on the slick rock. As he thought it, Taisce's feet went out from under him. The lantern flew from his hand. It hit with a clang, one of the glass windows shattering, but thankfully it didn't go out.

"I'm fine. I'm fine," Taisce gasped as Finn hurried to help him up. He'd landed hard but most of the damage was to his pride and his already aching leg. The floor was damp beneath him. Taisce fumbled for his handkerchief to dry his hands. The cloth came away dark. He held it up to the lantern. "This is blood," he hissed, wiping even more frantically at his hands but the stain remained.

He looked up again just in time to see Sef disappearing ahead. "Sef, wait!"

He didn't even seem to hear.

Taisce swore, scrambling forward. His hand scraped against the wall as the passage narrowed and finally leveled out. There was no sign of Sef but he hesitated to call out again. From somewhere deeper in the caverns another voice echoed back to him. This one was familiar though he hadn't heard it in quite some time. If it had been Rupert's voice it would have been a comfort. It wasn't. This was the voice he remembered from that night in his bedchamber. Norland. Taisce shuddered. Even in echoes he sounded like an unscrupulous reptile.

"Just a bit more, love."

No reply reached Taisce's ears. It was impossible to tell to whom he spoke but it didn't matter whether it was Rupert or someone else. Taisce didn't want to think about whose blood it was that he had fallen into, whose blood had been used to pull Sef to this place, but it had obviously been partially Norland's doing.

Taisce stumbled around the bend in the tunnel and stopped. He was faced with an enormous chamber. The ceiling curved so high above him that it was lost in deep, black shadow. Long alcoves had been cut into the walls, each set with glass panes to give the illusion of windows. Large metal candelabras sat in the corners but their many candles did little to break through the gloom in the massive room. It looked like a cathedral buried beneath the desert wasteland and Taisce couldn't help wondering how grand it would look with better illumination. The hand holding the lantern dropped to his side as he stared.

Finn faltered to a stop with an equally startled gasp. "What the devil is this place?" he whispered.

He came to stand just before Taisce and checked his belt. He'd traded in his battered old knife for a stiletto. It tapered to a mean point and Taisce knew the edge was just as keen. He'd watched Finn sharpen it over the fire just the other day. Finn had sliced his fingers before he finished, blood dripping onto the dry, cracked earth to prove how well he'd done his work. But he surprised Taisce by pulling something else from his belt.

"Where did you get *that*?" Taisce hissed, eyes fastened to the pistol in Finn's fist. The wood stock glistened in the low light.

"Provisions," Finn said simply. He gave the

weapon a pat before advancing.

Taisce eyed it warily. "I didn't give you permission to purchase any such thing," he couldn't resist whispering back. Then he pulled his own dagger. It seemed inadequate in the presence of a powder gun but it comforted him. Guns were known to miss. His dagger wouldn't have that problem if he was close enough to use it. He just didn't want to be close enough to use it.

There was no sign of Sef. Just as troubling was the sudden silence from Norland. Taisce was certain that had been Norland's voice he heard, but he didn't see the man anywhere in the cavernous room now.

"Where are they?"

Finn shrugged. They inched into the room together.

At one end of the cavern sat a large, flat stone altar. It had partially collapsed, one side slanting at an angle that gave Taisce a view of the dark smear atop it. Someone had painted a large circle and a series of strange symbols and words on the stone. At the sight, the air in his lungs disappeared. He crept closer and put out a shaky hand to touch the dripping words. His fingers came away wet with more blood. This had to be part of their summoning spell.

Taisce looked around for something to smudge the circle with. Maybe that would break whatever spell Norland had attempted to cast over Sef. He had smeared it a little with his touch but not enough, he thought.

There was a muffled noise from one side of the room and Taisce jumped. The woman's face was full moon pale in the dark. He recognized her immediately. He'd never known her name but it would be hard to forget the woman who had snuck into his bedroom with Norland that night. She slumped against the wall, clutching her arm in front of her. It ran with blood, badly wrapped with a scarf that did almost nothing to staunch the flow. He stepped forward to help her, hands out, without thinking. He realized his folly a moment later when he felt a blade against his throat.

"So good of you to join us, young lord. But however did you get here?" asked Norland. He twisted the dagger from Taisce's fingers and threw it away into the dark recesses of the room.

"Where's my brother, you serpent?" Taisce demanded. He willed himself still. To lean away from the knife at his neck would only bring him closer to the man at his back. He was already too close.

At times during the journey, Taisce had worried over Sef's similarity to Norland, but being in his presence again made the distinction quite clear. Taisce had never felt like he was really in danger from Sef. Norland was different. Even that night in his room, almost the first time he'd set eyes on the man, Taisce had felt like a specimen caught in a jar. There was no warmth in his gaze, only a kind of desire. To him, Taisce was an object to be used.

"Don't move or I'll slit his throat," Norland

warned as Finn inched closer. "Throw the pistol away like a good boy, would you?"

Finn locked eyes with Taisce, shoulders slumping as he set his new pistol on the ground and nudged it aside with his toe.

Norland sighed. "You can do better than that." When Finn didn't immediately oblige, he pulled Taisce in closer, drawing a purposeful line of blood on the side of his neck with the knife. "Get rid of it."

With a muttered curse, Finn kicked his gun away.

"You're vile." Taisce tried again to jerk free but Norland only tightened his grip.

"Careful, boy. You wouldn't want my hand to slip. Mina, love," Norland called, "how's your arm?"

"It hurts like a bastard," the woman, Mina, gasped. "He cut me deep."

Norland tutted and shook Taisce by the shoulder. "Your brother is a menace. I think now I should have brought you along after all. Hmm? I bet with a little effort you'd have been easy as anything."

"I would never have been taken in by miserable filth like you. Let me go. Rodent. What have you done with my brother? Where is Rupert?" Taisce could barely stay still. The touch of the man made his skin want to crawl away. If only the rest of him could follow so easily.

Norland hummed thoughtfully. "You've changed since last we met. Such vulgar words from that pretty little mouth. I like it."

"I do nothing for your pleasure," Taisce snapped.

Norland stopped his next struggles with a fist

wrapped in his collar. Taisce choked and went still. "Where is my brother?"

"Dead if there's any justice," spit Mina, still pressing one hand to the wound on her arm. "The shit tried to kill me."

"And what did *you* do to him?" Taisce asked.

"We only asked him to donate a bit of his noble blood to our mutual cause," Norland said. His smile flashed in Taisce's peripheral vision. "We hear the great monster prefers a pedigree in its victims. Who better to summon him than one of the old families?"

"What monster?" Taisce asked though he already knew. "What about the treasure?"

"So you've done your research, hmm? I should have expected that of you. Nose buried in a book, always such a good little student. Any subject but magic anyhow." He paused. "Look around you. This is a tomb. There's nothing but dust and bones. Not even a scrap of gold leaf. If there was treasure it's long gone."

"Then why—?"

"You ask too many questions," Norland said and his breath fanned Taisce face again. It had the hard bite of blood in it. "I want the beast. It's here. I can feel its echo, its power. I don't suppose you can with no magic. Were you jealous of the power we wield? Even Rupert can do a bit of feeble conjuring but not you. Do you envy us?"

"I don't know what you're talking about."

Norland released his hold on Taisce's collar and wrapped an arm around him instead. He held his hand out. Then, with a few sibilant words, crackling white light ran between his fingers like an electrical storm in miniature. "Would you like me to teach you?"

Taisce watched the spectacle encapsulated in Norland's dirty hand. Immediately his mind ran back to that night when Sef had fought the wolves. The raw power of it. Had Taisce been jealous then? He couldn't rightly remember anything but the surprise. Awe. And the answering call from deep within him. An echo that he couldn't quite place. What had he felt then?

Taisce shook his head. "I don't want anything from you."

"Pity. Then you can join your brother in being useful."

Taisce followed Norland's gesture and finally caught sight of Rupert. He lay slumped in a corner, nearly hidden by a pillar. His brother's stocky body was limp, his face a sickly gray in the flickering light. Taisce tried to take a step toward him.

"Not so fast, boy," Norland chuckled, tugging him back like a dog on a short leash. He made no comment when Finn went to Rupert's side, pressing a hand to his chest. "He's not dead. Only sleeping. There was no sense wasting his blood too soon. Now you can offer yours instead. Your blood for the safety of your brother. It seems an even trade, doesn't it? Your brother's blood doesn't seem to have been strong enough to call the beast all the way here. Maybe yours will do better."

"I wouldn't suggest it. He bites." The words echoed out of the darkness and everyone jumped, even Taisce, who recognized Sef's voice immediately. But the tone of it—the threat—that was entirely new. Sef stepped forward, eyes shining unnaturally bright like the flame of a candle. He staggered, catching himself on a stone pillar.

"Who're you?" Mina demanded. When Sef's head snapped in her direction she made a frightened squeak and stepped back.

Norland laughed. "You're not quite the monster I was expecting, but you'll do."

Sef swept the room with a look, taking in Rupert and Finn crouched beside him before swinging back to Taisce. His smile was a black pit. Taisce ached looking into it. "He's not a monster," Taisce spat.

"Oh ho! What secrets the little noble has," Norland said. "All this time I've spent searching for a way to bind the beast and you had him all along. How interesting. However did you capture him? What tricks did you use? Certainly not a spell."

"I would never..." Taisce stammered but he felt the traitorous rising of a blush along his neck.

The next snicker made it clear that his sudden color had not gone unnoticed. "What a wicked thing you've become. I had no idea," he purred. Then he nodded to Sef. "Come here."

Taisce waited for a clever retort from Sef. The lack of one was more troubling than the shadowed look in his eyes as he moved closer. "I dislike this place. What is it you've called me for?"

"I'll ask the questions," Norland said. "We have a contract to seal, you and I."

"Do we?" Sef circled the fringes of the room, slipping closer by small measures as he moved from shadow to shadow. "What is it you're offering?"

"I've got your plaything. Isn't his life a good enough prize?"

Sef tilted his head, pausing in his slinking approach. "You can't give me what does not belong to you. Haven't you heard the stories? Did you think I would be *easy*?"

"Then I'll slit his throat," Norland said and Taisce tensed as the blade pressed close again.

Sef's eyes flashed with strange light and one hand flicked out as if acting on its own will. Following the movement, the knife slipped from Norland's fingers and clattered to the floor out of reach. Sef glanced at it and then back.

"I'm losing patience. You had best talk fast," he said. He folded his arms.

Norland still clutched at Taisce's shoulders but the feel of it had changed. It had lost its power. Taisce felt more like a shield than a hostage now.

"I summoned you. I control you," Norland barked but it lacked conviction. He backed up a step and tugged Taisce with him, splitting the seam at one shoulder of his coat when he knotted his hands into the material.

Sef cocked his head. There was black amusement in the look. Calculation. This was the way he'd looked when they first met but it was only now that

Taisce recognized it. How long had it been since Sef had regarded him with such hard, unblinking eyes? When had his gaze changed to something else? Their eyes met again, just for a moment, but he didn't miss the softening. In the next second, it was gone as Sef's attention returned to Norland. His jaw clenched tight and something swam through his expression, something Sef had been fighting since they'd first set foot in the desert.

"We can't bargain if you have nothing of value. So far you've offered me things I already have. And threats." Sef's smile went sharp. "I don't like threats. Make me an offer."

It was Mina who finally answered. "The curse."

Sef raised an eyebrow and turned to her, eyes alight with curiosity at her sudden bravery. Or maybe it was foolishness. Taisce didn't miss the tremor in her voice when she spoke.

"Go on."

She swallowed. "I know who you are." At her words, Sef's face hardened. "I wasn't sure at first. But seeing you... I've heard about you, third son. We can break your curse."

"Impossible."

Norland regained enough courage to add, "Between us we can undo it."

"And what do you ask in return?"

At their offer Sef had gone even paler still. He barely seemed to be breathing. There was something wrong. Taisce couldn't say what it was that he felt, but it seemed to swirl around Sef like a whirlwind, growing darker with each passing moment. He didn't know what to do.

"Come closer and we'll discuss as friends. There's no need to fight," Norland said.

In those seconds of silence Taisce tensed, fear settling into the pit of his stomach. There was something wrong behind Sef's eyes.

"What do you say?" Norland asked when moments passed and Sef had said nothing.

"I would never have such shabby friends."

Sef's hand went out again and Norland was flicked aside like an insect. Taisce staggered as the man was torn away. Norland hit the wall with a thud and Taisce scrambled away in the opposite direction, retreating to Rupert and Finn.

. "He's unwell, my lord," Finn whispered when he came close. One hand was clamped to the wound in Rupert's side, trying in vain to stem the flow. "He's lost much blood."

Taisce touched a hand to his brother's forehead. It was frighteningly cold but his eyes fluttered, barely opening and rolling to take in his face. "Tash," Rupert said in a cracked voice. "I'm surprised to see you so far from your books."

Taisce smiled despite himself.

~~*

Sef was quite enjoying himself. With the flick of his wrist a chunk of masonry flew from the wall, narrowly missing the leech who'd been clinging to

Taisce.

By then the woman had regained her bearings. Her magic was weak but she had no intention of relying upon it, if the sword in her hand was any indication. She was quick with the blade, swinging it with tenacity. He took a moment to admire her skill. She was certainly better than he had ever been.

Not that it mattered.

On her next lunge, he knocked her aside with the brick he'd thrown at Norland.

Power burned in his veins. Here. At the source. Once he'd started it was easier to keep going, letting it flame straight through him, filling him and emptying him and whittling him down to nothing all at the same time.

Sef would tear the place apart stone by stone if he had to. Better that. Better that than the screaming, the feel of blood clinging to his skin. He could still feel it. His hands looked clean but that was only because the blood had soaked in long ago.

Norland cried out in the old tongue, his accent a sharp snap. He'd studied well. A sizzle of white light burst from his fingers and shot at Sef. He leapt out of the way a moment too late and it caught him in the arm, tearing through his shirt and the flesh beneath.

Taisce shouted. The fool was scrambling from the spot where he'd hidden with his nearly dead brother. Sef knew it must be Taisce's brother. They had the same feel about them even if they looked nothing alike. His brother was thicker and darker in almost every way.

Sef put up a hand and Taisce stopped, stuck fast in a momentary trap thick as honey. "Stay there," he said, absently, already turning away.

"I'll do no such thing!" Taisce snapped back. Always so stubborn. It might have made Sef smile if it wasn't so hard to concentrate when he was three places at once.

Every corner echoed with memories. He would never hate any place so much as he did this one. It wanted to crush him with the weight of his own guilt, his own fear. Norland and the woman weren't the only ones he fought. Something lurched at him from beside the altar and Sef sent out another burst of flame. It hit the wall, useless, the thing he'd seen evaporating like the phantom it was. Another shadow, a memory, one or both or neither. He couldn't be sure anymore.

He grunted, pulling at the walls, tearing great chunks from the stone and hurling them. They would hit something sooner or later. They would stop it. Dust sifted down around him.

"Stop it, Sef!"

He glanced at Taisce, still struggling to move in his trap. He looked afraid.

There was a crack like thunder and Sef staggered sideways. The gunshot didn't hurt. Strangely he felt nothing until Taisce called for him, crying out as Sef staggered again and fell.

Chapter Sixteen
IN WHICH ALL THINGS ARE BROKEN AND MENDED

Taisce pulled free, whatever sticky trap Sef had laid for him evaporating as he dropped to the floor. Sef gasped. He smiled with bloodied teeth when Taisce slid down beside him.

"No." Taisce's hands hovered over the gunshot wound in Sef's chest, desperate to stop the oozing blood. "What do I do?"

Sef hissed out another breath—his only answer.

The crunch of grit underfoot drew Taisce's attention up. Norland gestured with the pistol in his hand, Finn's pistol. He should never have brought the thing. Norland waggled it at Sef's head and made a sad little cluck. "I'd rather hoped you would be more useful," he said.

Time slowed as Taisce threw himself over Sef, covering him the only way he could. There was a wave of heat as the pistol fired a second time. A stutter of Taisce's heart. He screamed and it barreled from his lungs, a sound made material, threatening to split him open. He screamed and Norland flew backwards, arms thrown wide, carried by the force of Taisce's anger.

He'd done it.

How had he done it?

Taisce shuddered, falling over Sef, chest to chest, head throbbing. His stomach lurched. There was another clatter and he turned, searching for the source.

Mina had dropped her sword as she backed across the room. She didn't stop until she'd backed herself all the way to the wall where Norland had fallen. She tried to tug him back towards the tunnels. He shook her off.

"You." Norland put out his hands as if he could wring Taisce's neck from across the room.

"Nuh uh, you slippery little weasel," Finn said. Somehow he'd crossed the room unnoticed. Now he held Norland at bay with a stiletto at his throat and the gun, which he'd retrieved from Norland's hand. There was a moment as they stared at each other, testing each other. Finally Norland dropped his hands and stepped back. "That's right," Finn said, still guarded but obviously pleased with himself.

Taisce turned back to Sef. He'd gone very still, hands curled loosely over his chest. His shirt was nearly black with blood. Taisce moved his hands aside and opened the torn fabric. Uncovered, the wound looked worse. It pulsed with a slow flow of blood, the edges of the wound swollen and angry looking.

"What do I do?" Taisce wailed, surprised by the

tears prickling his eyes. He knew nothing of surgery and medicine. Medicinal herbs, yes, but there were none to be found here in the desert, buried beneath the earth in this would-be tomb.

Sef coughed and Taisce nearly screamed in fright. Like a spider, Sef's fingers scuttled up to grab his. He pulled Taisce's hands back to his chest. "It's stuck. Take it... out." He wheezed through pale, blood flecked lips.

"Take it out... Take *what* out?" Taisce stared at the wound. It still trickled deep red blood though it seemed to be slowing. He hoped that wasn't a bad sign.

Sef tapped a hand against his chest. "The bullet. Take it out." His voice was a cracked whisper.

Taisce snatched his hands back. "You—you can't be serious," he cried but he leaned closer to inspect the damage. He could see something, shining and metallic, against all the blood and... He looked away. "I don't think I can." He squeezed his eyes shut as tight as his lips, trying to hold in the terror and equally strong wave of nausea the sight had caused.

Sef coughed, spasming, head whipping back. Blood flew from his mouth and spattered the floor. A few droplets flecked Taisce's cheek. He'd barely fallen silent when Taisce scrambled over to where his dagger had fallen. His fingers were much too large to dig into the ragged hole but the narrow blade could.

He knelt at Sef's side, his fist pressed against his mouth to seal in the rest of his fears. Sef was so still. Still as death.

"Sef?" Taisce waited for the flutter of opening eyes, the crack of a defiant grin. "Sef?" he hissed with rapidly rising panic.

"I'm not dead," Sef groaned. "It's impossible... you fool."

Taisce bristled at the tacked on epithet, but it gave him the impetus he needed to press the tip of the dagger to Sef's chest. They winced in unison. Taisce bit down on his lip so hard he tasted blood. As the blade dug into flesh, Sef beat the floor with one fist, whining weakly. The dagger nicked the bullet.

"Lie still." Taisce leaned closer, pressing a steadying hand to Sef's shoulder though he knew he couldn't subdue the man if he thrashed in earnest. He tried again. This time the tip of the dagger dipped beneath the bullet so he could lever it upwards. Taisce pulled it the rest of the way free with shaking fingers. He sat back on his heels. The bullet nestled in his palm. So much blood for such a small piece of metal. A scrap.

The scuffle of feet echoed against the stone walls followed by a booming thud. Finn stumbled against a nearby candelabra. It tipped over with a bang and sent melted wax flying everywhere. Norland and Mina were gone, disappearing into the mouth of the tunnel. Finn tottered after them but he'd hit hard when Norland threw him. Taisce barely made it to hands and knees to give chase when Sef's eyes popped open. His right hand rose up towards the ceiling. As if pulling a rope, Sef yanked down and the sound of crumbling rock followed. A cloud of dust rolled into the chamber like a fog bank. Broken stone clattered.

Sef's eyes rolled up and he swallowed convulsively. "Ow." He pressed a hand hard against his chest. A rush of blood leaked out from beneath his fingers.

"What did you do?" Taisce looked from the blocked doorway to Sef. "What did you do?"

"Would you rather I left them to slit your throat some night?" Sef asked. He took another steadying breath, one hand still against the wound in his chest, then inched up to sitting. Sweat clung to his temples and drying blood speckled his lips, his cheeks. It ran down his chin in a thin trail, decorated his chest. So much blood. It looked almost black in the dim light.

Finn stumbled to a stop when he saw the mess of Sef. He stuttered, one hand out and pointing. "You should be dead," he said. From his tone it was hard to tell if he was surprised or disappointed that Sef wasn't.

Sef nodded. Taisce suspected there was disappointment lingering there too.

"They dead?" Finn asked with a nod towards the caved in path.

"Most likely."

"Good."

Sef smiled with blood-pink teeth and it wasn't so hard to understand why they'd called him a monster. And yet... the next moment the look had disappeared and he was the man Taisce knew once again. Filthy. Clothes ruined. Shamelessly staring with dark eyes until Taisce felt his face go pink.

"What is it?" Taisce asked finally, breaking away from Sef's watchful gaze.

He received no answer. Instead, Finn interrupted. "How are we to get out if the tunnel's collapsed? Rupert is still injured."

Taisce's heart sank. How could he have forgotten something so obvious? His eyes swept the room. Suddenly the enormous space felt terribly claustrophobic.

Sef chuckled but it quickly transformed into a fresh fit of coughing.

"And this one," Finn added.

"You two would be lost without me," Sef rasped when he'd caught his breath. He spit another mouthful of blood onto the floor, backhanding the residue from his lips. His chest was already healing to an angry pink scar. He wobbled to his feet, weaving his way between invisible obstacles. When he tripped, he crawled the rest of the way on hands and knees, evidently too tired to bother with the pretense of wellness.

"You should rest," Taisce said.

"I should," Sef agreed.

He tugged the binding free from Rupert's side despite Finn's protest. The gash was large. Taisce could hardly look at it. He'd seen too much blood for one day, more than he had ever wished to see in any lifetime.

A sudden glowing drew Taisce's gaze back to his brother. Sef's eyes drifted closed and his hands rested over Rupert's bleeding abdomen. His lips moved, forming a string of words in that strange language. A pale green twinkling, like stars in miniature, surrounded his clasped fingers, pressing into Rupert's skin. Taisce knelt at his side but he didn't dare touch or make noise, reluctant to disturb them.

"What is this devilry?" Finn asked in a hushed voice.

Slowly Sef drew his hands back, breathing hard.

Rupert's side was nearly healed. The dried blood flaked away like peeling paint as if the wound had never been anything more than stage makeup. Then Rupert made a low murmur. He blinked, eyes coming open fully and staying that way.

"What's happened?" Rupert asked in a dry voice. He sat up, barely seeming to notice his injury. "Where did they go? Have you seen them?"

Taisce didn't ask who he meant. It was obvious. "They're gone," he said.

Rupert scowled. "Made off with the treasure? Together?" He grumbled, a strange look passing over him as he fell silent. His lips moved in silent commentary, whatever it was something he didn't care to share.

There was an animal sound of pain as Sef stood. He looked pale and bedraggled, crusted with so much blood it was a miracle he had any left for his heart.

"We should clean you up," Taisce said but Sef shook his head.

"Who is this?" Rupert asked. He studied Sef

carefully, running his eyes over the man as if he were deciding his price. It was a shrewd look that was altogether new. Taisce didn't like it.

"Where are you going?" Taisce cried. Sef was already halfway across the chamber, heading towards a particularly deep pocket of shadow.

Taisce jumped to his feet, wincing at the sting of skinned knees. It was nothing compared to the others—even Finn had suffered a nasty gash along his temple—but he had completely forgotten them. Now the nick at his throat burned like fire and his palms were pink with abraded skin. His leg throbbed with slow but familiar pressure. His whole body cried out for sympathy but he ignored it.

Sef stepped into the shadows, hands out and searching as if he couldn't see. The shadows were certainly thick enough.

Finn helped Rupert to his feet, then his brother's weight landed on Taisce's shoulder. "Who is that, Tash?" he demanded. He leaned into Taisce so heavily he almost fell. "He glows."

Taisce shot a look at his brother. Perhaps the desert sun had gotten to him after all. "Whatever are you talking about?"

Rupert waved a hand at Sef's back. "You can't see it? No. Of course you couldn't. It's magic," he hissed. "Magic. He's brimming with it." He licked his lips.

"Get ahold of yourself." Taisce pulled away and let Finn take Rupert's weight instead. "What has come over you?" His brother's eyes had gone wide and unfocused.

"My lord."

"Not now." Taisce took Rupert's face in his hands. He'd grown thin while they were apart. The meaty width of his cheeks had narrowed, drawing out the line of his cheekbones, the angular jaw. His dark hair hung in his face and there were circles beneath his eyes, dark smudges that had little to do with weariness and everything to do with illness.

"My lord?"

"What is it?" Taisce snapped, finally turning to Finn.

Finn pointed at the wall where Sef had been. He was gone.

Taisce spun, searching for signs of him. When he called Sef's name the only answer was an echo. He rushed to the spot where Sef had been last, feet sliding cautiously over the pitted stone floor. One step into the dark. Two. Finally he felt the rough edges of stone relief beneath his finger tips. And something else. He inhaled deeply. There was a draft of fresher air here. He turned into it.

The passage was hidden from view, disguised by the darkness and the elaborate curls of an ancient motif. It was only when Taisce looked back that he realized he'd lost sight of the others. In this spot he was hidden completely.

"My lord?"

"I'm here," Taisce called back. He felt strangely distant though they were only separated by a handful of steps. "There's a passage."

He waited for the sound of answering footsteps

before he headed on into the passage. It was the only logical direction that Sef could have gone. The tunnel was illuminated with the barest of gray light reflected from the cavern he'd just left. Hardly enough to see by. He was glad that Finn had thought to collect the lantern before following. Taisce didn't like the idea of getting lost in this maze without a light.

~~*

Taisce's voice came after Sef, each cry sounding more and more frantic. Sef paused.

It would be easy to leave them to fumble alone through the tunnels. A part of him wished he could, wished he would. Being alone was so much simpler. Quieter. There were no choices to make when he was alone. Nothing to feel.

Sef found them without difficulty. He'd mapped these tunnels as a boy and they were still ingrained in his memory even after all these years, as familiar as his own body, his hands.

"Wrong way, milord," Sef said. Taisce started at his sudden appearance, making an amusing squeak. Sef beckoned them the way he'd gone, leading them in silence. It was hard enough to walk straight. He couldn't be asked to play tour guide as well.

"What is this place?" the brother Rupert asked. They had a similar way of speaking, a tone that implied they were used to being answered when they deigned to ask a question. But, where Sef liked the flavor of arrogance on Taisce, it sat ill on Rupert.

Almost petulant. Sef ignored him and his question went unanswered.

They emerged into a store room whose contents had long since crumbled to dust. Sef held his breath. There was nothing here, but the stench of decay still swam around him. It clawed at his lungs like panic. Rank. Acid. A rotten corpse.

A touch at his shoulder made him jump. Taisce. The boy looked at him with large eyes in the yellow darkness. The storeroom had a single window, once covered by glass and shutters, but those had been broken away centuries ago. Now the little porthole let in the late day sun, diffused and weak.

"Are you in very much pain?" Taisce asked. His eyes hovered just below the healing bullet wound as if he couldn't bear to look any higher.

Sef had almost forgotten that particular injury in light of the others he had to focus on. "Always," he said. Then he pulled away. Things would only get worse. That was what they did.

Sef steeled himself to head on, shrugging off the echoing in his ears. It had been centuries. There would be no one there. *Could* be no one there. He was safe.

He kicked the door wide. The passageway was empty. He had expected that, yet it was a surprise. Empty windows let in light like liquid gold, pouring across the tiled floors, picking out the inlaid designs as they moved on to the main hall with its high ceiling. Somehow the mosaics had survived the centuries when nothing else had. Sef raised his hands to the wall, running them over the time-smoothed edges of the tiles. Weathering had muddied the colors but he remembered how beautiful the great tree had looked once, small chips of precious stone embedded between tiles so that, in the right light, the leaves of the tree had looked like they shivered in a gentle breeze. He lay his cheek against the wall and for a moment Sef lost himself, his current self. This place was his heart. Time could not change the fact that it was his home. He was meant to be here. He turned away from the mosaic. A short hall led to a door and the desert beyond—the exit Taisce had wanted. Sef turned the other way and mounted the center staircase, heading up.

The creamy stone walls were bare. Not a single banner or tapestry remained. Creeping plants had taken root in the cracks of the stone, creating an uneven and tangled carpet underfoot. All Sef saw was death. All he smelled was decay. Dust.

He shook his head. It wasn't there. He knew it wasn't but...

Taisce spoke behind him but Sef couldn't hear the words. Sef slipped from his grasp and kept walking. Down another hall. Up a curved set of stairs. He couldn't look out the windows. The view would be wrong. Barren. Empty. Desolate. Not the greenery and life he remembered. Not even the choking pillars of smoke that he remembered from the time when everything else was gone. There was nothing there now. He didn't want to see it.

The hall was the same as the others had been. Pale

stone like bleached bone. Someone had cleared away the bodies or perhaps time had done that for them. Had the corpses crumbled to dust already? How long would that take? Had they been dragged away by animals? Sef smiled a little to think that his long ago attackers might have been feasted upon by wild animals in his absence. They deserved it. They deserved more. He had never claimed to be a forgiving sort.

The doors along the hall were mostly broken or missing, the heavy wood warped and cracked, metal hinges hanging from the wall like clawed fingers. One doorway at the end of the hall, more familiar than the rest, drew him closer. The remains of his door lay in pieces, somehow still resting where they had fallen when the people came for him. He stared at the shards for a long time before he inched closer. The past held him in its palm. The feel of it. The smell. The rope pulled tight around his throat. He gasped.

Something brushed his arm. Sef lashed out at it, terrified. Finn stopped his backhanded swing before it hit Taisce, and he pushed Sef away so hard he slammed into the wall. Sef dropped his gaze to the floor. He couldn't look at Taisce with his startled eyes and his hands up to guard against the blow. He couldn't apologize. His voice had run dry. Maybe they weren't even there.

Sef stepped over the wreckage of his door. Old soot painted the walls of the room, scorched stone running up to the high ceiling. There was little else left inside. The bed had gone up like a pyre. His bedchamber was as much a husk as the rest of the castle. He didn't know what he had expected to find there. Solace? Some kind of peace? Whatever it was, he didn't find it.

Taisce had followed him into the room, though he kept his distance. He turned in a circle and paused, eyes caught on something Sef couldn't see. He crouched over a pile of broken masonry that might once have been part of the window—Sef couldn't quite remember now. There was the drag of metal and Taisce held up a battered sword, the blade tarnished and dull but familiar all the same. Sef shuddered. All at once his dreams came back to him with perfect clarity. He knew how this was meant to go, had known all along and had forgotten somehow.

"My sword," Sef said.

"Hmm?" Taisce glanced at him, the look still wary but curious. He moved closer to the window, hair shining, eyes flashing bright as stars when they caught the light. He fingered the blade gently, inspecting the hilt, the time worn inscription that he wouldn't be able to read.

Those were the eyes Sef had seen so many times in his restless sleep. The glow of gold. Just that way. He'd completed the circle even without intending to.

Sef dropped to his knees.

He didn't want it. Even after last night, explaining everything, he had wondered if he would feel different in the moment. If he would welcome it despite everything. He didn't. It was a relief actually.

Taisce turned to him, eyes large with concern. The sword still hung from his hand as though he'd forgotten. "What's the matter? Is it your wound?"

He had the most ridiculous urge to laugh, but instead he shook his head. Then he pulled Taisce in for a kiss.

~~*

"What has come over you?" Taisce cried as he tipped over. He landed sprawled atop Sef, sword clattering against the floor as it fell from his hand, and then he was too busy to worry about it. Sef tasted faintly of blood but even that didn't matter. Not when he was being kissed like he was life itself.

Finn yelled from the doorway, drawn by Taisce's cries, and Rupert followed slowly in his wake still looking gray and tired. "Tash?"

"We're fine," Taisce said, breaking the kiss to answer. Sef made a regretful noise. His forehead rested against Taisce's cheek, his breath a faint tickle against his throat.

Finn hovered in the doorway. He looked in need of a hat to wring. "But..."

"Go."

When they'd gone out again, Taisce turned back. "What was that for?"

Sef squeezed his eyes shut and shook his head. Not a no. Just an expression of doubt. When he opened his eyes again there was a question there. "Did you mean what you said before? About returning with you? Did you mean it?"

"Of course I meant it." Taisce frowned.

"Then don't touch that sword. Please. Put it anywhere but in your hand. Throw it into the nearest sea when you find one."

Taisce turned to look at it, the sword sitting in a patch of disappearing sun where he had dropped it. It must have been a beautiful weapon once. For the brief moment that Taisce had held it in his hand he had felt something, the faintest vibration, like touching his hand to a sleeping heart. And then he understood. "It was yours."

"Yes."

"And that's what I was supposed to... to use."

"Yes." The corner of his mouth quirked up. "But please don't."

"How do you even *know*? It's been years, you said. You could be wrong," he insisted. This was why he hated magic. Everything was a trick sooner or later, like a nesting doll, one truth hidden within another and another. Even Sef. *Especially* Sef. But that didn't change how much he still wanted him. He reached out to rub a patch of dried blood from Sef's cheek before he leaned in for another kiss. "Yes I meant it. I want you to come back with me. To Blume. To my home. We can find somewhere to dispose of the sword together." He smiled against Sef's lips.

"And then I can begin showing my gratitude."

Taisce scowled and pulled back. "I told you that you didn't owe me anything."

"Oh, believe me, this is as much about pleasing

myself as you." He caught Taisce's hand and pressed a kiss to the palm before twining their fingers together. His eyes softened. "You make me feel… peaceful. Despite everything. I hadn't expected that, had forgotten I even could feel that way." With his free hand he traced the outline of Taisce's cheek, his jaw, the beginnings of a frown line around his mouth. "I love you. And after I tried so hard not to. You certainly do make a mess of my plans."

"Is *that* what all of that was supposed to be? A plan?"

"Absolutely."

Taisce sniffed derisively. "I thought you were just a miserable person who enjoyed tormenting me."

"I am that too. But unfortunately you're stuck with me now since I've grown attached. Back to Blume, was it? I haven't been in decades." His arms tightened, almost crushing them together.

"You'll really come with me?"

"Anywhere." He paused for a moment and then a slyness crept into his expression. Taisce had seen that look too many times already to trust it. The suspicion was confirmed as Sef's hands slipped along his spine and settled at his hips. His green eyes darkened. "I plan to make myself indispensable. You'll be lost without me."

It was possible that he already was. Taisce leaned in to meet him, pressing their lips together. "Shouldn't you clean off? You're still covered in blood."

"After. I'll be getting much dirtier first."

"And you're injured."

"It hardly hurts at all anymore, though you're welcome to check for yourself if you wish. Be gentle with me." He grinned and that broke the last of Taisce's resolve.

"You're impossible. They're right outside the door," Taisce whispered as he slid Sef's ruined shirt from his shoulders.

"Then you'll have to be very quiet. We have a lot of time to make up for."

On that, they were agreed.

Fin

ACKNOWLEDGMENTS

Thank you to everyone who helped to make this book possible. It's been such a long road to get here and I couldn't have done it without your support along the way.

To Ellie, for loving my pansexual disaster.

To Murphy, for all the What Is Love jokes.

To Skye, for making sure my commas were in the right places.

And to everyone who ever asked how the book was going or helped me celebrate when I had news.
Thank you so much.

ABOUT THE AUTHOR

J. Emery is slowly writing their way through every fantasy trope imaginable. And if they can make it weirder and queerer while they do, that's even better as far as they're concerned.

They spend their free time watching anime, gaming, and drinking large quantities of tea, occasionally all at the same time. They have also been known to document their ridiculous levels of terror while watching horror movies on twitter as @mixeduppainter. Sometimes they even discuss upcoming projects.

They have also written and self-published two queer short stories: *An Offering of Plums* and *Help Wanted*.

STILL NEED MORE?

To receive updates and special bonus content, including side stories, visit the address below to sign up for my newsletter. I promise not to abuse this newfound power.

Thanks for reading!

-

https://mailchi.mp/ccb68f4efead/mixeduppaintersignup

ALSO BY J. EMERY

Ashveil Academy Series
Help Wanted

An Offering of Plums
Forgotten Monster

Made in United States
Orlando, FL
04 December 2022